A WOMAN LEARNS DEEPLY HIDDEN FAMILY SECRETS WHEN SHE INHERITS BROUSSARD COURT APARTMENTS IN NEW ORLEANS FROM A GREAT-AUNT SHE DIDN'T KNOW EXISTED.

Madame's extraordinary powers, helping those in need as well as punishing evil doers, are held in awe throughout her neighborhood and even in the greater city of New Orleans. Madame, however, is old and sees the mists forming telling her she will soon die. She leaves her considerable holdings to her only known relative, Addie Zappo, who is completely unaware of her great aunt and the power she wields. Already Madame has set in motion events that will bring together the lives of four unsuspecting women in unimaginable ways, but it will be up to Addie, the New Witch, to ward off the evil already gathering to strike at the women.

"*The New Witch*" grabs you and lets you be that fly on the wall as the abused wife meticulously plots her escape and covers her trail on her way to her new hideout in New Orleans. Gibson is a master of engagement of the reader and will not turn you loose until she takes you on a ride. She is wonderful story teller who will throw you in the current of her words and wash you down- stream to the end of the book."—*Chap Harper, author of Beer, Bait, and Ammo.*

i

THE NEW WITCH

Nancy Smith Gibson

Moonshine Cove Publishing, LLC
Abbeville, South Carolina U.S.A.

FIRST MOONSHINE COVE EDITION MARCH 2017

ISBN: 978-1-945181-08-5
Library of Congress PCN: 2017902776
Copyright © 2017 by Nancy Smith Gibson

Front cover design by Moonshine Cove staff; front cover illustration uses public domain images.

This book is dedicated to my children

Lisa Gibson Sanderock
Robin Gibson Beard
Holly Gibson Thorwarth
James Joel Gibson

With many thanks for their love and support

About The Author

From the time she learned to read, author Nancy Smith Gibson has had her nose stuck in a book. *I can do that!* she thought. So when she found herself in an empty nest (except for cats and dogs) she proceeded to do just that. She is author of the contemporary romance/mystery *The Memory of All That* and the historical/mystery/suspense series *Tales From the Brazos: The Marriage Bargain, Betrayal on the Brazos, Gussie and the Cherokee Kid,* and the upcoming *The Scandalous Inheritance*. Other works include *Mrs. Mommy*, *Wherever Life Leads*, and plenty more to come.

Mother of four, grandmother of four, great-grandmother of one, she believes in ghosts, divine order, UFOs, the power of gemstones, and things that happen in threes. She lives near Hot Springs, Arkansas, where she enjoys genealogy, jewelry making, road trips, and lunching with friends . . . and, of course, writing.

Keep up with what Nancy Smith Gibson is working on now at her website:

www.nancysmithgibson.com

ACKNOWLEDGMENT

My thanks go out to the following people, without whose help this book might never have come to be.

Michelle Devon
Whose suggestions, advice, and editing helped me along the way.

Accentuate Writers Forum
And their input on the story line.

The Hot Springs, Arkansas, Writers Critique Group
Whose constant support sustains me.
They can always be counted on to tell
me if a scene is boring!

THE NEW WITCH

CHAPTER ONE

Evelyn had the grocery ads spread out on the kitchen table when her husband came down for breakfast. "I'm going to the market. I thought I'd fix a pot roast for supper. Did you like the one from last week?"

"Yeah, it was okay," he said, although he'd eaten seconds.

She tugged at the sleeve of her sweater to cover the bruising that circled her wrist. Subconsciously, she reached for the scarf that hid similar marks around her throat and pulled it higher to hide the discoloration.

"Is there anything you want me to get?"

"Get some pork chops. You don't make quite as big a mess with those." He added more items. She wrote his requests on the list as though she intended to buy them.

"I'll be going to the library, too, to return some books."

He acted like he hadn't heard her, but she knew he filed the information away. He always had to know where she was.

After he left for work, she took time to clean the kitchen. It wasn't unusual for him to return with the pretext of having forgotten something. She didn't know what he thought he would catch her doing. After half an hour, she was fairly certain he wouldn't return. She took a garbage bag into the bedroom and packed. Now that she had started, she moved quickly.

There were no suitcases in the house. She guessed he thought that would stop her from running. She hurriedly filled the bag with a couple of dresses, a pair of dress shoes, plenty of underwear, slacks, blouses, makeup, tampons, aspirin. She added a towel and some washcloths and pulled the drawstring closed. She almost ran as she carried the bag to the garage and threw it in the back of her Escalade.

Back inside, she grabbed her purse that contained the money she accumulated by hiding it around the house. She also gathered all the jewelry he had ever given her. She knew she was more fortunate than most women in her situation. Appearances were important to her husband, so he made sure she drove a nice car and had nice clothes and jewelry. It was unfortunate that every item of clothing she owned had a high neck and long sleeves to hide the bruises that usually covered her arms and chest.

She suspected the almost-new Escalade had a tracking device on it, but that was okay; more than okay, because she planned for that to work to her advantage. The last thing she retrieved was the title to the car. She discovered months before where Ed kept it but left it untouched until it was time to leave.

Before she left, she went to Billy's bedroom. Standing there with all his mementoes, she allowed one tear to trickle down her cheek for the son she loved so dearly. If it hadn't been for Billy, she would have left long ago.

She walked to his dresser, just like he'd left it when he'd enlisted. Running her fingers over the basketball trophy he had been so proud of, she said final goodbyes.

He had stuck the picture of him on one knee, in his basketball uniform, holding the ball, into the mirror frame. His face was stern, without a hint of a smile, as though he hated to be there.

How could he have been happy playing, with his father criticizing every move he made on the court? I'm sorry you didn't have the loving father you deserved, Billy.

She stuck the picture in her pocket and took a final look around. After she kissed her fingertips, she touched them to his senior picture on the bureau.

I thought I said goodbye at your funeral, but this is really it. Goodbye, my darling son. Goodbye.

* * *

She took the highway northeast toward Kansas City. With any luck, she would dispose of the car before he had a clue she was gone. She turned off her cellphone. He usually called her at home during the day. If he didn't get an answer he would call her cellphone. If he found it off, she hoped he would assume she was in the library, where visitors were required to turn them off. Sometimes she had intentionally forgotten to turn it on again. The first time this happened, he yelled at her and told her how stupid she was, how she couldn't do anything right. The second time earned her a slap. She hoped those two times would convince him she was only absent-minded this time.

In a town along the way, she stopped at a Walmart long enough to buy a duffle bag and transfer her belongings. She would attract less attention with a duffle.

When she reached Kansas City, she drove until she found a strip of highway lined with used car lots. She drove by several times until she saw what she searched for. When she entered the lot adjacent to the Cadillac dealer, she was immediately met by a salesman.

"What can I do for you today, ma'am? You need a second vehicle? For your son or daughter, perhaps?"

"I'd like to sell my car. How much can you give me for it?"

"Well, ma'am. Let's see." He walked around the car, looking carefully for dings or signs of a wreck. He slid into the driver's seat and looked at the odometer. He popped the hood and examined the motor. Closing the hood, he asked, "Why do you want to sell this car? Are you having trouble with it?"

"I've never had a minute's trouble with it. I have some unexpected expenses and need money more than I need the car."

"Let me get my manager and see what he says."

When he returned, she heard him say to the man with him, "It's a real cream puff, and she needs the money."

She knew they would lowball her. She had researched on the internet and knew what the car was worth, but she wasn't in a position to haggle for long; time was important. She needed to be away from there before Ed realized she'd gone. When the manager finally named a price, she was pleased it was not much below what she'd expected.

"I'll take it on one condition."

"What's that?"

"I don't have a bank account in Kansas City, and I need money now. I'll take it if you'll pay me in cash or drive me to your bank and authorize them to cash the check so I can leave with cash."

"No problem, ma'am. I'll be glad to take you to our bank."

In his office, she pulled out the title, and he asked to see her driver's license. When he compared the two, he frowned. "The title says E.A. Simmons. Your license says Evelyn Simmons. You are the same person?"

"Yes, I'm Evelyn Ann Simmons. The title was made that way because it was how my name appeared on the checking account."

He grunted, accepting her explanation, and continued with the paperwork. He had no way to know E. A. on the title stood for Edward Allan and her name was Evelyn Carol. He had her sign the title and some other papers and handed her the check.

"Here you are, Ms Simmons," he said. He turned and took a key off the board behind his desk. "If you're ready, I'll drive you to our bank."

She retrieved the duffle bag from the Escalade while he pulled his car alongside. Ten minutes later, they entered the bank. He escorted her to a teller.

"Hi, Jennie. This is Ms Simmons. I bought a car from her. She wants to cash the check I gave her. Will you take care of it?"

When the teller saw the amount on the check, her eyebrows went up. "Would you like a cashier's check for this?"

"No, I need it in cash, please. Hundreds will do for most of it, but I would like about a thousand in twenties." The teller counted out the money. "Do you have a brown paper bag I can put that in?"

Jennie looked under the counter and came up with one. Evelyn put two hundred in twenties and a stack of hundred dollar bills in her purse and stowed the paper bag in the duffle bag.

"You be careful with that, ma'am. That's a lot of money to carry around."

"Yes, I will."

The car dealer said, "Is there anything else I can do for you?"

"Yes. Would you call me a taxi, please?"

He pulled out his cellphone, called information and dialed the local cab company. He relayed her request to be picked up at the bank.

"They want to know where to, ma'am?"

"The airport." He relayed the information.

Good.

She figured when Ed found the car, and he would, she would have three witnesses — the manager of the car lot, the bank teller, and the cab driver — tell him she went to the airport. She told the driver to drop her at the departure terminal of American Airlines.

Let Ed pester them to figure out which plane she took. She entered the building, and after she got her bearings she walked to the waiting area with rows of seats. She chose one away from others. She used her cellphone to call information several times. She asked for numbers for a couple of motels in Milwaukee and for American Airlines in that city. She called airlines there and asked a few questions — more to run up the time on the phone than to gain information — and called motels. She placed the cellphone on the seat and walked away.

Her next stop was the restroom, where she placed her credit card on the floor by the sink, as though it had fallen. She hoped a dishonest person would find it and use it across the country to further confuse the trail she was giving Ed.

She exited the doors by the luggage carousel. She cautiously approached a taxi, checking to be sure she it wasn't the same driver who had delivered her. When the fatherly-looking man asked, "Where to, lady?" she asked for his advice.

"I need to buy a dependable car, not a junker, but not brand new. Maybe a Toyota or a Honda. Can you take me to a car lot where I could get a reliable one?"

"Sure, lady. I'll take you where we bought my wife's car. They treated us right there. Honest folks." He wheeled into traffic, chatting all the way about his wife, her car, their kids and their cars. "You moving here?"

"Yes, and the first thing I need to do is get some transportation. Then I'll look for an apartment."

The used car lot he dropped her at was exactly what she had in mind, and she left with a Toyota only a few years old. She paid cash for it, which would make the salesman remember her. She was sure most people, even if they paid for the car in full, would write a check. She had asked the salesman what part of town she should look to find an apartment.

After she drove through a fast-food place, she got on I-70 and headed east. She drove an hour, and then pulled off the interstate at small towns along the way. At the third one, she found what she was looking for, a small beauty shop in front of a house. The sign said OPEN but there were no cars in front. She pulled in, hoped for luck, and went through the door. The woman dropped her *People* magazine and hopped up when Evelyn entered.

"Do you have time to take me without an appointment?"

"I sure do, honey! Sit right down here," the woman said. She turned the chair around for Evelyn. "What do you want done to that pretty blonde hair?"

"I want it cut short. It's hot, and I want it real short for summer. And I want to change colors. I think I want a medium brown."

"My name is Sue, honey, and I can do that." She gathered up the hair that reached to Evelyn's shoulders. "We'll have it off quick as a wink, and you'll be just as pretty as a brunette as you are as a blonde."

While she tucked a towel around Evelyn's neck, she had to pull the scarf away. Evelyn heard the beautician suck in her breath when she saw the ugly purple and yellow splotches on her neck and shoulders. Evelyn had kept it hidden from everyone she knew all those years, but she was starting a new life.

"You're running away, ain't you? Don't tell me. I know. I won't say a thing. If he comes looking for you, you ain't been here."

Evelyn didn't say a word. She didn't know what to say, and she didn't want to get into a conversation with Sue about her problems. It didn't matter. Sue talked enough for both of them. When she was finished, Evelyn's hair was brown with auburn highlights. The new style was shorter than she had ever worn it, and she couldn't help but stare at herself in the mirror.

Sue threw her arms around her, and they gently hugged. She held Evelyn's hands and said, "You take care of yourself. This is on the house. No, no, I won't take a penny. You see, I was in your shoes one time and someone helped me. I'm a great believer in paying it forward and backward and every which way, so when you get to where you're going and get on your feet, you help someone who needs helpin.' That'll be enough for me."

* * *

Back on the road, she reached St. Louis late that evening and spent the night. The next morning, she headed south on I-55. If she hadn't been nervous about getting far away from Ed, she would have enjoyed the scenery. As it was, she passed through miles of delta land, white heads of cotton showing among the green leaves, almost without seeing it. When she reached West Memphis, she decided it was time to change cars. Ed might have discovered what car she was driving. Although he was probably looking for her up north, it was better to be safe than sorry. This time, she took a chance on being truthful, sort of. The big car lot she picked had late-model cars of all kinds, but the salesman had a problem understanding her needs.

"Lady, if there's nothing wrong with your car, and you don't want a newer one, why do you want to get rid of this one?"

"I'm embarrassed to tell you, but I'm running away from my boyfriend. See here?" She pulled the neck of the sweater down over her shoulder. "See this?" she pushed up the sleeves. "He did this, and he may be looking for this car and me. I just want a different one."

Once Sue had been broken ice, she had no trouble using her injuries to her advantage. When the salesman saw her bruises, he grimaced and looked at the ground, a muscle in his jaw jumped as he held it tight. He dropped his head and murmured an expletive.

"If I can get to Florida, where I have family, I'll be safe. I don't want to spend any more money than I have to."

Finally, the man understood and sympathized. He traded her car in on another Toyota of a different color, but same year and less mileage. It cost her two-hundred dollars difference. When the transaction was completed, she left.

She spent that night in Vicksburg, and the next day she reached her destination, New Orleans, the city full of possibilities, the city where she could hide from Ed.

Hopefully, it would be the city where she would be safe.

When she arrived, she drove all over town, looking for a place to light. She had it all planned to this point, but since she had never been to New Orleans, and the internet could only tell so much, she had no idea where to look for a place to stay. She had to be careful with her money. She had ideas about how to earn more, and she could sell her jewelry — her engagement and wedding rings alone should bring a good sum — but she needed to be wise with the remaining cash.

She found herself in an older part of the city, not on the tourist paths, but close, when her stomach growled. She realized she was hungry for the first time in days. She had eaten because she knew she should, not because she wanted food. Now the thought of a meal sounded good. There was a parking place right in front of a little café called Simon's Place.

The red brick building sat on a corner, and the door was kitty-cornered to the quiet intersection. A folding blackboard sat on the sidewalk to announce the special of the day: jambalaya. She went in and took a seat, glancing around at the homey-looking place.

Evelyn studied the menu, trying to figure out what the strange names were: jambalaya, gumbo, etouffe, muffaletta.

How am I going to figure out what to order?

It was almost like a foreign country.

An old woman entered the almost-empty café. "Simon, how you be? The spirits done sent me to you. I come for a glass of your lemonade and one of your fried pies."

The big black man spoke with evident pleasure at seeing the old woman. "Madame! It is an honor to have you visit! We have peach pies. The apple is all gone."

"*La pêche,* she is best anyway. Bring me one and a glass of lemonade with jest a l'il bit of ice."

She sat at the table next to Evelyn's.

Evelyn tried not to stare, but she couldn't help looking at the woman. She was dressed in a white blouse and a long skirt the same brown as her skin, her head wrapped in a turban of red, green and yellow. A multitude of necklaces hung around her neck. She had never seen anyone dressed like that.

The woman looked back at Evelyn, her brown eyes twinkling.

"I 'magine you're new here. Can you make sense of the food you see on the menu?"

"No, I can't. I was trying to decide what to take a chance on. I'm so hungry, I probably could eat anything."

"If you haven't tried Cajun food, maybe it be best to start slow. Simon, he makes a powerful good ham sandwich. You like that, *chère?*"

"Yes, a ham sandwich sounds delicious."

Simon approached with Madame's order. "Simon, you make this here lady one of your bodacious ham sandwiches. She's not tried Cajun food before. Give her a little bowl of sumpin' to start getting her taste educated."

The women talked while Evelyn waited for her food.

"You ever be to N'Awlins before?"

"No. I've never been this far south." Evelyn hoped the old lady wouldn't ask where she was from.

"You never have any gumbo or jambalaya?"

"No, I haven't. I'm looking forward to trying some."

Simon brought her sandwich and a small bowl filled with some sort of rice dish with onions, peppers, sausage and shrimp.

"This here's jambalaya," he said. "Most folks around here like it real spicy, but I was light on the red pepper for you."

Evelyn liked the jambalaya, and the ham sandwich so thick it was difficult to bite into.

She was glad the question of where she was from didn't come up. For some reason, she didn't want to lie to the lady Simon called Madame, but she didn't want to tell the truth, either.

They were finished eating when Madame said, "You wouldn't happen to be looking for a place to live would you?"

"Why, yes. Yes, I am."

"I rent a few apartments down in the next block. I have one empty right now, and I be needin' someone to move in. It's all furnished and everythin.' You come see. You'll be likin' it." She folded her napkin and placed it beside her plate.

Evelyn paused. It was a coincidence, the old lady with an apartment for rent when she needed one. She liked the neighborhood, with its brick sidewalks and trees along the small businesses that lined the street.

Madame saw the hesitation and said, "You don't know me, but I be safe. My house is safe. Tell her, Simon, tell her it be a good place to live."

Simon's smile lit up. "That be so, Miss. Madame's place is the safest place in the city. No harm'll come to you under her roof. You be one lucky lady; she likes you."

"I guess I can come see it, before I decide."

"That's right. We can just walk. If you take it, you can move your car to the garage in the back." The old woman stood and picked up her cane, an ornately carved piece of dark wood with what appeared to be a carved snake twisting around it, its head forming the end of the handle.

Evelyn opened her purse to pay for her meal but Simon waved his hand to stop her. "Madame, she always eat free here. An' you, this is your first meal here. It's free as a way of saying welcome to the neighborhood. Any friend of Madame's is welcome here."

* * *

When Evelyn first saw the flat, a second-story apartment that overlooked a secluded courtyard, she felt she had come home. It was furnished with pieces that looked like they had been there for over a hundred years. Perhaps, she figured, they had been. A beautiful walnut secretary sat against one wall, with a sturdy chair ready to pull up to the fold down shelf. A comfortable armchair, covered in faded chintz, was placed next to a table with a lamp, all ready to settle down with a good book. Tall ceilings allowed heat to rise, where it escaped through transoms. It felt like a home, not just a rented *pied-à-terre*. Covered parking in the back of the building would keep her car out of sight.

"Oh, this is lovely! But I doubt I can afford it."

When Madame quoted the monthly price, Evelyn was stunned at how low it was.

"I'll take it," she said, before the old lady changed her mind.

CHAPTER TWO

*"Dani, fetch me a loaf of bread from the corner grocery, an' I'll give
you a nickel."*

*"Take this package to Sister Jones's house for me, Dani. Here's a
dime for your trouble."*

*"Dani, would you go to the park, and tell the children to come
home? I'll give you a quarter when you bring them back."*

A quarter was a lot of money. The coins went into a jar Dani
kept in her grandmother's dresser drawer.

When she had first moved in with her grandmother, most of the
things she wore were from the church's mission to the poor.
Grandmother spent what little money she had on Dani's underwear
and socks. At least those were new, but everything else had been
someone else's first. When she was small, it didn't matter much, but
as she grew older, she saw the differences in how other girls
dressed.

Dani didn't spend her coins on sodas and candy, the way most
kids might. She knew she couldn't go into a regular store and buy
new clothes with her nickels, dimes, quarters and dollars, so she
shopped at thrift stores.

After saving up a few dollars, she got on her old bike — the one
the church gave her one year for Christmas — and went shopping,
with a basket to hold her purchases. wired onto the handlebars

One day she discovered a marvelous new shopping venue, yard
sales. This had opened Dani's eyes to a whole new world. Memphis
was full of yard, rummage, garage and estate sales. Instead of
paying a dollar or two at a thrift shop, she could find clothes for a
quarter or fifty cents. She would pick up a copy of the *Thrifty
Nickel* every week and scan ads for sales in her part of town.

"Look, Granny, what I found today at a rummage sale."

"Now don't that look pretty? We can sew up that seam and it'll
be good as new. My, what people do get rid of when it can be
fixed."

"Granny, do you have a button in your box that matches these? It
was only a quarter, and the only thing wrong is a missing button."

Dani's grandmother taught her to sew when Dani was young, not long after Children's Protective Services took her from her drug-addled mother. By the time she was eight, she could sew a button or fix a dragging hemline. When she was ten, her grandmother taught her to use the sewing machine. Actually, she taught Dani to use two sewing machines. First, she learned to use the treadle machine that originally belonged to Grandmother's grandmother.

"You've got the pedaling down pat, child. Now let me show you how to fill a bobbin."

She learned how to slip the belt on and off and how to sew a straight line without putting the needle through her finger.

"I can sew straight, Granny. See? Teach me something else."

"You knows all about that ol' treadle. It's time you started on the electric one."

By the time Dani was in eighth grade, she had also learned several things about fashion. She knew that the differences between what was in fashion twenty or thirty years ago and what was in fashion today were slight and could be corrected with a little alteration. Sometimes the things that were in fashion twenty years ago were made better. Plus, they were unique and original, because they weren't found in stores. Decades-old clothing was considered vintage, and therefore, desirable.

By the time Dani entered high school, she had her own style. It drew favorable comments from classmates and teachers alike.

"Where did you get that cute jacket, Dani? I'd like one," girls would say.

"Oh, at a little shop over ..." she would vaguely wave her hand. "It was a going out of business sale." *Yeah, an estate sale that only lasted one weekend.*

The clothes that brought Dani the most compliments were the things she constructed herself. She took parts of one thing and added to something else and came up with an original design.

"Those jeans are so cool, Dani. Where did you get them?"

"I made them. See, I took a leg from one pair and replaced the leg of another pair. I took these patches and put them all over."

"Will you make me a pair, Dani? Please? How much would you charge for them?"

Even the boys came to her. "I have all these NASA patches my uncle gave me. Can you put them on my jacket for me?"

"Can you make jeans out of a bunch of different ones for guys, like you do girls?"

She soon sold ten pair at fifty dollars apiece. Of course, every pair was unique but in the same style as the others, which was what Dani's customers liked. No one could turn up in exactly the same jeans as someone else, yet they were all wearing the same style.

Even the teachers liked the skirts and blouses Dani dressed up with ribbon, buttons, and beads. She would buy clothes of good style and fabric even if she didn't have something they matched or they weren't her size, and add her magic touch to them.

When a teacher complimented her on her blouse, Dani said, "I have one in size twelve, maroon cotton with ribbon, and three different kinds of beads. Would you like to see it?"

"I'd like to see anything you have in size twelve. I love your style."

That was her first sale to a teacher but not the last.

When Dani turned sixteen, she landed a job at Dairy Queen and saved her money. She wasn't going to be one of those girls who hung around the neighborhood, flirting with the boys, doing nothing and going nowhere.

"Granny, do you think I could go to college? My guidance counselor says my grades are good enough."

"Honey lamb, you can do anything you set your mind to."

"Maybe I can get a scholarship to Memphis State. I want to be a fashion designer."

Every minute she wasn't in school or sleeping, she spent working or making clothes. Everywhere she turned she found new ideas.

One day she came home with a surprise. "Granny, come look! I bought a car!"

"Lordy, child! A car?"

"Yes, ma'am. I need one. Now I won't have to use my bike or catch the bus. I can go to estate sales all over Memphis, even in the rich areas. With a car, I can find shops where I can sell my designs on consignment. I gave $1200 for the car, and I'll bet I make that much back by having it. I can take you to buy groceries or to your doctor's appointments. The car will make life easier for both of us."

Things were going well for Dani and her grandmother, but one night in her senior year, her world crashed.

She worked the late shift that Saturday night. When she got off, she walked around to the back lot where employees parked their cars. A carload of boys pulled in. "Hey, girl! Y'all closed? We want some hamburgers and fries!"

"We're closed for the night. Come back tomorrow."

They were too drunk to listen. Finally, one of them said, "She said go someplace else, fellows. Let's take her with us to show us the way."

Two of them jumped out and grabbed her and pushed her into the backseat. She screamed, but it did no good. One of them even said, "That's right, I like it when you fight back."

They raped her, all four of them. Then they took her back to the Dairy Queen and shoved her out beside her car.

She lay on the hot pavement for a while, all the fight, all the anger, all her optimism for life draining out of her like the blood and semen escaping her body. Nothing was left in Dani but despair. After a while she got up and got her keys out of her pocket — thank heavens they were still there — and drove home. She woke her grandmother, who held her and cried with her. It wouldn't do any good to go to the police, Granny said.

"They'll say you was willin.' They'll just say you was out partyin' an' just wanted some money from them."

"But I wasn't, Granny, honest," Dani sobbed into her shoulder.

"I knows, sweetheart, I knows. You's a good girl. You don't do none of that stuff, but that's what them boys'll say. And who do you think the police is gonna believe? Four white boys or a pretty black girl?"

She tried her best to stop thinking about that night. In the daylight, when she was busy, she could push it out of her mind. At night, it was a different story. She cried herself to sleep and woke each morning remembering terrible dreams in which she relived the rape.

When she missed her next period it was soon obvious she was pregnant. She thought about having an abortion. She had the money for it in her bank account, so that wasn't what stopped her. It was the thought of taking a life, part of her, her baby, and doing away with it. Although she lived through the shame of being raped, she didn't think she could handle an abortion. She considered giving up the baby for adoption. She did some research on the computer she

24

bought a year before at an estate sale to help her with schoolwork, and found that although there were many childless couples looking for newborns to adopt they overwhelmingly wanted white babies. The black couples wanting a newborn wanted a black newborn. Nobody wanted a half-white half-black baby. Maybe it was because her own mother didn't want her enough to straighten up and keep her, but Dani was determined that her baby would be loved and wanted, as well as cared for in every way she knew how.

"Don't you worry about it none," her grandmother said. "We'll make it fine, and your baby's gonna have a lovin' mama and a lovin' granny. I done started gettin' my Social Security, and I can take care of the l'il thing for you while you works. You'll be graduatin' from high school shortly, and maybe you can work full-time after that, until it gets close to your time, so's you can buy what all you needs."

Her hopes of college were gone.

When she graduated, no one knew she was pregnant, so she was spared the comments of her classmates. Unfortunately, graduation also ended most of her customer base. She once hoped to use her savings for college and supplies for more creations, but now she knew she would have to use it for the baby. She soon needed maternity clothes, and using her talents she was the best-dressed pregnant lady in town, at least in her opinion. When her pregnancy started showing, her friends and neighbors hinted around, trying to figure out who the father was, but Dani didn't confide in anyone. As far as she was concerned, the baby had been divinely conceived, that terrible night at last pushed so far back into the recesses of her mind it never surfaced.

Dani knew the chances were even between having a boy or a girl, but her heart told her it would be a girl. When she went to the sales she bought a couple of things for a boy, but lots of things for a girl. She learned how to take out the milk stains that marred the little dresses and onesies she bought. She even picked up some slightly larger girls clothes and did her magic on them. She would have the hippest little girl in town, attired in snazzy jeans, beaded shirts, and dresses adorned with ribbons and embroidery, a walking advertisement for her designs for little ones.

Then the baby was born. A boy.

She crooned to the tiny figure she held in her arms.

"Sweet son, I'm going to have to think of a name for you. I don't think Danielle Rose fits a boy." She tucked the blue blanket around him and held him to her cheek. "It will have a be a special name for a special little boy."

Danielle was Dani's first name, although she had gone by Dani for so long everyone she knew thought it was her real name. Rose was her grandmother's name, and she wanted to honor the person who cared for her, loved her, and sheltered her when her own mother wouldn't. She didn't have a clue about what to name a boy. She thought about Daniel as a name, but the only Daniel she knew was a bully, and besides, if she named him the same as someone in her class, people were sure to think Daniel was his father.

She had no role model to name him after. She never knew who her father was, and there wasn't a grandfather in the picture either. The only man in the family was her uncle, her aunt's husband, and he was a creep. He had been nosing around, trying to come on to her, even before she got pregnant. After a while her expanding belly marked her as easy. She did her best to avoid being caught alone with him, and one time she had to threaten to kick him in the balls if he came any closer. Grandmother knew him for what he was and stayed close to Dani whenever he came around. No role model there.

She thought about men she didn't know personally, famous people. She guessed she could name him after the President, but somehow that name didn't fit the tiny baby. She thought back to when she was a young girl, wishing for a father. She used to imagine she had one; it was just that he had to be away working all the time, making movies. Finally, after the office lady had been back twice to find out the name to put on the birth certificate, she thought of the person she used to pretend was her father. She had seen lots of his movies on TV, and watched him being interviewed a couple of times too. She thought he seemed like a nice man, strong and even-tempered, wise in his choice of roles he played. She never saw him as a deadbeat or thug. She also knew he owned a restaurant down in Mississippi, not that far away from Memphis.

"His name is Morgan Freeman," she told the office lady. "Morgan Freeman Washington."

The next few years were good ones. Dani forgot all about having wanted a girl. She loved Morgan intensely and delighted in

26

everything he did. They didn't have a lot of money, but Dani was frugal and they got by. She was even able to save some money. Every bit of extra went into the bank. The old car finally started giving her some trouble, so she traded it in at the used car lot for another one, not quite as old. She received a promotion to shift manager at Dairy Queen, and that meant a little more to put back. Sometimes she worried about whether it was too hard on her grandmother to watch Morgan, but she was assured that he was no trouble at all.

"Morgan don' give me no trouble, child. He plays all around with his lil cars and trucks, buildin' roads and such with his blocks. An' he fetches stuff for his granny," she said, looking toward the grinning boy, "Don't you? Don't you worry none about me and Morgan. We do fine."

Most evenings after supper Grandmother would go to bed early, while Dani sat at the sewing machine and worked up new garments to sell. Morgan would play at her feet and tell her about his day.

"We walked down to the corner store today, Mama. I carried the bread back home for Granny."

"You're a big help to Granny, Morgan. I'm so proud of you!"

"Yessum. I'm a helper. You want me to do something for you?"

"You can take the whisk broom and get all these scraps up off the floor and put them in the trash. There's a good boy."

Business was growing slowly. Selling at other people's shops meant she had to split the profit with the shop owner. She wished she could afford a store of her own, but rent in a good area in Memphis was high. And if she had a store, she would have to quit her job. She couldn't make it without that income and the health insurance that went with it. Even so, she was building a stock of clothing for when that day came. It would come, she knew. She didn't know how she knew, but she did.

When Morgan was four years old he came into the bedroom one morning and shook her awake. It was her day off. She was sleeping in, after staying up late the night before sewing.

"Wake up, Mama. Wake up. Something's wrong with Granny. She won't wake up."

Dani knew before she reached the other bedroom that it would be bad. Her grandmother had been feeling poorly for several days, but refused to go to the doctor. Now it was too late.

Years before, Granny had purchased a burial policy, so there was very little expense to be paid for the funeral. Before the funeral home even arrived, Dani retrieved all the money her grandmother secreted around the house. She hid in several places, all of them easily found by anyone who searched, and Dani thought it likely her uncle would start searching as soon he heard about the old lady's death. She gathered all the money together and, on the way to the funeral home that afternoon, she deposited it in her bank account.

Before she left the house she looked in the top dresser drawer, where Grandmother kept her important papers, and stuck the folder into her own purse for safekeeping. She called her aunt to tell her about her mother's passing and made an appointment to meet her at the mortuary that afternoon to complete the arrangements.

She stopped at Kwik-Kopy on the way and made a copy of the will to give to Aunt Janice. She knew what was in it, because her grandmother told her many times what Janice was to get. It was all ready to give to her: a ring Janice had always admired, a broach with garish green stones, which Janice swore were real emeralds, a pair of earrings, and underneath all that, a hundred dollar bill. Dani got everything else. The furniture and household items, which weren't worth much, the two sewing machines, which weren't of value to anyone but Dani, to whom they were precious. It all went to her.

The funeral was to be in three days, and Dani spent every one of them getting ready to leave. She had to be careful her aunt and uncle didn't find out. They were already griping about the fact that Dani got all the furniture, although what they would want with the shabby stuff she didn't know. If they knew she was going to sell it they would demand half the money. They assumed, and Dani didn't correct them, that she and Morgan would continue to live in the house.

She was afraid of her uncle. Without her grandmother there as a witness to what he might do, she didn't know if she could fight him off. He kept making references to coming over after the funeral and helping Dani go through her grandmother's things.

The funeral was at ten o'clock. By noon they were back at Saint John the Baptist Methodist Episcopal Church where the ladies auxiliary served lunch. By one-thirty Dani and Morgan were ready to go back home.

"Dani, honey, we'll just come along with you and help you go through Mama's things," her Aunt Janice said.

"Yes. We're family and we need to be there for you in your time of need," her uncle said piously as he tried to put his arm around her shoulders.

"There's no need," she replied as she evaded his grasp.

"There's all the need, sugar. We're family. I'd never forgive myself if I didn't help my niece with the sad chore." Janice wiped an invisible tear from her eye. "Mama would never forgive me if I abandoned you now when you need us most."

"Well, if you really don't mind helping…"

"Not at all. Not at all," boomed he uncle, smiling broadly. "Would you come tomorrow morning about ten? Sister Johnson and Sister Long are coming by this afternoon, and we wouldn't be able to do much." This was a lie, but if he thought other people would be there, maybe it would discourage her uncle from showing up unannounced.

"Of course. We'll be there. Now don't trouble yourself until we're there to help. No sense doing everything yourself when you have us to lend a hand."

When she and Morgan returned home, she told him to change into jeans and a tee shirt and bring her his suit. "Hurry, now. And if Aunt and Uncle show up, don't say anything to them, not anything at all."

All their clothes were packed in bags and boxes, as were the mementos she was taking, and all her sewing supplies. When he came back and handed her his suit she said, "Now run next door, quick as a wink, and tell Turrell it's time to come help me. Hurry!"

While she was waiting for the teenager to come help load the car, she called Big Eddie, the Furniture Man. He came by the day before and gave her a price on all the furniture in the house. She explained that it needed to stay until after the funeral, but when she called he needed to bring a truck and get it as fast as possible. "Big Eddie? I'll be ready for you to pick up the furniture in half an hour. Bring plenty of help so you can get it quickly."

When Turrell came, she had him put as many boxes as would fit in the trunk of the car, along with the electric sewing machine. The treadle machine went in the back seat — barely. She had measured ahead of time to be sure it would. She didn't know what she would have done if she couldn't have gotten it in. It was too precious for her to leave behind. A lot of the clothing she put in black trash bags, which could be maneuvered around everything else. When at last everything was in and the doors really would close, she turned to Turrell. "Thank you so much. I couldn't have done it without your help," she said as she handed him a twenty-dollar bill.

As Turrell returned home, Big Ed pulled up with his truck and two helpers jumped out. "Everything else is yours," she said.

It only took about forty-five minutes for the house to be completely empty, as if they had never lived there. Big Ed pulled a roll of money from his pocket and counted out five one hundred dollar bills. "But you said you would give me seven hundred dollars!" Dani was angry.

"You took the sewing machines. I had counted those in the price."

Dani knew she had emphasized the fact that the sewing machines were going with her, but Big Eddie knew he had her. "You want me to unload all this, lady?" He started to put the money back in his pocket.

"No. You're cheating me. You know that and I know that. But what goes around comes around, so you better watch out for who cheats you, Big Eddie."

She took the money and called Morgan to come get in the car. "Let's go, sugar. Let's go start a new life — after a couple of stops."

She took the keys to the house by the rental office and told them she had moved out. "We'll have to check for damage before we can return any deposit."

"That's okay, just keep it," she said. When they looked at their records they would find that Granny had lived in that house for twenty-five years. If she had put up any deposit it would be small, and she was sure they would find something they would have to fix.

"We need a forwarding address for you, Miss Washington."

"I'm moving to Chicago. I don't have a place yet, but I'll send it to you when I get settled."

Yeah, when pigs fly.

Next she stopped at the bank and closed her savings account. She let the checking account go low, so she left that. She knew she didn't have any checks out, and she didn't want to get in a conversation with the bank about a forwarding address. She had picked up her check for last week's work at the Dairy Queen the day before and cashed it instead of depositing it like she usually did, but she didn't give notice when she was there. She was afraid it would get back to her aunt and uncle. She would call DQ tomorrow from somewhere on the road. They had been good to her there, and she hated to leave them like this but it couldn't be helped. The day before she also filled out a notice at the post office to hold all her mail until she sent them a forwarding address.

All of this done, the only thing left was shutting off the utilities. She had a phone book with her and would call tomorrow to take care of the matter. It was time to get on the road. She wouldn't get very far today, but she had time to get out of Memphis and out of Tennessee before they stopped for the night.

"Are we really moving to Chicago?" Morgan asked.

"No, sugar. We're moving someplace a whole lot better. We're moving to New Orleans."

CHAPTER THREE
Nine months ago

"Those are such dweeb classes," her sister Julia said one night at the dinner table. "Why don't you take something fun?"

Their father smiled and said, "Now, now. Not every girl can marry a man who will support and take care of her. Diane needs to take classes to learn things that will help her get a good job."

Their mother smiled and put her hand on his arm, looking at him adoringly. Diane knew they expected Julia to marry well, but plain Diane would have to take care of herself.

Diane wasn't anything special. She knew it, and knew her parents agreed with Julia. She took all those business classes — keyboarding, accounting, computers — because she knew she was going to need them someday.

"They may not be exactly *fun*," Diane replied, "but they're interesting to me. I like the classes I'm taking." She willed away the ache she felt at her father's statement.

Diane had started to think of herself as a dweeb at a very young age. She knew it was so because her big sister, Julia, who knew everything, said she was. Julia was all the time saying, "Diane, you are such a dweeb!" and Diane knew by the way Julia said it that it was a bad thing to be. Julia was the exact opposite of a dweeb. She was head cheerleader, homecoming queen, and voted most popular girl in the senior class.

When Julia graduated from high school, she took a job as hostess at the country club. She didn't have any experience at the job, but she didn't need any experience to seat people at tables. She figured it was a good place to meet a rich man. There was no talk of going to college, since her grades were barely good enough to graduate from high school.

"I don't think I could run the office without Diane's help," her father said, exaggerating her usefulness. "When I retire in a few years, she'll be able to take over the business."

Not a chance. No way am I going to stay here in Julia's shadow.

She worked after school, on Saturdays, and every summer, at her father's insurance agency and put the money she earned in her savings account. Although she didn't tell anyone except her best friend, Connie, she was saving the money to leave town as soon as she graduated. Although she could have gone to college — her parents would have paid for it — she was tired of school and ready to start a new life out from under Julia's influence. To be a new Diane.

"I am so ready for this," Diane said as she and Connie packed their belongings into their respective cars and headed for New Orleans, keeping in touch with each other by cell phone on the way. They figured New Orleans was a good spot to start their adulthood. It was only a short day's drive from home, but as different from north Louisiana as another city in the same state could be.

They stayed in a Motel Six the first night and found a furnished apartment the next day.

"This looks the same as a cheap apartment back home," Connie said, looking around the small flat. "I thought New Orleans would be different."

"It will be," Diane replied. "Once we get out there and see what the city has to offer. It's going to be very different. I know it. And we can fix this place up to suit ourselves."

The next day they looked for jobs.

Mrs. James, head of personnel at the Preferred Insurance Company's head office, the second place they applied, interviewed them together. She questioned them about their duties in their respective jobs: Connie's at a pest control company and Diane's at her father's insurance office.

"Sit right here while I go check your references," she said after forty-five minutes.

When Mrs. James returned, she hired both of them. "This is your lucky day, ladies. A file clerk didn't show up for work today, it's her third time to do that, so she's just lost her job. And we were already short one person. I'm impressed with the office experience each of you has, and with the classes you took in school. I'm hiring both of you, but you won't work in the same department."

Diane's job was okay — boring but okay — and Connie was satisfied with hers. Connie made friends quickly, but Diane was her usual shy self. She always thought of herself as plain, and she was definitely not outgoing. Moving to New Orleans was the bravest thing she had ever done. Her goal of becoming a 'new Diane' wasn't much happening.

"You're going to have to stop comparing yourself to Julia," Connie told her. "Not many girls can live up to her."

Julia, who was tall and slim with blonde hair and turquoise eyes, was outgoing and popular. She looked like their mother but taller. Diane took after her father, brown hair and blue eyes — kept hidden behind glasses — but short, like their mother.

"I know, I'm trying."

After a couple of months, at Connie's urging, Diane got contact lenses to replace her glasses and a permanent wave to turn her straight hair into a mass of curls. The humidity so common to New Orleans kept it curly without any work on her part.

Connie said, "Now you look kind of like Meg Ryan."

Diane didn't see the resemblance.

One Friday after work, the women in the department where Diane worked said, "Come and join us. We're going to Le Chat Noir to have a drink and listen to the singer-piano player. Everyone says he's great!"

"I'm just eighteen and I can't drink."

"Oh, pooh," one of them replied. "You can drink a soda, if you don't want anything stronger. Don't be such a stick-in-the-mud."

So the group went into Le Chat Noir, The Black Cat, to listen to the pianist and Diane was immediately enthralled. The music reached her spirit, her heart, her very core. When she moved closer so she could hear better and see in the dim light, she saw a man with curly blonde hair, maybe in his mid-twenties, sitting at the baby grand piano. He sang for the first time since the group of women came in. The song was "Just the Way You Are Tonight," and Diane fell in love.

Diane found out his name was Scott Ballew. He played there four evenings a week, from Wednesday through Saturday. She started to drop by every night when he worked, buying a diet soda, and listening to him play. After a week she got up enough nerve to speak to him.

"That was great. I love Cole Porter music, and you play it so well."

"He's one of my favorites. Of course I have a lot of favorites," he said. He paused to take a drink of water from the glass the bartender kept on the piano. "Who else do you like?"

"Oh, lots of composers. Most anything from the thirties or forties, and some from the fifties and sixties."

"How about the Beatles?"

"Oh, yes. Certainly the Beatles." He played and sang "Yesterday".

From then on Diane bought her soda when she came in and went to the piano and chatted with Scott. He asked her to sit at the little table next to the piano with the RESERVED sign on it and visit with him when he took his break around ten o'clock. When he went back to playing she left to go home and get enough sleep so she could work the next day. If not for work, she would have stayed until the bar closed at two in the morning.

This went on for several weeks until Diane, despairing that Scott would never ask to see her outside Le Chat Noir, decided to ask advice from a couple of girls she worked with.

Yesenia said, "You need to go see Madame an' ask her for help."

"Who is Madame?"

"Girl! Madame is just about the most famous hoodoo woman in N'Orleans. She can help you get him. She can do anything!"

Jeanine agreed. "She can whomp up a spell or potion for anything a body would want. She helped me out when I needed it. I had an eye for Tyrone, but he didn't pay me no mind, so I went to Madame for a spell, and now we're married."

"That's true," said Yesenia. "You go see Madame and she'll fix you up. He won't be able to resist you."

* * *

"I think it is a terrible idea. You need to forget it!" Connie told her as they shared lunch in the small park across the street from their office building.

"Jeanine and Yesenia say Madame Badeaux is the real thing. It's going to work, you watch and see."

"If you can't interest a man without resorting to hoodoo, he's not the right man for you. You're going to spend all your money and maybe hurt someone, too."

"If I was pretty, like you, I might could interest a man, some man," she paused as she ate another bite of her po-boy, "But I want *this* man. This particular man. We are so perfect for each other. We like the same music and books. We can talk about anything. It's like we have known each other forever."

"Then what's the problem? He already likes you without putting juju on him."

"The problem is he doesn't ask me for a date."

"Where did you meet this man? Is it someone we work with?"

"No. Connie, I've told you about him before. It's Scott Ballew, the man who plays the piano and sings at Le Chat Noir several nights a week. I drop in there and we talk while he's playing."

"Yes, you've told me about him." Connie shrugged as she took a swallow of soda. Diane's stories of the terrific pianist hadn't impressed her.

"Does he act interested in you at all?"

"Sometimes when I get there he's sitting at the table next to the piano having a drink. When I speak to him he says, 'Sit down, Diane. Sit down and visit with me,' and I do. If he's playing, when it comes time for his break he says, 'Stay and visit with me during my break.' But he doesn't ask me out. If I were pretty he would, I know he would."

"So what are you going to ask Madame Badeaux for? A spell to make you pretty? A spell to make him see you as pretty? A spell to make him fall in love with you? What?"

"I don't know. I'll explain it to Madame and ask her what is best."

"We'd better hurry if we are going to get back to work on time."

They got up and put the wrappings from their lunches into a trash barrel.

"I still think you are making a mistake to turn to hoodoo," Connie said as they crossed the street. "I won't wish you luck, but I'll wish that everything works out for the best."

* * *

A tinkling bell announced Diane's arrival at the small shop. Off the tourist paths, in a section frequented mostly by locals, the place gave no welcome to entice customers to enter. The windows on either side of the door were filled with a hodge-podge of items. She noticed candlesticks, boxes, figurines, green and blue bottles, and pieces of wood of unknown use or origin. The only light in the place came from small lamps on the countertops, shaded with beadwork or filmy cloth. Diane was wondering if the place was deserted until a voice spoke from the shadows.

"You have come for help. Yes?"

Diane walked further into the shop, stopping when she saw a wizened old woman behind the counter. If she were less polite, she would have called her a crone, or even a witch. Although she had put on a brave front to Connie, she was shaking inside as she thought about what she was about to ask of this woman.

"I need a spell, or a potion, or something."

"And what makes you think I can provide such a thing?"

"My friend, Jeanine, came to you and you helped her with something to attract a man. A certain man. And now they are married and happy. So I thought you could help me, too."

"Ah, yes. Jeanine. And of course it worked for her. My spells always work. Do you have a man in mind for this plan?"

"Yes, certainly. We know each other, we talk and laugh together, but he doesn't ask me out. He is very good looking, while I am very plain, as you can see."

"Do you work together, you and this man of yours? Or do you live near each other?"

"No. I work at an insurance agency, and he plays the piano in the evenings at *Le Chat Noir*. I have been going there for weeks and we have become friends. He says, 'Come stand here by the piano and visit with me, Diane,' so I do. And sometimes we sit at the table that is reserved for him, and we talk."

"And why does he not ask to see you away from *Le Chat Noir*, out to some other establishment on a date, do you think? Is he married, perhaps?"

"He doesn't wear a wedding ring. And I think — no I'm sure — we have talked of both of us being single."

"Some other reason, then, hmmm?"

"I think it's because I'm not pretty. He is so good looking he could have any girl he wants. Why would he chose someone plain, like me?"

The old woman moved down the counter into the glow of the lamp. A turban wrapped her head in brightly colored cloth, while the light played on her wrinkle-covered skin. Around her neck hung multiple strands of beads, shells, glass, and what Diane thought looked like bones.

"Tell me what you want of me. Do you want a potion to make him love you and only you? Or do you want a milder potion to entrance him? Do you want a spell to make yourself pretty? Think very carefully about this. I make strong juju. You must be sure of what you want and the dangers, as well as the benefits, of having such a thing granted to you."

"I was hoping you could tell me, help me decide, what I need, Madame."

"Hmm. You are wise to depend on my advice. Some girls come into my shop and want what they want. They do not listen to me. The results are sometimes not what they expected."

"I will listen to you."

"Well then, you do not want the potion and spell to make him love you and only you. I told a girl this once, and she ignored my words. She insisted that was what she wanted. They married and he loved only her. He no longer loved his parents and his brothers and his sisters. They had a child and he did not love the child. He followed his wife around wherever she went. She could never be alone. He loved her so much he wanted to be by her side at all times. It like to drove her crazy. She fell out of love with him, and she paid me to take the spell off him. It was a very difficult spell to reverse, and it cost her big."

"Then I do not want that spell."

Madame Badeaux turned and reached into a basket behind her. She drew out a small red bag with a long drawstring. Diane watched as the old woman gathered items from the jars, boxes and baskets that lined the shelves. She placed on the counter beside the bag a piece of root that looked strangely like two people holding hands, a wrinkled black bean, dried leaves of various kinds, and small stones. One of the stones glinted red when the light struck it, and another appeared to be a smooth opaque blue. Finally Madame placed them one by one into the bag and pulled the drawstring closed.

"This here be your mojo bag. Put the strings around your neck and wear it all the time. If you want to wear a low-cut dress, put the bag in your pocket, but it be best worn around your neck so it will be close to your heart." She reached under the counter and drew out a small brown paper bag. Reaching high, she pulled down a basket filled with what appeared to be dried mistletoe and put three handfuls into the sack.

"Each night for three nights, use this to make a tea. Be sure you do not drink this tea, for it be poison. Draw your bath and pour in the tea. Soak in the bath water, and splash it all over you, but don't get it in your mouth or eyes. Do this for three nights in a row, no longer."

She again reached under the counter and got another small brown paper sack, in which she placed a small amount of dried leaves from a jar on the shelves. "Go to the market and buy some fresh parsley to mix with this jasmine. Put some in your shoes when you go to see your man." She paused and studied Diane's face.

"Now all that is fine and good, but you must use a spell for the best results. Do you have something you can write on, so you can do it just so when the time comes?"

Diane dug into her purse. "Oh, yes, Madame. I'll write it here, in my notebook."

"First, you have to find just the right spot in your house. It must be a place where you can leave a candle safely burning for three days." She went to a far corner and brought back a large red pillar candle. "You put this on a plate, so as to catch any drippings, and so it will be secure and can't be knocked over." She put the candle in the gathering of items. "Then you get your Bible to hand. You do have a Bible, don't you?"

"Yes, Madame, certainly."

"You turn to "Song of Solomon," the fourth chapter, and you read that whole chapter out loud three times. Then you lay the Bible on the table next to the candle, face up, still open to that place, with the top of the pages pointing east. Each day for three more days you read that chapter out loud one time, and you put the good book back just so, with the top pointing east. At the end of the three days, you can blow out the candle and close the Bible and put it away. Don't do the spell any longer than that." She reached under the counter and pulled out a larger brown paper bag and put all the items and sacks into it.

When Diane heard what it would cost her to gain what she so desired, she was glad she had thought to empty her meager savings account and bring with her, but her hand trembled as she counted out the bills.

"I see you shake, chère, at spending so much, but me, I guarantee my spells. If he don't desire you, you come back and I'll give you another mojo, free. All these things are to work on you, to make you desirable. If that don't work, we do a spell on him, to make him see you, see the real you, the inside and outside of you." The old woman grinned widely. "An' if that don't work, we do a powerful spell to make him fall in love with you." Her expression became grave, "But we try to get him to fall in love on his own, without hexing him. It is better that way, to give him little nudges to do it on his own. Give these things time to work. Don't be in no hurry. The good things, they will come."

Her sudden cackle startled Diane, and she gathered up her purchases, murmured words of thanks, and left. The old woman frightened her, but that was okay if the potions and spells worked. She could stand being a little scared to get what she wanted.

CHAPTER FOUR

Addie waited for another shoe to drop. It would. She knew it would. She just didn't know when. Her life came in patterns, in cycles. When she dropped a glass and broke it, it was a sure thing she would drop two more things and break them. If a crazy driver ran a stoplight and almost hit her, she better watch out because two more crazy drivers were going to show up in her life. Maybe not today, or tomorrow, but sometime this week, they'd be there, so she'd better be careful.

Of course it worked for good things, too. If she found a dollar bill in the pocket of a jacket she hadn't worn since last winter, then she would find more unexpected money. It might only be a dime she found on the ground, or a check in the mail for a two-dollar rebate, but hey, money is money. It's the pattern that's important.

Of course, not everything in the world happened in threes, but Addie could usually tell when something was the start of a pattern. She would get a funny feeling, sort of quivery, the kind she got when she was a little kid when it was almost Christmas and she thought she couldn't wait another day, or the kind of feeling she had waiting for the announcement of who made cheerleader. When Addie got that feeling she knew more was to come, and something important, too. So she was waiting for the second thing to happen, and from the way her insides jumped around it was going to be something big.

The first thing had been her boyfriend breaking up with her.

"I just don't think this is working out," he told her. She had that quivery feeling, knowing there would be more to come. Addie wasn't surprised he thought it wasn't working out. She didn't think it was working out either. Tom didn't understand about the Rule of Threes, or coincidence that wasn't really coincidence, but a sign. He thought she was flaky; she thought he was uptight.

They didn't live together. Addie couldn't stand to even stay one night in his apartment. She thought it was like being in a hospital. Tom had everyone pull their shoes off when they came in the door. Everything was white and the furniture was chrome and glass. The only color in the place was in the few splashes the pictures made. There were no knick-knacks, no books, and no interesting things to puzzle over or make up stories about. She found his apartment cold and boring.

On the other hand, Tom didn't see how Addie could live in the clutter of her home. Her house held all the memories and mementoes of her life and her mother's life; framed pictures of her grandparents, her parents and herself were here and there throughout the rooms; a couple of her childhood paintings were framed and hung in the upstairs hall; shelves held curios and keepsakes.

Whenever something would catch her interest, Addie would search out books about it. She was currently interested in Irish faeries, leprechauns, gemstones and jewelry design. Books on these subjects sat in piles near where she tended to sit and read. Yard sales drew her like magnets, and the treasures she found at them adorned the rooms. Baskets held unusual balls. Teapots were filled with flowers from the grocery store. Old quilts were thrown over chairs and beds. Tom called it cluttered. Addie called it eclectic.

The way she dressed was a point of contention between them. She liked bits and pieces from various decades. The vintage clothing store was one of her favorite places to shop. One time when they met Tom's friends for dinner she wore a dress from the '40s with a piano shawl as a wrap. Tom thought it not appropriate. Well, tough! Addie figured it was her body and she would adorn it as she saw fit.

He was a three-piece suit kind of person. Addie couldn't define her style. He called it 'hippy,' but she didn't like many of the fashions from that period and seldom wore them. He couldn't understand the distinction between the clothing of the '30s, '40's and '50s and that of the '60s and '70s.

Addie couldn't figure out how they stayed together so long. Her friend, Gina, talked her into a blind date with Tom over six months prior, and they just kept on going out until they somehow drifted into a relationship. It wasn't like they were madly in love or anything. It was more like they were too lazy to find anyone else.

So they were over. Finished. Kaput. Addie wasn't sad over this, only waiting for the next thing to happen — number two of three.

She was thinking about that while she drove to meet her best friends, Gina and Karen, for dinner. She wondered what the pattern would be. It couldn't be breaking up with boyfriends, because she didn't have any others. She hoped it wouldn't be breaking up with friends in general because she had been friends with Gina and Karen since high school. They had remained close through college and now they met at the Lamplighter for dinner every other Thursday night to stay caught up on each other's lives.

* * *

Gina raised her glass of wine in a toast. "Here's to the new Human Resources Manager of Superior Manufacturing. May her light shine."

Karen grinned while the other two women tipped their glasses toward her. "Thanks, ladies."

"Have you moved into your new office yet?" Addie asked.

"Yeah, I moved in today. Of course I didn't have much to move. My secretary helped me."

"Your secretary? Well, la-di-dah. Aren't you something?"

"What about that jerk who was telling everybody he was going to get the job? Are you having any trouble out of him?"

"Not really. He's telling everybody I only got the job because the company had to fill quotas on blacks and women, but everybody knows what a jerk he is. He didn't get the job because he stands around and talks while he pushes his work off on other people."

"He won't be around long then, if he doesn't do his job."

"I only hope I don't have to fire him. I will if I have to, you understand, but I hope he moves on along on his own. How about you, Addie. Are you looking forward to the end of school?"

"Sort of. I love my kindergarteners, but it will be nice to have the summer off. I feel so restless, though, that I don't have a clue about what I want to do this summer. Probably just lay out at the pool and get a tan." She stretched out her arms. "I think I look better with a tan, and I always get so pale during the winter months."

"You be careful, girl. You white folks sho' do sunburn easy," Karen said in a put-on dialect.

"Yes, Addie, especially blondes. Don't get burned. It can lead to skin cancer," added Gina. She sat her glass down. "Has the next thing happened yet? After breaking up with Tom, has the second thing happened yet?"

43

Karen and Gina knew all about Addie's theory of things happening in threes. They had learned about it in the tenth grade when their Algebra teacher, Mr. Wyatt, wasn't watching where he was going when he walked into the classroom and ran into a student, which caused Mr. Wyatt to drop his books. Later, in the lunchroom, The teacher turned quickly and hit the edge of his tray against the counter and everything spilled. Addie liked Mr. Wyatt, and thought she was helping when she went over to him and cautioned. "Mr. Wyatt, that's two times today you've run into something. Please be careful when you drive home tonight. Things happen in threes, and you sure don't want to run into something in your car."

He laughed and said he would be careful, but that afternoon the car in front of him stopped suddenly. Because he wasn't paying attention, he ran into the back of it.

Mr. Wyatt told the science teacher, Mrs. Busbee, what Addie said, and then the whole class had a lecture on coincidence being just that, coincidence. There was no truth, Mrs. Busbee had said, in the theory that happenings occurred in sets of three.

Her classmates took to teasing Addie about it and some of them had even called her a witch, but one day Gina told a bunch of guys who were giving Addie a hard time to knock it off or she would let the principal know they were the ones who took the fire hose down and strung it down the hall, so they shut up and left Addie alone.

Another time Karen asked Addie a question about whether or not her boyfriend would cheat on her again, and Addie said yes, he had done it twice and he would do it again, so Karen broke up with him. She discovered later he had already cheated the third time. She just hadn't found out about it yet. From that time on they hung together and both Karen and Gina had seen lots of instances of Addie's 'Rule of Threes' coming to pass.

Addie had grown up knowing the Rule of Threes. Her mother told her about it, and cautioned her to watch for it. Her mother had learned from her mother, Addie's grandmother, and passed the knowledge along. Addie saw the proof — the sad absolute proof — five years ago. Her mother's old dog laid down under the oak tree in the backyard one day and died. Two months later her mother's cat — a big old tabby that never left the porch — went out under the oak tree, laid down in the same spot as the dog, and died. Her mother said then, "It's a sign. I'm going to die before the year is out." And she did.

Sean, who waited on them each time they ate at The Lamplighter, came by their table. "Are you ready to order, ladies? We have something extra tonight that's not on the menu. The manager's brother, who has been cooking at a restaurant in New Orleans, is here visiting. He's made a big pot of jambalaya. We're serving it with a soaked salad and French bread and calling it the New Orleans Special."

"What in the world is jambalaya?" Gina asked.

"It's rice cooked with onions and bell peppers and lots of spice and other stuff. It has shrimp and smoked sausage and chicken in it. It's spicy, a little hot, but not too hot."

"That sounds so good I'm not even going to ask what a soaked salad is." Karen handed her menu back to Sean. "Give me the New Orleans special." The other two quickly repeated her order.

"You know, my grandmother came from New Orleans originally. I wish I knew more about the city and the cooking," Addie said, unfolding her napkin.

"Didn't she ever tell any stories when you were little, about her life there?"

"She died before I was born. My mother said she would never talk about her life there, only that she was an orphan with no family left. She fell in love with my grandfather, and he brought her home with him. She never went back."

"New Orleans would be a fun place to visit. Maybe we can all go on a vacation there sometime," Gina suggested. "Remember the fun we had when we went to Atlantic City?"

The three women spent the next hour reliving the good times they had on various trips they shared. When Addie left, she forgotten all about watching for another event to happen that would be number two out of three. She turned her car radio to a station playing Golden Oldies and heard Linda Ronstadt singing "Blue Bayou," but it didn't really register until later, when she opened the used book she pulled out of the sack of paperbacks she bought at a yard sale. When she settled herself in bed and read the first line, "The air was hot and humid in the Big Easy...," she knew that she was going to have something to do with New Orleans. The three clues were there: food, music, and a book. They all pointed the same direction. But how does that tie in with ending my relationship with Tom? Or does it?

She still felt like two more important changes were coming, big ones. But she couldn't know when. She turned off her bedside lamp, snuggled into her pillow, and fell asleep to dream about New Orleans.

CHAPTER FIVE

Parker fit his key into the lock of the massive iron gate. It swung open on well-oiled hinges and as easily closed behind him. He tested it to be sure it was secure before proceeding. Madame Badeaux had assured him the premises were safeguarded by a very powerful spell of protection. This assertion might have meant more if he had been born and raised in New Orleans, but to him it sounded more like a warning about his landlady's mental state than an assurance of security.

When the brick walkway widened into a courtyard, Parker looked around and thought about how lucky he was to find the place when he arrived in the city two years before. Although Madame Badeaux's declaration of safety seemed weird to him when he first arrived, her mention of spells and signs, omens and portents were only charming eccentricities of a fascinating old woman. Of course he didn't believe in her magic. He was a modern man, after all, and not caught up in all the mumbo-jumbo that seemed so prevalent in New Orleans.

Those occurrences people called magic were only things they did not understand. Madame called the computer a 'magic box,' and maybe it was. He worked with computers all day, putting in information, telling the magic box what to do with the data, sending it across the room or across the world with a push of one finger. He figured there was nothing to say that wasn't magic, at least to someone's viewpoint. However, he drew the line when it came to believing in the things that were Madame's specialty.

Parker always thought of himself as a very commonsense person. His friends saw him that way, too. He was not gullible, not easily fooled, didn't believe everything he heard. That was why it was so hard for him to understand his involvement and interest in all these people who believed in the weirdest things such as spells, potions, signs, and magic stones. He just couldn't understand himself.

When he lived in Dallas, which was all his life until two years ago, he was the person he thought himself to be. Then he became bored. Everything was the same-oh, same-oh and Parker was tired of it. When his company offered him the chance to move to New Orleans he jumped at the chance. Now the people who surrounded him believed in things he knew couldn't possibly be true. He was a skeptic, he told himself, a cynic, a modern, educated man who didn't believe in a bunch of mumbo-jumbo.

Why, then, did he never speak up and tell these people the spells and magic they believed in were fake? Probably, he thought, because he had become enchanted with Madame, but not in the magical sense. She was a fascinating woman, a mix of cosmopolitan sophistication and primitive beliefs. He could sit and listen to her stories of New Orleans in 'the old days' for hours. He could well imagine her as the toast of the town, the life of the party, every cliché he had ever heard about the flappers of the twenties and glamorous belles of the thirties and forties. When she told stories of lovers reunited, children cured, or vengeance gained with spells, a bad man who met his just end with a little help from a hex, or somebody kept safe with a charm, Parker was captivated.

It would have been ungracious to tell her he didn't believe in anything she was telling him. When her friends and neighbors, the people he met at Simon's Place and at the bars farther on down the street, made it plain they respected Madame and all she could do, then how could he, in good conscience, tell them they were wrong? He couldn't bring himself to tell them all those things they told stories about would have happened without Madame's spells, and their subconscious was doing whatever was being done, curing an ailment or finding a lost item, and the lover would have come back anyway, without a spell.

Madame was a nice old lady, and she became his friend, so when she asked him to help her catalogue her leaves and roots and bits and pieces of God-knows-what in his 'magic box,' Parker was glad to help her. Each day he spent his hours working with computer programs: math, databases and schedules. The magic of computers was enough magic for him, and that wasn't magic at all once someone understood how they work.

When he came back to his flat each evening the few blocks that separated the modern, workday world of science and knowledge from the old quarter filled with superstition and spells acted like a gate and closed as he entered into another realm. He was happy to help Madame put her work in order, even knowing she wanted to do so because she felt her death was imminent because the omens foretold it. He felt like he was the sorcerer's apprentice, although he laughed at himself at such a thought. There were neither sorcerers nor apprentices around there.

It was like living in a book, a novel written about a hoodoo shop, the old woman who was the proprietor, and the people who came and went. Parker wondered if she were a witch, and if so, if she was a good witch. Each day after work he returned home to hear a new chapter. A wealthy woman came in today? She wanted a potion to make her husband fall back in love with her? A young man needed a spell to help him study for final exams? A businessman needed help in overcoming fear of public speaking? And what, Madame, did you give them? Each day a new story, a new character, a new chapter.

He often ate dinner at Simon's Place, where he heard new tales, new scenes, new dialogue in the book of life.

"Did you hear what Ramon's wife did when she caught him with that redheaded waitress from the Brown Jug Bar?"

"Non. What she do?"

"She done cut up all his clothes and threw them out the window into the street."

"Um-um. I knowed he was gonna get caught. That wadn't the first time he go cattin' around."

Every day a new story.

"Jacques Pickard's chillun onto him to move in with them. They say he too old to live alone."

"They make him do that, he just die. He like his lil place and bein' alone. All the neighbors around watch out for him."

No need for TV with these stories being played out.

"Dorie Saucier's son visited her again the other day."

"What did he take this time?"

"He took his mama's watch and rings and some money she had in a dresser drawer."

"Did she call him out?"

"Nah. You know she didn't. She did that one time and he told her if she was going to accuse him of stealing he wouldn't come see her no more."

He was never interested in his neighbors when he lived in Dallas. Even the people who lived in the apartments on either side and across the hall were strangers to him. He assumed they lived as unexciting lives as he did. He was only slightly interested in what went on in the lives of his friends. Like Parker, they went to work, met a couple of nights a week after work for a beer, went home, went to bed and started the same thing over again the next day.

No wonder he was bored in Dallas. Nothing like this every happened there. If there were stories around him in his hometown he never heard them. In Dallas he lived in a cocoon; a boring shell where nothing ever penetrated. Here, he was in the middle of life.

He was learning more about mystical things, too. For the last few weeks he helped Madame catalogue the inventory of her small shop. Each day she cleaned and straightened and made handwritten lists. Each evening he put the list into an Excel document and printed it for her. He made one for leaves and roots, one for bottles of liquid, and one for what she called 'gris-gris.' He made labels, which she stuck onto the boxes, baskets, and containers that held the accumulation of seventy or more years. She was working on rocks and stones. After that she was contemplating writing down what each item was used for.

"I will start with the colors of the candles," she told him. "They are the easiest to explain. Then I can move to the stones. They, too, are not hard. But the rest? Hmmm. That will not be easy."

She seemed to realize her mortality. Her age, which must be at least ninety, weighed on her mind. She repeated the stories about her past — about her grandmother and parents, and especially about her sister and brother.

Parker enjoyed hearing her stories and helping her on her project. He wanted something different, after all, when he left Dallas and his family to move to New Orleans. His life in Texas was too routine — boring if he told the truth. He reached the age of thirty while living in the city where he was born, about five miles from his parents and maybe six miles from his brother. None of them could understand why he accepted the transfer.

"Those people in New Orleans, those Cajuns, they're funny people," his dad told Parker.

"It's so humid there, uncomfortable, I understand," said his mother.

"You'll last maybe six months. Then you'll be back," said his brother Mark.

But it had been two years now and he still enjoyed living in the Big Easy. Of course, everything was different in New Orleans. After all, in Dallas he never would have found a shop for spells, hexes and potions as his next-door neighbor. Neither was there jazz on the street corners, dancers on the sidewalks, or lines of people led by a man with an umbrella celebrating the life of a person recently deceased. Every day was unique — a treasure. Like going into a junk shop and finding a valuable antique; he never knew what treasure a day would hold, so he had to be alert, ready for the possibilities.

Yes, he was lucky, lucky to have found a place close enough to work that he could walk the dozen blocks, lucky to have an apartment opening onto the bricked courtyard where he could laze in the sun or shade, lucky to have nice, quiet neighbors and a fascinating landlady.

The woman who lived in the apartment above him, Evie, practically never came outside. Madame introduced them when Evie first moved in almost a year ago. Parker drove her places she needed to go a few times, and occasion bought things for her at the market, but usually anytime he saw her she scuttled back inside when she noticed him. She was a slim woman, probably in her forties, with short dark hair. He thought she might be attractive, but he couldn't really tell, since she always wore a floppy hat and sunglasses whenever he took her any place.

The apartment above Madame's flat was vacant, after the young couple living there moved out. Madame's apartment was a twin to his, and L-ed to the right around the courtyard, while his L-ed to the left. The way he had found this place was one of the mysteries that seemed to surround Madame Badeaux. He was new in town and looked at an apartment a couple of blocks from his office. It was a real dump and he knew he didn't want to live there, so he started to walk. There, in this dingy shop window was the sign that read 'Apartment For Rent.' He went in and asked to see it. The flat she showed him felt like home the minute he walked in the door. The rent was reasonable, so he took it.

Later, when the couple in the apartment above hers moved out, he suggested she put the sign back in her window. "I never put a sign in the window," she said. "You never know who you might get that way. I wait until the spirit sends someone to me."

"But that's how I found my apartment, I saw the sign in your window."

"Non. I never put a sign in window." She smiled at him. "The spirits sent you to me. They knew I would need you to help with my inventory, to put the lists in the magic box."

At the time he thought the years had affected her memory, but then again, maybe it was something else entirely.

He rented the place furnished, having only to provide sheets and towels and some dishes. The furniture was an eclectic mix, some pieces of which, he was sure, were valuable antiques. It had a well-lived-in, comfortable air about it, welcoming him each time he returned home.

He grabbed a beer out of the refrigerator, taking a long cool swig on his way to the bedroom. Although his workplace was not formal enough to require a tie, shorts and a tee shirt would have been entirely too casual, so he changed into his favorite apparel and slipped into sandals. His mother had been right when she commented on the heat and humidity in New Orleans, but he was adjusting. Although the apartment wasn't air-conditioned, the high ceilings swept by ceiling fans and the shade trees in the courtyard kept his living space comfortable.

He took his beer out into the courtyard where he settled into a blue wooden chair under a tree. When he looked up, the woman in the upstairs apartment jerked back from the window where she had been watching him.

Maybe she's in the witness protection program. She acts like she is in hiding. Another puzzle.

After sitting in the shade a few minutes, he decided to go to Madame's shop and see if she needed him to record any more items into the computer for her.

* * *

Madame looked up. *The mists. I'll have to stop working soon.*

The light through the grimy front windows was almost gone. The small lamps scattered about the store were not much help. She looked up to the old-fashioned chandelier, as if by looking she could make it work. If truth were told, she could probably conjure up a spell that would do just that, but it was too much trouble just for more light. She seldom used any magic for herself, anyway. She saved it for the paying customers or people who really needed it.

The chore she had set for herself for the day was straightening up all the stones she had stored in baskets and boxes. She plucked the occasional amazonite from the turquoise, the agate from the jasper, and put them in their proper place; how they got mixed up she didn't know. She turned, from time to time, to the paper and pen on the counter where she was making a list of all the stones she had, and another of those she needed.

The tinkling bell over the door announced a visitor. "Ah, Parker. I thought *peut-etre* you were a customer. But this is better, that it is you."

The sandy-haired young man grinned at her. "It's always good to know you want me, you sexy thing!"

The old woman laughed at their ongoing joke. "La, Parker, if you had seen me seventy years ago, you would say 'sexy thing' for certain."

"Madame, seventy years ago you would have been an infant."

"Seventy years ago I was in my prime. But enough of this. Here are the lists of the stones I have, and the ones I need. This evening I will start writing the magic properties of each so you can put them into your magic box."

"Sure thing, Madame. I'll go ahead and print out labels for the ones you have on hand, like I did for the leaves and roots and things. When you have the magic properties all finished I'll enter that into the computer too."

"You are doing well. We may yet finish this job before I die."

"Your niece you're going to leave all this to, she doesn't already know all this stuff?"

"Non. When my sister, her grandmother, left this city she left behind this life and all the knowledge that came with it. She followed her young man where he went, and she wanted no hint of the old ways attached to her. She wanted to be like other people, not special, like our family has always been."

"So this niece doesn't know she has any talent in this area? Or does she? Have talent in the magical arts, that is."

"This I do not know. I don't even know if she has ever heard of me. And there is something else I do not know if she is aware of."

"What's that, Madame?"

"You can see the color of my skin. I am the color of coffee with plenty of milk. Ma soeur, my sister, Adelaide, had much fairer skin.

Where my eyes are brown, hers were gray. Her young man never met the rest of the family, and never knew Adelaide was mulatto. It may come as a shock to my niece the news she is a woman of color."

"No kidding! She may have a lot of adjusting to do. Isn't there another relative you might want to inherit all this, someone here in New Orleans who knows and understands the culture?"

"Non. She is my only relative, the only child of my sister's only child. My brother, Jean-Paul, never married, and he was killed in World War II. Non, it is my niece who must carry on the family tradition."

"And if she doesn't want to do that?"

The old woman shrugged her shoulders. *"C'est la vie.* Come, it is time to quit work for the day. You have already put in your day of work at your office." She walked to the front door, locked it and turned the sign to CLOSED. She went to each of the small lamps, switching them off while she worked her way to the door behind the counter. "Come, Parker, let us rest our weary bones."

CHAPTER SIX

The mists swirled around her all the time now. She first saw them weeks ago but they had grown thicker and more visible, if only to her, incessantly. It was the spirits, of course, come to take her to the other side. Her parents were there, and her siblings, as well as her grandmother and those ancestors she never met. They were telling her the time was close when she would cross over into their world. About a month ago she awoke one morning to find a picture herself, her brother and sister, long dead, lying on the kitchen table. They were young then, when the picture was taken, and did not know what the future held for them, but the picture's mysterious appearance told her she would see them again, soon.

She spent much time thinking about the people who came before her. There was her grandmere, slave on the great plantation up the river, mistress to the owner. She bore her master a son, who was doted on by his father, because his wife only gave him daughters. When the man died his will had stated that her grandmere and her son be freed. Not only that, although a treasure beyond counting, they were to receive ownership and title to a house and land in the city of New Orleans, where the family, both white and black, had been accustomed to staying for weeks at a time. Along with this, they were to have a sum of money. The amount named had been enough to keep them going until the son could begin to support them. This had made the man's white family angry, and they said Grandmere practiced hoodoo on the man to make him do this. It made no matter, Grandmere and her son moved to New Orleans to live in the grand house where they once were servants. The white family grumbled, but they truly believed in the hoodoo and were afraid to do or say more, lest Grandmere put a curse on them.

The son grew up to be a fine man, educated and wise. His mother had taught him all she knew about hoodoo, and at her instruction he wrote it all down in journals, as she never learned to read or write. When the time came, he married a fine looking mulatto woman and they produced three children.

Clotilde was the oldest, and as such, her grandmother had taught her all the old ways. Although the books there for her to consult, especially after her grandmother passed on to the other side, Clotilde absorbed the knowledge as if by osmosis, the knowing becoming part of her being. She was a beautiful child, and even a more beautiful woman, and she had many lovers, both black and white. She did not have to resort to love potions or spells to make them fall in love with her, although the other women, the ones who were jealous and spiteful, had started rumors that she had done so. When the time came for her to settle on just one man and be faithful to him alone, she picked a tall, handsome black man named Joe Badeaux. She assumed he would be faithful to her, also. She was wrong.

There were many stories flying about the city concerning what happened to Joe Badeaux. Some say he moved to California with the woman he had been sleeping with, as she disappeared at the same time he did. But those who knew what Clotilde Badeaux could do insisted she turned him into a dog — the dog that had appeared about that time and hung around wherever she was went, whining and begging to be petted. The dog finally became rabid, and the police shot it and carried the body away to the dump.

By this time Madame Badeaux had been living in the flat she still occupied to this day. Her father built the shop and the apartments around the courtyard for rental income, but then the Great Depression came, and they lost the fortune which allowed them all to live a life of luxury. Her father died of a heart attack at the news all his money was gone, and her beautiful but shallow mother took to her bed. Despite Clotilde's best spells and potions to revive her, she had passed on into spirit to be with her beloved husband.

Clotilde evicted the tenants living in the apartments her father built and each of the children moved into their own flat, leaving one they rented out. They sold the big white house where they were raised for a fraction of its worth and divided the money equally among them.

Clotilde chose the apartment that opened into the shop facing the street. The artist who rented the shop for the sale of his paintings slinked away owing rent, so she distributed the paintings he left among the three flats occupied by the siblings and took over the shop for herself. She put the accumulation of ingredients for her potions and spells, which she and her grandmother collected, into the shelves lining the shop, and soon enough people started coming to her for their needs. She took in a few coins for a spell to make a person lucky in love, another few for a potion to dissolve a wart, and two dollars for removal of a curse. Word of her successes spread and soon she began keeping the shop closed much of the time, only opening and taking clients when the spirits told her to do so. Even then, she made enough money to support herself and put money into savings, at first hidden in her apartment, then later, when she deemed the banks safe, in an account.

The second child was Adelaide, fair of skin and sunny in disposition. Her light brown hair fell in loose curls and her gray eyes smiled at everyone she met. Where Clotilde was the color of coffee with cream, Adelaide was cream with only a hint of sweet chocolate. When the big house was sold and Adelaide received her portion of the money she spent part of it to go to secretarial school. She was determined to leave the French Quarter, the old part of New Orleans, and take a place in the new, modern world.

Even though times were hard and jobs scarce, due to the skills she learned in school she had found employment as assistant to the manager of a fine hotel. She looked and spoke like a white person and the family name, having been that of the white plantation owner, was well known in town, so no one thought to ask her if she were a person of color. One day, when she was filling in at the front desk, she checked in a handsome young man visiting from Connecticut. He flirted with her and she with him. Later, when she was working in her office instead of the reception desk, he sought her out and found her occupied at bookkeeping duties. He asked her to dinner, and thus started their courtship. When a month later he completed his business in New Orleans and returned to his home state, he took her with him as his bride. She was honest with him about some things. Both her parents were dead, her father had been in cotton, they were rich but lost it all when the cotton market crashed along with everything else in 1929, so she was no longer wealthy and had to work for a living. She was, however, not truthful when she told him she had no relatives living, and she completely omitted any mention of the fact she had black blood. Adelaide related all this to Clotilde.

"This is my chance, my way to get away from all this. I love you and Jean-Paul but I don't like this place, the atmosphere that hangs so closely around everyone and everything in this city. I want to forget my old life and make a new one."

And so she left. She sent letters to Clotilde from time to time. She told about the new house she had, and the automobile her husband bought for her to drive. She included a snapshot of her baby daughter, Carol, after she was born. But she never put a return address on the envelope, or mentioned where she lived. Clotilde saved all the letters in a stationery box kept in the bottom of the big cabinet in the living room. When the time came that she determined to find out about Carol and any children she might have had, Clotilde pulled out the letters and let the private detective she hired read them for clues. He was able to make out the postmark, even after all these years, and used that to find her grandniece.

The baby of the family, Jean-Paul, was the one who had been most destroyed by the death of their parents and their way of life. He adored his beautiful mother and imitated his businessman father. Each day he accompanied his papa to the cotton exchange, to the club, to the docks: everywhere his father went, so went Jean-Paul. He learned the cotton trade just as his father had at his own father's side. But where the plantation owner's death lifted his son into a better, richer life, that son's death plunged Jean-Paul's life into confusion and despair. He no longer would live the life of a gentleman, but would be required to find a more ordinary occupation to support himself. He spent a decade knocking around the city, doing whatever jobs came his way, and romancing whatever woman came into his view.

He was a handsome young man, tall and graceful. Where Adelaide was fair, he was dark, much darker than either of his parents. Some people whispered that his mother must have taken a lover for her child to be so much darker than she or her husband, but Clotilde did not believe this. She remembered how devoted her mother was to her husband. She would never have cuckolded him. It was simply the genes of some distance ancestors making themselves known.

Jean-Paul was without ambition, and he simply did not know where to use his talents. When the Japanese bombed Pearl Harbor and America went to war, he saw it as an opportunity to see more of the world than New Orleans and to prove himself, so he joined the Army. Eighteen months later he died on some island in the South Pacific. Clotilde never knew which one.

Madame sat in her favorite chair, looking at the picture and living in those memories when without warning a picture, one of the ones the artist left behind, came crashing to the floor. She knew then the end was near. Rising, she picked up the picture and leaned it against the wall. Retrieving some paper and a pen, she wrote a letter to the niece she had never met. Placing it in the cabinet where all the journals were kept, she felt a sense of calm, of completion. There was no more she could do to ensure the girl carried on the family heritage.

The next day, a candle she set to burning on the sideboard went out by itself, without the slightest puff of breeze to cause it. *The second sign.*

That night she dreamed of a black candle, sputtering in the dark. The next morning when she arose and looked in the mirror, she saw her sister and brother standing on either side, behind her. She went to the chifferobe, took out the clothes she wished to be buried in and placed them across a chair. She took a piece of paper, on which she wrote the name of her attorney and the name of the funeral home where she had made arrangements, and left it on the kitchen table. She straightened the sheets and coverlet, then bathed and dressed — she did not want to be found in her nightgown — and laid on her bed.

The mist enclosed her and, after a while, if someone had been watching they would have seen a smoky miasma rise from her body and join the cloud surrounding her, then float toward the ceiling and disappear.

* * *

A year after escaping her husband, Evelyn was mostly acclimated to living in New Orleans, but for some reason something had her pacing the floor today. She, who kept all her nerves bundled up inside when she was living with Ed, was as jittery as could be. She looked down into the courtyard where the man who lived in the apartment below her, Parker, was sitting in the blue chair and drinking a beer. That's what he did most evenings. He seemed like a nice young man, but for some reason whenever he looked up she stepped back so he wouldn't see her looking at him.

Something was going to happen. Madame Badeaux was the one who said such things, but today Evelyn knew it, too. She felt it in her bones, as her grandmother used to say. Something big was going to happen.

* * *

After he finished his beer, Parker decided to walk down to the next block and eat supper at Simon's Café. He was in the mood for a muffaleto, and Simon made the best ones around. He'd knock on Madame's door and see if she would like to accompany him. He knew she would keep him entertained with her stories, and introduce him to anyone in the café he hadn't met. There was no one in the neighborhood Madame didn't know.

"What's the matter, Francois? Did she kick you out of the house?" he said to the Siamese cat sitting outside Madame Badeaux's door. The cat, usually quiet, was using his typical Siamese voice to express his displeasure at being outside the door when he wanted inside under the breeze of the ceiling fan. When she didn't answer his knock he became concerned and entered her flat.

That was when his world began to change forever.

CHAPTER SEVEN

Simon spread the flour on the board where he was rolling out the dough for fried pies. Using a small plate for a guide, he quickly cut circles and put them aside, and gathering up the dough that had been between the circles, he kneaded and rolled it out again. While he rolled and cut, he thought about Madame and what a loss to the neighborhood her death was. She was a special old lady, a touchstone around which everything around here revolved. And she was gone. Before he moved to this place, before he opened his café, he never believed in magic or spells or any of the other trappings of the hoodoo Madame was said to practice. After five years of seeing what she was said to accomplish, he was at least willing to consider the possibility of such things.

He went to the funeral service and afterwards came back and opened the café to the people who followed the funeral procession through the city streets. He had made a huge pot of gumbo earlier in the day, and told his assistant cook, Leroy, to have it hot when they returned. The stories he heard that day about Madame's powers astounded him, even though he had already heard of many things she had done.

The people crowded into his place, wanting not so much to eat his free food — although everyone acknowledged he was a superb cook — as much as they wanted to share their stories. An old man told about his mother going to Madame Badeaux just before he went off to war in World War II and asking for a spell of protection for her son.

"Madame wove powerful magic," he said, and he came through many battles without a serious injury, although those around him died. "And she wouldn't take any money from my mother, either. Not a penny."

"Then why didn't she protect her own brother?" someone asked. "He died in that war. Why didn't she put a spell on him to protect him?"

"Because he ran away and joined the Navy before she knew about it. When he finally wrote, he was far away and she didn't know where he was. He told her he had to get away from New Orleans and apologized for not telling her what he planned to do. The government used to censor letters during that war, you know, so she never knew where he was and couldn't do much to protect him."

"I heard she tried," said another man. "My father told me she took her brother's picture and did a spell to protect him, but by that time he was already dead. She was too late."

Everyone chimed in with their stories of how she cured sick children, found lost items, brought back wayward husbands and lovers, and helped cure infertility. Simon heard how Madame never charged these people, knowing they could not afford to pay to have their child healed or their wandering husband brought back. She made her fortune, if you could call it that, when the news of what she could do spread to the wealthy people of the city. They came to her for help with things they did not want the people in their world to know about.

Businessmen came to her for an advantage in deals they were cooking up. Wives came to help them regain money they lost gambling. Women came for help in getting a married lover to leave his wife. Many people came for spells to hide things from others, secrets they wanted kept at all costs, or else their lives would be shattered. These people she charged handsomely. They could afford it. Madame became rich enough she kept the door to her little shop closed and locked most of the time and had the heavy wrought-iron gate installed in the entry to her courtyard. She said the spirits would see to it that the people who really needed her would get to her or she would find them, and every once in a while a wealthy client would make arrangements to meet with her for help.

"One thing about Madame Badeaux," said Mrs. Purifoy, "she wouldn't sell curses. I knowed somebody who tried to buy a curse put on her sister-in-law and Madame wouldn't do it. She said 'fore long Fate would take care of it." She paused to take a sip of her iced tea.

"Well, she mighta not sold curses, but she sure 'nough made it hard on people who got on her bad side," commented Mrs. Purifoy's sister, seated next to her.

So the stories started about how it was best to be on Madame's good side. Anyone who cheated her or was rude to her experienced unpleasant things. It might have been as minor as tripping and falling flat on their face or developing very severe adult onset acne to having the roof of their house cave in or their car have every possible thing go wrong with it. It was not wise to cross Madame.

"She put terrible curses on people who were bad evil," added Mr. Tremont. "Remember that man who molested his little daughter. Remember him? He got that strange disease that the doctors could never diagnose, and his pecker turned black and fell off. He ended up killing himself."

"And remember that woman, about twenty years ago, who was poisoning cats?" said Angie Hobart. "Somehow she got food poisoning so bad she almost died, and her daughter came and moved her to a nursing home because the woman was always so sick to her stomach she couldn't take care of herself. The daughter didn't want her mother in the house with her family, because the mother was so mean. Remember her?"

Royce Benoit held his glass up to signal Simon to pour him some more tea and said, "Madame was a sincere believer in the rule of tens; that is, whatever is put out in the universe — whether it is good or bad — comes back multiplied by ten. She used to tell me that all the time."

The group gathered in Simon's café were divided as to whether Madame helped along the payback to those who did bad things, or whether karma took care of the situation without Madame's assistance.

The newest arrival to the neighborhood, a pretty black girl who had a shop on the other side of Madame's, spoke up. "I've just been here six months now, but I wouldn't be here at all if it wasn't for Madame. I was looking for a place to live and have a shop, but everything I had looked at was too expensive for me. I looked around here because most of these shops have apartments above or behind them. I came to look at the shop beside Madame's and she was sitting on that bench that is between our two places. The landlord was supposed to meet me there, but he was late and Madame invited me to sit down and visit with her while I waited. My little boy was with me, and she reached in her pocket and pulled out a little ball and gave it to him to play with. We visited for some time and she learned all about me and what I wanted to do. When the landlord finally got there Madame looked at him and said,

'JayMar, this woman will make you a very good tenant. You be sure you treat her right, understand?' and then she said something in French. I don't understand French, but it some of it sounded sort of like 'mal' and 'diction.'

"Anyway, the rent he quoted me for both the shop and the apartment was less than what I thought I would have to pay for just one or the other, and he did all the repairs that it needed. When I needed washer and dryer hook-ups he put them in and didn't charge me anything for doing it. After hearing all of you talk today, I guess he was scared of her and wanted me to be happy."

"La malediction, that's what she said, chère?" asked old Mrs. Bonnet.

"Yes! That's it."

"The curse. She threatened to put a curse on him if he didn't treat you right. And JayMar'd know, all right. His cousin, Tonio, overcharged Madame one time on some work he did for her, and he didn't get another job for six months. Finally he went to her and apologized and gave her back some money — he had to borrow it from his girlfriend — and then people started hiring him again. Yes, JayMar Davis knows he'd better treat you right. I hope he don't go up on your rent now that she's gone. He got that job takin' care of all that rent property, done changed his name from Jamar, a good name his mama done give him, to that fancy JayMar and now he thinks he's somethin' else. Uh-huh. I hopes he keeps on treatin' you right now that Madame's passed."

"Who's gonna get all her property now that she's gone?" asked Jefferson DuMont.

Parker, the white man who lived in one of Madame's flats and often brought her to Simon's Café, said, "She has a niece, a great-niece actually, her sister's granddaughter, who lives back east somewhere. She inherits everything."

This caused a stir among the crowd, and as Simon walked about refilling bowls and glasses he heard the questions people were asking themselves.

What do you suppose the niece is like?"

"I wonder if she has Madame's skills."

"Adelaide had a grandchild?"

"I didn't know she ever heard from Adelaide after she ran off. I wonder how Madame found the granddaughter?"

Simon didn't know the answer to any of the questions, but he knew one thing. The granddaughter's coming was bound to change the neighborhood. Whether it would be for better or worse he didn't know. He went to refill the glass of the pretty girl who spoke about Madame helping her.

"Hi. I'm Simon Bondurant, the owner of this place," he said as he poured her lemonade.

"My name is Dani Washington. I own the shop next door to Madame's place," she answered. "And this is my son, Morgan." She indicated the little boy sitting beside her.

"Welcome to the neighborhood, Dani. I'm sorry I haven't said hello before this."

"I haven't been in your restaurant before now. I spend all my time on my business."

"I hope you can come in again. It's a pleasure to have you in the area."

He moved away to fill the glasses of others who had come to celebrate Madame's legacy."

He hoped JayMar Davis didn't go up on the rent and make Dani move. He would like to see her again. He was happy when she returned his smile

CHAPTER EIGHT

The rule of threes was following through in her life. Boy was it! Now she could see the pattern that started when Tom broke up with her — letting go of old things, old boyfriend, old job, old home. Except she thought there were more than three things she was letting go of. The first had been her relationship with Tom, of course, and she recognized right off that the ending of that was the start of a pattern of threes. A month later the town redrew the school district lines, consolidated kindergarten classes, and informed Addie her contract would not be renewed for the following year. Last hired, first fired. So that was number two.

Figuring out what was number three was harder. She had let go of her home and most of her belongings. She was letting go of the town where she was born and lived all of her life, excepting the time she was in college. It felt like she was letting go of her best friends, Karen and Gina. Sure, they would still be friends, but it wouldn't be the same when she lived 1400 miles away. There would be no more every-other-Thursday-night dinners at the Lamplighter. No more shopping together. No more spur-of-the-moment trips and giggling confidences shared. She could see right now she would have to get a cell phone plan with lots of minutes, because Addie couldn't imagine not sharing every minute of her adventure with her two best friends.

Somehow she knew when the phone rang that morning six weeks ago that something important waited on the other end of the line. When it rang she had that quivery feeling that sometimes caught her unaware.

"You are Adelaide Carol Zappa, are you not?"

"Yes, I am."

"And you are the daughter, the only child of Carol Henson Zappa, now deceased, and Martin Lewis Zappa?"

"Yes."

"And your mother was the only child of Gregory and Adelaide Henson, both deceased?"

"That's correct."

"Then I have found the right person. My name is Pierre Arceneau, and I am an attorney. I have called to tell you that you are the sole heir of your grandmother's sister, Madame Clotilde Broussard Badeaux, late of New Orleans, Louisiana."

"Er, Madame, ah," Addie stammered and sputtered.

"Yes. You would probably say Mrs. Badeaux, but Madame preferred the French word, as do many in our city. Clotilde was the older sister of your grandmother, Adelaide. Their maiden name was Broussard. Madame was married, many years ago, to a Badeaux."

"She must have been very old."

"Indeed. She never told her age, but she was at least well into her nineties, perhaps even one hundred or more. She was very active right up until her death."

"I never heard of her. My grandmother died before I was born, and my mother said my grandmother never talked of her family. In fact, I am sure Grandmother told everyone she was an orphan."

"That is true. Her parents were deceased when she married Mr. Henson and left New Orleans, but she had one sister, Madame Badeaux, and one brother, Jean-Paul, who was killed in World War II. Therefore, you are the only living descendant of Madame's family, and she has left everything to you in her will."

"To me? Her will?" Addie thought she sounded more tongue-tied than one of her kindergarten students.

"Yes. We can go over the document in more detail in person when you come to New Orleans, but basically you have inherited a building with four apartments and an attached shop. Madame lived in one apartment and renters who have been there for some time occupy two more. One flat is empty at this time. All are in good repair. They are all furnished, some with pieces which are valuable antiques. They came from the old Broussard home, which was sold in the thirties. My information tells me you are single. Is this correct?"

"Yes, I'm single." She wondered what that had to do with anything. *Did I inherit a man, too?*

"Then Madame's apartment may be quite satisfactory for you to live in. All the flats except one are one bedroom units, you see."

"You said there is a shop. Do you mean a shop that sells things? Or do you mean a workshop?"

"A shop that sells things, though I cannot tell you what Madame sold from that shop. It faces the street, and although the building is not in the main tourist shopping area, it is a good area with many active businesses around it."

"What happens if I don't want to move to New Orleans?"

"That would be a problem. You see, Madame's will states you must come here and live in her apartment and take care of the property for one full year before it becomes yours. There is money allotted for your move and for any repairs that should become necessary, but you can't dispose of anything until you have lived here in her home for a full year."

"So what happens to it if I don't move there?"

"It will be sold and the proceeds donated to charity."

"I'll have to think about it and discuss it with friends. Give me your name again, and your phone number. I'll be in touch within a few days."

She hung up after getting the information, but she knew without a doubt that fate, karma, whatever, was sending her to New Orleans, to the home of her grandmother's family. That was number three.

Of course she talked about the whole thing with Gina and Karen. They even had a sleepover at Addie's house and spent hours imagining the life she might lead in the Big Easy. They squealed like teenagers as new, exciting thoughts dancing through their heads.

"You have to stay a year, but nothing says you might not want to come back here after the year is up," said the ever-practical Karen. "You can put all your furniture in storage and rent out your house. That way, if you don't like it in New Orleans you can sell everything down there after a year and come back home."

"That sounds like a good plan, but I have a strong feeling I'm supposed to be there. I don't want to have to worry about too much back here."

"So, the spirits are telling you that you'll like it?" Her friends liked to tease her about the spirits telling her what to do.

Addie grinned. "Well, I guess you can say that. I just have a feeling New Orleans is where I belong right now."

Eventually, Addie sold most of her belongings and boxed up the rest. She decided to keep her house and signed up with a rental agent who would be in charge of finding a reliable tenant, collecting the rent and having any needed repairs done. She filled her car with as much as she could pack into it. All of her clothes, her jewelry making supplies, some of her books, treasured garage sale finds, photos, and various other items she couldn't do a year without filled it completely. She rented a storage locker and put the rest in it. If, at the end of the year (or before then, for that matter) she wanted the rest of her belongings, she would call Karen or Gina, both of whom had keys, and they would UPS the remaining boxes to her.

Three days ago she started her journey across the country, pausing along the way to see new vistas. Late in the afternoon of the third day she reached Slidell, Louisiana, and checked into a motel. Tomorrow she would cross Lake Pontchartrain and find the office of Arceneau and Arceneau, Attorneys-at-law. And after that she would begin her new life.

CHAPTER NINE

That morning when Addie woke and checked out of the motel in Slidell, she called the office of the attorney, Henri Arceneau, and he told her how to take the bridge over Lake Ponchartrain into Metairie, and which streets to take to get to New Orleans proper and his office.

The meeting with him didn't produce much new information. Mr. Arceneau had already covered everything with her by phone and mail during the past six weeks. He had asked if she needed a plane ticket to New Orleans. If so, he would provide one, but she said no. She had a car that could make the long trip and that way she could bring everything she wanted. He sent her a generous check. To use for the trip, he said.

She understood she would have to live in Madame's apartment for a year, and she could use the shop if she wanted, or rent it out. Mr. Arceneau would pay for any repairs to the property, and the utility bills came directly to him to be paid, as they had for her aunt. The money for that came directly out of Madame's savings and investments. The rent from the apartments would go directly to her, and she could spend it any way she wished, or save it. There were four apartments surrounding a courtyard, one of which was hers, two were rented out, and one was vacant. She could rent the other one or not. It was up to her.

Mr. Arceneau said a young man, Parker Hyatt, who lived in one of the apartments, agreed to watch out for the property since Madame's death. He knew of Addie's imminent arrival and would take off work and meet her at the flats whenever Mr. Arceneau called. The attorney handed her a set of keys and told her Parker had a set also.

"He is a reliable young man, and your aunt trusted him. He can show you around and introduce you to the people in the neighborhood. He does something in the computer field, writes programs and data bases, or something like that, I think. He helped your aunt with her business before she died."

"And what kind of business was that, Mr. Arceneau?"

"I think she sold herbs and things. I really don't know." He looked down and nervously shuffled the papers on his desk. "Mr. Hyatt can probably tell you more than I can about that subject."

* * *

Addie leaned up against her car as she studied the shop directly across the narrow brick street. It was a small store and the windows on either side of the front door were covered with dust so heavy it was barely possible to make out the gold lettering: BADEAUX. That's all it said, BADEAUX. There was no clue as to what was sold inside, although there was a jumble of items displayed behind the glass. Mr. Arceneau had been very uncomfortable about the subject. She wondered if it was possible her aunt was dealing drugs out of the nondescript redbrick building. She sure didn't want to get mixed up with anything like that, and for the first time since the whole crazy business had started she felt some apprehension about her leap of faith into a new milieu. *Surely an old woman of that age wouldn't be dealing drugs. But she made money, good money it seems like, in some way.*

The shop could be made to look nicer by cleaning the windows and putting attractive displays for people to see, and it needs a new coat of paint on the door and windows. She looked at the store to the left of her aunt's. Someone had made the effort to paint the wood trim around the windows and the front door a bright, light blue, sort of an azure color. It was very attractive. When she read the placard in the window and noticed what was for sale there, she smiled.

DANI'S DESIGNS, read the sign propped in the window. She could see she would be shopping there in the near future. The windows were full of clothing. One window displayed women's clothing, while the other one held little girl's apparel. Yes, Addie would have to explore there as soon as she was settled.

To the right of her aunt's bedraggled place of business there was a brick walkway, perhaps six feet wide, which led toward the rear. *That must be where the courtyard is located.*

About ten feet back there was a tall, heavy wrought iron gate, ornately decorated with swirls and circles of metal. Mr. Arceneau said she would need one of the keys on the ring he gave her to get in through that gate.

Well, time to get on with it. Time to see my new home.

She crossed the street and approached the imposing gate. As she sorted through the keys, a voice greeted her from inside the courtyard.

"Hi! You must be Adelaide Zappa. Here let me get that gate for you," said the man coming from farther down the walkway. He turned a latch on the inside and swung the gate open.

"Come in and see your new home." He pushed the gate closed and checked to see that it latched. "I hope you had a good trip, no problems or anything."

"Hi." She stuck out her hand, "Just call me Addie."

"I'm Parker Hyatt," he said as he shook her hand.

"I had an enjoyable trip but I'm glad I'm finally here. I've been wondering about this place ever since the attorney called."

"Come on into the courtyard and I'll show you everything."

They walked another ten feet or so to where the walkway opened into a large brick-paved square. On both the left and right sides, as well as straight ahead, galleries ringed the area both on the ground floor and upstairs. Windows and French doors opened at intervals onto the shaded walkways on both levels. Addie marveled at the bougainvillea, which was growing two stories high and sprinkling the ground underneath with bright pink flowers. In another spot a tree extended its shade over a table and chairs painted the same bright blue she had seen on the shop next door.

"This is Madame's flat. Well, that is, your flat, here on the left. It turns the corner back there and takes up half the back. Mine is just like it, over there on the right side. There's an opening between them in the back. You can unlock that big wooden door and have access to the car shed. Above me is another apartment just like yours and mine. A woman named Evie White rents it, but you won't see much of her. She's almost a recluse, but not quite." He motioned to the gallery above the apartment that was to be Addie's. "The one above you is a little larger, since it extends over the shop. It isn't rented out now. Madame was very particular about who she rented to, and it was kind of eerie how she found renters. I'll tell you about it sometime. She used to say the spirits told her who to rent to."

"That's funny. I sometimes say the spirits tell me whether to do something or not. It's just a feeling I get about whether something is right or not. My friends tease me about it."

"Huh! Madame wasn't sure if you would inherit any of her gifts or not. It looks like you might have."

"What gifts?"

"Let me show you around now, and we'll talk about that when we can sit and visit. There is a lot about Madame you'll want to know. That is, if your family didn't tell you about her."

"No, my family didn't tell me anything at all. I didn't even know she existed until the attorney found me." Addie put her hands on her hips, "This is all very mysterious. First Mr. Arceneau wouldn't talk about her, and now you won't. I'm getting a little bit scared, like maybe I shouldn't have decided to move down here after all."

"It's nothing like that. Nothing bad. Madame was a kind, wonderful person. It's just that she was a very interesting character and can't be quickly described in a few words. I'll tell you all about her over supper, I promise." He took a few steps toward her apartment door. "Here, let me unlock the door for you."

Addie fell in love with the place as soon as she entered the door. The living room was filled with furniture from at least a century of styles, or maybe more. Addie wasn't an expert on periods of furniture, she simply knew there was old, really old, and newer mixed together. Although newer was probably not the right word, she figured. She doubted there was anything there from later than the 1940s. She could hardly wait to browse through the eclectic mix of items scattered around the room. The high ceilings — to let the heat rise, she had read while researching New Orleans on the net — gave a feeling of spaciousness to an already large room.

Parker gestured toward a door on the right. "That leads to the bedroom and bath."

Addie opened the door and found another large and shadowed room. A big bed, canopied in white, stood against the far wall. Parker walked over to it and pulled on some gauzy fabric. "This is mosquito netting. You can pull it around the bed at night to protect yourself, especially if you leave the French doors standing open for the air. The mosquitoes can be quite annoying here."

"Yes, we have them in Connecticut, too. I take vitamin B-1 and they don't bother me."

"Really? B-1, huh? I'll have to try it."

"Well, they don't sting me, but sometimes they sing in my ear. The netting will probably be very handy." She looked around the room, admiring the beautiful paintings that adorned the walls. A large ornate armoire sat against one wall. "That's a gorgeous piece of furniture."

"Yes. I think that is one of the pieces that came from the original home place."

"And you'll tell me about it later. Right?"

"Right." Parker grinned, "Here's the bathroom." He opened a door to reveal a big, claw-footed tub with an oval pipe suspended from the ceiling to hold a shower curtain. An old-fashioned showerhead extended from the white ceramic tiled wall. A white pedestal sink, an old one, Addie was sure, not a modern reproduction, and a white toilet, completed the fixtures. The room was large enough that a big glass-doored cabinet held towels. Parker opened another door. "And here is a walk-in closet. If you are like my mother you can easily fill that up." Addie saw it was still full of her aunt's clothing. She would love trying on the fashions from by-gone days. This was like having a whole vintage clothing store at her fingertips.

"Let me show you the kitchen." Parker led the way back through the living room to the room on the far side. It was old-fashioned, but not as bad as Addie had thought it might be after seeing the other rooms. The refrigerator was modern, and the range, too. The cabinets were old but in good shape, and painted a shade of green that was popular in kitchens of the 1930s. She wondered if that was the last time they had been painted. A large round oak table and chairs sat in the middle of the room, and there were several freestanding cabinets. She could see dishes in the one with glass doors, and the one with open shelves held beautiful serving pieces.

"Through here is the shop," Parker said. He turned the knob and opened a door on the far wall. Addie followed him into what appeared to be a storeroom. There were several trunks against the walls, and she saw another door leading toward the front of the building. Entering the next room she realized it was the shop she saw from the street. It was so dim she could barely see, and an unusual scent filled the air.

"Are there any lights?"

"Sure." Parker turned to a small lamp on the counter and turned it on. She could see a little better, but not much. She looked up at the ceiling and saw a huge chandelier, dripping with hundreds of crystal drops.

"Can't you turn on that light?"

"It hasn't worked since I've lived here, but there is another lamp I'll turn on." He moved around the counter to the other wall and switched on another small lamp.

"What is that smell?"

"That would be Madame's herbs and stuff."

Addie put her fists on her hips. She might as well find out right now if she wanted to stay or not. "What kind of herbs? I'll tell you right now I'll have nothing to do with marijuana or anything else like that to smoke. No drugs of any kind! None! Nada! If that is what she was doing, selling 'herbs and stuff' like that I want nothing to do with it. If people around here are expecting to come to me for that, I'm out of here. You tell me right now. What did my aunt sell in this shop?"

Parker grinned. "I'm not sure you are ready for this. Think you can handle it?"

"Of course I can. What are you grinning about? What did my aunt sell?"

"She sold potions and spells. She undid hexes and bad mojo. She sold protection against the evil eye. She would spin a spell to help you find a lost item, heal a rash, or catch a man. She cured people of illnesses brought on by someone putting a curse on them. To people in the know, she was famous. Her death was a blow to this entire neighborhood."

Addie stumbled back and sat on the high stool behind the counter. "Voodoo?"

"No. Hoodoo, not Voodoo. There is a difference you know."

Addie thought for a minute. "Yes, I know, now that I think about it. When Mr. Arceneau contacted me about Aunt, er, about Madame's will, I tried to find out anything I could about New Orleans. A program I watched on the Travel Channel touched on the differences between Voodoo and hoodoo. Voodoo is a religion, right?"

"I don't know a lot about the differences, but yes, I think Voodoo is a religion, but people who practice or believe in hoodoo believe in the Bible and are usually Catholic, sometimes Protestant. Madame believed in using her gift for good, never for evil."

"Well, that's a relief!"

"I don't know how much of a relief it's going to be to you. Everyone around here is waiting to see how you measure up in the mixing of potions and the casting of spells."

CHAPTER TEN

Addie stepped out into the courtyard and Parker thought some of Madame's lingering magic must have propelled him back in time by fifty years. She came floating across the enclosure like someone out of an old movie, in fluffy petticoats that extended her skirt around her, her hair heaped upon the top of her head and held with ribbons that spilled down the sides, entangled with the curls. Tiny straps were tied in bows on her shoulders, and Parker wondered if he untied them, what would happen to her dress.

"Hello. Am I late? Have you been waiting long?" the vision asked.

He jumped to his feet. *Come on Parker, snap out of it! It's not like you've never seen a good-looking woman before.*

"You aren't late. You're just right. Have a seat." I'll get something for you to drink while I tell you a little about your aunt. I probably won't get a chance at Simon's."

"Who's Simon?"

"Simon is the owner of Simon's Place. It's in the next block." Parker motioned to the west with his hand, "It's the place where I and lots of neighborhood people eat. They serve great Cajun food, and non-Cajun too. I used to take Madame there for supper often."

He realized that most of the neighborhood would be present when they found out Madame's heir was dining there, and he wouldn't have a chance to tell her the story he promised her. "I have iced tea, lemonade, and beer."

"Lemonade sounds great, thank you."

"I'll be right back." He hurried into his kitchen by way of the French doors that stood open. A minute later he returned with her glass, and his refilled. He placed it in front of her and took a deep breath. Parker had thought all day about how much to tell Addie about her heritage. Some, he thought, but not too much at one time. I don't need to overwhelm her. She'll learn it all sooner or later.

"Are you ready to learn about your aunt?" He settled back into his chair.

"Definitely. You've been putting me off all day."

"Only because I thought it would be better to sit down like this and talk, instead of trying to tell the story while we worked."

"Okay. That's fair. So now, what's the story?"

"Your aunt's name, as you probably know, was Clotilde Broussard Badeaux. The Broussard name is an old one here in New Orleans, she told me. She was raised in a big white house, some might say a mansion, in the rich part of town. She had me drive her by it one time, to show me where it was. I can show you, if you like. It was where her father was also raised. He was an educated man, a man of means, who dealt in cotton. Not that I am well versed in the cotton industry, but from what Madame told me, I believe he worked in the cotton markets. That is, he bought and sold cotton and cotton futures.

"Madame's grandmother, her father's mother, was alive until Clotilde was in her teens. She taught Clotilde all she knew about hoodoo. The grandmother was a well-known practitioner of hoodoo, as was Clotilde after her. The grandmother didn't read or write, so she dictated the directions and recipes for the spells and potions and such to Clotilde's father, and later to Clotilde, to be written in a journal. I don't know for sure, but I think the journal is somewhere in your apartment. Madame would have kept it close to her. She once told me that its existence should be kept a secret, that some people would kill to get possession of it."

"Then why did she tell you about it?"

"These last few months, I think Madame knew her time was running out. She trusted me with a lot of things. She had me make inventory lists of her roots and herbs, so you would know what each one is, and she repeated these stories about her past. She didn't tell me everything, mind you. There are still a lot of mysteries about Madame's life."

"Okay. Go on with the story."

"The stock market crash in 1929 wiped out their fortune. Most, but not all, of their money was gone. When he heard the news, her father had a heart attack and died. Her mother took to her bed and died not long after, of grief, Madame said.

"Clotilde realized she and her sister and brother could not continue to live the lifestyle they were used to living. Her father had this apartment complex built for income property and Clotilde made the people living here move out. Some of their servants lived in the apartment over yours for a few months, then it was rented for the income. Her brother, Jean-Paul, had the flat I am living in, while her sister, your Grandmother Adelaide, took the apartment above mine.

"At the time an artist was renting the shop, but by the time the Broussard family moved here, he had moving out owing back rent. He left a note telling Clotilde she could have all the artwork in lieu of the unpaid bill. Those are the paintings in your apartment, as well as the other flats." He stopped to take a sip of tea.

"I noticed the paintings. They are very good. I wondered if someone in the family painted the."

"Sometime during that time was when Clotilde married. His last name was Badeaux. He turned out to be a bad one, cheated on Clotilde, which was the wrong thing to do to someone who practices hoodoo. He disappeared. Some people say she turned him into a dog."

"Why did they say that?"

"Because a dog showed up about then and stayed right by Madame's side, licking her hand and cowering down, whimpering, like he was begging for forgiveness."

"So, did she forgive him and turn him back into a man?"

"No. The story goes the dog went mad and had to be shot."

Addie drew back, eyes wide.

"Madame didn't tell me that story. I heard it at Simon's after her funeral."

Addie took a sip of her lemonade. "Go on with the story of her life."

"They say Madame was a very beautiful woman and had many lovers. She practiced her hoodoo for others. The people in the neighborhood, the ones who needed her, she never charged, but the rich people and the tourists, she made another fortune from them. Whatever Madame chose to invest in prospered. Either she made the business flourish with spells or she knew what to invest in. The people who followed her lead prospered, too. I'm sure you will hear lots of stories about this, so I won't repeat the ones I've heard. People will tell you themselves.

"They sold the big white house for far less than its value, having moved as much of the furniture as they could here into the apartments. The chandelier in the shop was from their old home.

I'm sure it was something to behold when it was clean and brightly lit."

"Mr. Arceneau said to let him know what needed to be repaired, and that is one thing already on my list. I'm sure it will be beautiful when it is restored to its full glory." Addie took another sip of her lemonade. "Go on with the story. This is as good as any novel I've ever read."

"Jean-Paul squandered his share of the money on women and wild living. When World War II broke out, he joined the Army. Madame didn't know about it until she got a letter from him many months later from somewhere in the Pacific, and by the time the letter reached her, Jean-Paul was already dead.

"Adelaide, your grandmother, took her share of the money from the sale of the house and went to secretarial school. From there she went to work in one of the big hotels, which is where she met your grandfather, who was in New Orleans for several weeks on business. When he went back home she went with him. Madame said Adelaide wanted nothing to do with hoodoo, didn't like living here, and wanted far away from all the memories and this culture."

"She died before I was born, but my mother didn't mention anything about hoodoo, or potions or spells or anything like that. She did pass on beliefs that Grandmother had, like things happening in threes, and watching for coincidences and signs. My mother was a big believer in those, and I am too."

"Madame wondered if you had inherited any of her gift, as she called it. And, as I said, everyone around here is wondering the same thing. I want to warn you about tonight. You are going to stir up a lot of conversation at Simon's."

"How do they know I'm going to be there?"

"Simon's is where I eat several nights a week, and with you being new, they expect me to bring you there for supper."

Addie laughed, "Okay, I'm ready to meet the neighborhood." She picked up her small purse and stood up. "Let's go get it over with."

Simon offered his arm and she linked hers through it. He expected her to be wearing high heels, but she had on flat heeled shoes adorned with jewels. They added to the impression she had stepped out of another time period. Enchanted, Simon escorted her to the gate, where he showed her how to open it from the inside without a key.

While they walked arm-in-arm down the sidewalk she asked, "So how did Mr. Arceneau know how to find me? I meant to ask him, but I forgot."

"Your grandmother wrote to her sister from time to time and told her about her life. She didn't put a return address on the letters, but they had the town name on the postmark. Madame hired a private investigator to find out about any heirs, using those envelopes as clues. He found you." *And I'm so glad he did.*

CHAPTER ELEVEN

Simon had already served up a day's worth of jambalaya by the time lunch was over, and was almost out of the black olive mix for muffalettas. The arrival of Madame's heir was proving to be his busiest day since Madame's funeral. The neighborhood was buzzing with talk ever since the news spread that Madame had a great-niece who would be coming to claim the estate, and Simon's was the place they met to share the latest news.

The grapevine carried the stories, passed down from parents and grandparents, of Madame's sister Adelaide, fair skinned and light haired, who worked at one of the big hotels where she met a young man from Back East and accompanied him back home without revealing her heritage. She had 'passed,' they said, as in 'passed for white,' not that she had died. No one knew what had happened to Adelaide, except evidently Madame, since she left everything to the niece, Adelaide's granddaughter, in her will.

They had what they considered a direct line of information: Madame's attorney was Pierre Arceneau, of Henri and Pierre Arceneau, attorneys-at-law. Pierre Arceneau's maid was Sophie, sister of Solomon, who worked at the hardware store in the next block. He was only too happy to pass along the news of the heir.

Then there was the receptionist at the offices of Arceneau and Arceneau. She was cousin to Donya, who was a hairdresser at a high-class beauty salon. Old Mrs. Saurage's granddaughter, Twanette, swept up hair and washed towels at the salon, and heard all the gossip that went on there, so she passed on all the pertinent information — along with all the other gossip — to Mrs. Saurage.

If that wasn't enough, Henri Arceneau's cook was Rosetta, who was aunt of Simon's assistant cook, Leroy. She probably heard less than anyone about the matter, but she is the one who heard when the heir was expected, since Monsieur and Madame Arceneau discussed whether it would be advisable to have a dinner party to present the heir to the upper-class community or not, and had consulted Rosetta about a possible menu. They decided to delay a decision, because, after all, no one knew what type of person this Adelaide Zappa might turn out to be, and though it was wise to stay on her good side, in case she had power equaling that of Madame Clotilde Broussard Badeaux, nothing would be lost by waiting until they met the woman before making a commitment.

Simon decided to cook another pot of jambalaya plus one of red beans and rice, even though it wasn't Monday. After some thought, he decided to make some chicken and dumplings, too, in case the newcomer didn't like the typical New Orleans cuisine. Actually, he had been thinking about expanding the menu as well as the restaurant. The shop next door was vacant, after the gift shop which had occupied the premises went out of business. How anyone thought they could succeed in this area selling items made in China he didn't know. Simon intended to contact the landlord and see if he could afford to rent that space and pull down part of the wall separating the two stores to make room for more customers.

Leroy's working out real good as assistant cook. Maybe we ought to start calling ourselves chefs instead of cooks. It sounded better to the tourists that were beginning to come in increasing numbers. Leroy prepared over most of the dishes they served, which left Simon time to explore new possibilities, like the chicken and dumplings he planned to serve that evening. Every once in a while he would get a group of tourists that included someone who couldn't or wouldn't eat the gumbo or jambalaya, which was his main claim to fame. He wanted to find a good recipe for Natchitoches meat pies too. With Leroy to cook, he could afford the time to drive up to Natchitoches to see if he could find a local cookbook with a good recipe. Failing that, he would buy some pies to bring back and sample to figure out the ingredients.

Leroy wanted to add steaks to the menu, for a higher-priced dish, served with dirty rice and soaked salad. He said his Aunt Rosetta taught him how to cook a powerful good steak using a flat iron. If Simon could expand the size of his restaurant, maybe he could make the other room a little fancier for some patrons of the evening meal. *Serve dinner in there and supper in here.* He smiled at the thought.

The place stayed mostly full the past couple of days, since everyone had figured out the heir was due to arrive at any time. Late that morning, however, someone spotted a young woman with a mass of red-blonde curls leaning up against a dark blue Toyota and staring at the front of Madame's shop. After a few minutes she had gone to the gate of the courtyard and was admitted by Parker. That was when tables filled with people, most of whom had no intention of ordering a meal. Finally, he rounded up all the beer, iced tea and lemonade drinkers and had them share tables at the rear of the room. He put one pitcher of tea and one pitcher of lemonade out and told them when it was gone they would have to pay for more. That was all the free refills they were going to get. The beer drinkers would have to pay for all refills.

People came and people went, but along about the middle of the afternoon the crowd had thinned considerably, having been assured by Simon that, if there was any news, he would lend his cell phone to Mr. Bayard and show him how to use it to call Mrs. Pettit, who would then call others so they could come back.

Finally, about half past six Parker entered escorting the young lady, and all conversation stopped.

CHAPTER TWELVE

When Addie and Parker entered Simon's Place, conversation stopped and a sea of faces turned toward the door. She smiled and clung tightly to Parker's arm as she glanced around the crowded room. Unsure of what to do, since it was obvious those faces were looking at her, she waited for Parker to make the first move.

A tall man in a white chef's coat approached them.

"Addie, this is Simon Bondurant, owner of this fine restaurant and chef extraordinaire. Simon, meet Madame's niece, Addie Zappa. She has arrived to take up residence and needs some of your superb cooking."

"Miss Zappa, I am proud to have you in my establishment. Please come this way. I have held a table for you." Simon escorted them to a table in the center of the room. *I might as well put them in the middle so more people can get a good look at Madame's heir.*

People gossiped ever since the word got out that she was coming. The big question in the neighborhood was whether the niece had the hoodoo power that Madame commanded. The next question was whether she was a nice person or not. What would they do, the locals asked each other, if she was powerful but also evil or power-hungry?

By the time some of the people worked themselves into a state worrying about a hoodoo woman who would make their lives miserable with her demands and curses, Simon decided he had to step in and stop that sort of talk.

"Why in the world," he asked them, "would you think any niece of Madame's would be as evil a person as you are trying to make her out to be? Wasn't Madame nice to all of you? Did she ever do anything bad to anyone who didn't deserve it?"

"You're right, Simon," Mrs. Molyneux said. "I'm sure she'll be as nice as Madame."

Shamefaced, they backed down and no more talk was heard about a mean, evil witch moving to the neighborhood.

Simon led Parker and Addie to the table with the RESERVED sign on it. He started to pull out the chair for Addie, but Parker beat him to it.

Placing menus in before them, Simon asked, "Can I get you folks something to drink?"

"Iced tea for me, please Simon," Addie said. "Unsweet, with lemon."

"Sweet tea, thank you, Simon," said Parker.

Addie looked around the room and the other occupants tried to look like they hadn't been staring at her. She picked up the menu and holding it in front of her face she spoke softly to Parker.

"Is it my imagination, or has everyone been staring at me since I walked in the door?"

"I warned you," Parker whispered. In a normal voice he asked, "Do you need me to tell you what some of the items on the menu are?"

"I already see what I want. Maybe next time you can describe what some of the other dishes are."

Expecting her to order the chicken and dumplings or some other dish common all over the country, Parker asked, "So what do you see that looks good to you?"

"The jambalaya. A restaurant at home served it once. It was really good, and I've been wanting to have it again."

Simon appeared with their glasses of tea. "Have you had time to decide what you want to order, Miss Zappa?"

"Please call me Addie. I'll have a bowl of jambalaya."

"Would you like a salad with that?"

"The time I had jambalaya before they served a salad with lettuce that was all wilted. I liked it, but I forget the name."

"Was it soaked salad or wilted lettuce salad? I have both."

"What's the difference?"

"Wilted lettuce uses a little hot bacon grease, mixed with a little sugar and vinegar, to wilt the lettuce, and bacon is crumbled on top. Soaked salad is lettuce, tomatoes and olives marinated in olive oil mixed with vinegar and spices."

"Yes! Soaked salad, that's it. Although the other one sounds good too. I'll try it next time."

"How about you, Parker?"

"Make it two, Simon."

"I'll have these right out to you folks."

Parker took a sip of his tea. "I've told you about your aunt. Now it's your turn. Tell me about yourself."

"Well, I was named Adelaide after my grandmother, who died a couple of months before I was born. My parents were divorced and I never knew my father. I had a great mother, though, and I was happy growing up. My mother died about five years ago, and I still miss her.

"I was a kindergarten teacher for two years, until not long after the school year ended. The town of Greenview redrew the school district lines, consolidated some schools, and I lost my job. I love children, and I loved teaching. When the attorney, Mr. Arceneau, called me I was trying to decide whether to look for a different kind of job in Greenview or whether to move to another town to teach."

"Instead you moved here," Parker said, smiling.

"Now it's your turn. Are you from New Orleans?"

"No, I was born and raised in Dallas. I got bored living there, and when a spot opened up here I transferred. I write computer programs and train people to use them. What I do is pretty boring to most people, but I like it."

Simon returned with their salads and a basket of thick-crusted bread that smelled of butter and garlic.

"Oh, Simon. This looks so good. Just as good as I remember it."

"I hope you enjoy it."

"I'm sure I will."

Parker and Addie started to eat their salads when a tall, slim, redheaded woman slid into an extra chair at their table.

"Oh, Miss Zappa. Please, can you help me?" she asked, wringing her hands.

Addie put down her fork, startled. "If I can."

"My name is Sally Flournoy. I've lost a ring. It was my mother's engagement ring and it means the world to me. I was working the other day and it felt loose on my finger so I pulled it off. I put it down somewhere, but now I can't find it anywhere. I'm so afraid it either fell to the floor and got swept up or gathered up with some trash." She paused and wiped a tear that was rolling from the corner of her eye. "I am so upset I can't sleep. I can't get any work done. Please, can you do the things Madame could do? Can you make my ring appear?" Her voice broke.

Addie reached over and placed her hand on the distraught woman's hand. "No, I'm sorry, I don't have the same abilities that my aunt did. I don't know anything about hoodoo or things like that."

Sally Flournoy dropped her head and put her other hand over her face.

"I can tell you what I do when I lose something, and it always works for me. I can't guarantee it will work for you, though."

Dropping her hand from her face, the distressed woman looked at Addie with a glimmer of hope and squeezed Addie's hand. "Please tell me. I'll try anything."

"I find a quiet place — usually at home with no one else around. I sit down, close my eyes and calm myself. I tell myself to not be upset, that it is going to show up and everything is going to be okay. Then I talk to my guardian angel. Everyone has one, you know."

"Uh-huh. I've heard that." Sally's eyes were open wide.

"Sometimes I talk out loud and other times I just talk in my head. But I say something like, 'I know you know where my ring is, and you know how important it is to me. Please show me where to find it. I know you are going to show me, so thank you very much for helping me.' Now here is the important part, and it's harder to do."

Sally leaned forward, an intent expression on her face. "I'll do it, whatever it is. I'll do anything to find my mother's ring."

"You have to let go worrying about it. You have to be confident your guardian angel is going to show you. When you know for sure something good is going to happen, you don't worry about it not happening, do you?"

"No. I guess not."

"Well, know you are going to find the ring when the time is right. Feel happy about it."

"Oh thank you, Miss Zappa. Thank you!" She stood to leave.

"One more thing…"

"Yes, I almost forgot. What do you charge? What do I owe you?"

"Charge?" Addie said, startled. "There's no charge. What I was going to say was when you find your ring, be sure to tell your guardian angel thank you."

"I will, Miss Zappa. I will. Thank you!"

"It's Addie, and you're welcome."

The woman rushed back to her table and Addie resumed eating her salad.

"It's started already," Parker said.

"This is what you meant?" Addie paused in her eating and looked at Parker. "People would be asking for help?"

"Yes." Parker wiped his mouth with his napkin and started to say more when Simon arrived with their bowls of jambalaya.

"Here you are, Miss Zappa — er, Addie. I hope you enjoy it."

"I know I will, Simon, thank you."

"What else were you going to say?" Addie asked while she stirred her jambalaya, picking out a perfect spoonful of rice and shrimp.

"Everyone is curious about you. They all want to meet you. I just hope they don't bug you too much, not only with requests for help, but just in general."

"I'm flattered they are interested in me. They're going to be disappointed, though, when word gets around that I can't conjure up lost items or do spells or anything, like my aunt used to."

"Until then, you're going to be busy answering questions and telling them you don't do hoodoo."

Addie's attention was on her meal, but Parker noticed Simon trying to keep people from approaching their table. When they finished their meal, Estelle, the waitress who had worked for Simon the longest, approached to clear their plates.

"I hope you enjoyed your jambalaya, Miss Zappa," she said.

"Please call me Addie. Everyone should call me Addie. I enjoyed my meal very much. I'm looking forward to eating here often."

"My name is Estelle. I hope you feel right at home both here and at your aunt's place. The neighborhood is real happy you've come."

Simon approached the table and frowned at Estelle, who scurried back to the kitchen with the dishes.

"I've been trying to keep people away so they didn't disturb your meal. I'm sorry Sally Flournoy slipped through."

"Simon, if it's all right with Addie, I think we might as well let them through and get it over with," Parker said.

"My goodness," Addie said, eyes wide, "Of course let them speak to me if they want to."

"You're sure?" Simon asked.

Addie took a deep breath. "I'm sure."

Simon walked back to take his place behind the counter, nodding his head to people along the way.

An older man with silver hair was the first person to approach Addie.

"We thought highly of your aunt, Miss Zappa. She came down hard on folks what didn't do right. She'd put a hex on 'em and that'd straighten 'em out, all right. She protected us, that be so."

"Please call me Addie, Mr......?"

"Tremont. My name is John Tremont, er, Addie."

Addie extended her hand. "I'm glad to meet you, Mr. Tremont."

"Well, I just wanted to make my welcome."

When he left, Addie heard him talking to the people a couple of tables away. "She seems real nice," he said.

Angie Hobart was next. "I just wanted to welcome you to the neighborhood. My daddy wanted to be here awful bad. Madame did a spell of protection over him and he's sure that's what brought him home safe from the war. He's feeling poorly or he'd be here tonight. We're all so happy you're here."

The stream of people grew. After several more people, Addie whispered to Parker, "I'll never remember all these names."

"Don't worry. I'll help you put names and faces together."

The restaurant slowly emptied as people finished eating. When they started for the exit they came by to tell Addie how much they thought of her aunt and to welcome her to the neighborhood.

At one point when there was a break in the line, Simon approached the table, chuckling. "Those tourists over there asked me if you were a movie star or sumpin, the way people are comin' over and speaking to you."

"What did you tell them?" asked Parker.

"I tol' 'em your auntie was the hoodoo queen of New Orleans and she done passed. You're her niece and the new hoodoo queen," Simon said to Addie.

He left, still laughing.

"Is it me, or does Simon's dialect get stronger from time to time?" Addie asked.

"Yeah, he puts it on thicker when there's tourists around, but sometimes he talks like that around everyone."

An elderly woman slowly made her way to their table, leaning on her cane.

"Miss Addie, could I ask you sumpin?"

"Addie, this is Mrs. Raynard. She is one of the elders of the community."

"Yessum. I be elderly all right. And I'm havin' trouble sleeping. Is there anythin' you can do to help? A spell or potion or sumpin? Your aunt used to give me some herbs an' stuff to put under my pillow what would help me sleep."

"Mrs. Raynard, I don't know anything about herbs. I do have something that may help you, though. You can try it and tell me if it does you any good or not." Addie reached into the pocket of her dress and pulled out a purple stone. "This is an amethyst. Put it under your pillow and see if it helps you sleep, like the herbs used to."

"Oh thankee, ma'am," the old woman said as Addie place the stone in her hand. "I do appreciate it."

"Be sure to let me know if it works or not."

"Sure 'nough. I'll do that," she said, then turned and slowly made her way toward the door.

The place was almost empty when Parker rose and helped Addie move her chair away from the table. Simon approached them.

"Parker, the meal is on the house tonight. It's my way of saying welcome. Besides," he said to Addie, "your presence filled the house tonight. It was a good night for business."

"Thank you, Simon. That is kind of you."

"Yes, thank you Simon. I hope I will be bringing Addie to Simon's Place often."

"Well then, I'll let you pay next time."

On their way home, Addie's arm again looped through Parker's, she said. "I enjoyed that so much. I was kind of nervous about meeting the people who knew and respected Madame, but everyone was so welcoming and nice."

"They are naturally welcoming and nice people, as long as a person treats them right. They could see what kind of individual you are, and they are ready to accept you."

The streetlight illuminated the sidewalk. The sound of a song wafted through the air, trumpets and trombones echoing, swirling on the hot summer atmosphere like the scent of roses that accompanied the music.

"This is like a fairy tale come true. The sound of music, the scent of flowers, a lovely walk back to a marvelous apartment." She looked up at Parker. "And a handsome man on my arm. A perfect evening."

CHAPTER THIRTEEN

Addie stood in the shop, surveying the work she completed the day before. She would never have believed so much could be completed in the month she had been there. Of course Madame's legacy guaranteed Addie's wishes would be carried out as soon as possible. The workmen in the neighborhood jumped at the chance to please Madame's successor. Parker told her some people were referring to her to as 'the new witch.'

She asked Parker how to find someone to do painting, fix electricity and build shelves. He referred her to Hebert's Hardware Store in the next block. Addie walked down over there and introduced herself to Mr. Hebert, who was only too happy to find workmen to do the jobs she needed done.

"They will be glad to have the work," he said.

The electrician was first. Addie asked him to repair the chandelier in the shop. While it was down she washed and dried each of the crystals. When they were clean they cast sparkling glints of light all over the shop. She also had him check the wiring throughout not only the shop and her apartment, but all the other apartments, too. Mr. Arceneau suggested it when she called him to get the okay on her plans.

"Madame didn't have anything redone in decades. It's past time for that important safety issue," he said. "Take care of it in the shop and in all the flats and have the bill sent to me."

Addie had extra outlets installed; everyone had so many more appliances and gadgets than they used to, and it wasn't safe to have extension cords running all over the place.

Evie tried to avoid it when Addie told her the repairman might work as much as a full day in her apartment. She didn't need any work done, she said, and she didn't want some strange person coming into her space. She wrote articles she sold for publication on the internet, and she needed to stay at her work.

Hiding, she's hiding from someone.

Those initial thoughts were reinforced by Evie's behavior.

"This will probably interrupt your work, your writing, but it has to be done. Why don't you come to my apartment that day. With the wireless router Parker installed, you should be able to work as well as in your place, and you won't have any strangers around."

Evie had thought for a moment, then said "You're sure it won't bother you? I wouldn't be in your way?"

"Not at all. You need to give me a list of where you want more places to plug stuff in. Parker has already given me his. After the electrician does the work in my apartment he'll do yours and Parker's, then the vacant apartment. He'll be through in the shop and storeroom after he puts up the new light.

"I don't know how my aunt could find anything in there with the one dim light. He's going to put up lights tomorrow when he comes, then do my apartment. I'll let you know the day before he needs to start on your place. You can bring your laptop over and write."

"Sounds like it would work, if you are sure I wouldn't be putting you out any."

"I'm sure. I'll try not to bother you myself. I need to move my aunt's clothing and finish hanging all mine up, so I'll be working in the bedroom, mostly."

The day went well. Evie sat in Addie's living room and wrote articles to be published on the web while Addie put her clothing in the closet, armoire and drawers, pausing from time to time to try on some item of Madame's. At lunchtime they ate together in Addie's kitchen and talked.

"I did some writing for the internet before I moved here," Addie said. "I was a kindergarten teacher, and I published some ideas for helping a child get prepared for going to school, and extra activities, things like that."

"That's what I write too!" Evie said. "I used to be a first grade teacher, years ago, and I write articles about extra things to do at home, games to play and such, to help children learn."

"You know, there's a site where you can post lesson plans, don't you? And you can sell all sorts of things to other teachers. It might be a place for you to make some more sales."

They spent a pleasant hour discussing articles for and about children and other subjects both women.

All the electrical work went smoothly. The electrician upgraded the service considerably during the time he worked on the property.

By the time he completed all his tasks he was acting very strangely. He was nervous and jumpy. Parker said later that he told people that Madame's ghost was still in the place, wandering around.

Addie had the storeroom painted a clean, bright white and new shelves built. She transferred the contents of the shelves in the shop into the storeroom. It took her a full day, since she stopped and looked and thought about all the unusual names on the items she was moving and what they might be used for.

When I have time, I'll read up on hoodoo and figure out what Madame did with all this stuff.

It was time to think about how she wanted the shop arranged. She stood as if she had just entered the shop by the front door, pretending she was a customer. The shelves on the back wall were fine, as were the ones on the left wall. She had the walls painted a soft ivory color. She needed the counter on the left side moved, so she could put a worktable behind it, by the window. She wanted to be able to see out as she designed and made jewelry.

Six weeks after she arrived, Addie was cleaning all the glass in the shop: the fronts of the counters, the door and the front windows. The door stood open to let the air circulate through the shop into the storeroom, and continuing on into the kitchen and living room where the French doors stood open to catch every wisp of breeze. Each time she finished cleaning one surface, before going to another surface that needed to be polished, she stopped to marvel at how everything looked. The chandelier sent sparkles of light flashing around the room as the soft drafts moved the crystals. Furniture polish made the old walnut wood on the shelves and counters gleam as it must have done almost a hundred years before. The pleasant scent of the herbs that had previously filled the room lingered on, or maybe drifted in from the storeroom. Soon, her original designs of jewelry would fill the glass-front cabinets and be shown to the outside through the soon-to-be gleaming front windows.

She jumped as a small ball of fur, yipping madly, ran into the shop, followed by a little boy.

"Stop, Spike, stop," he yelled.

Addie couldn't help laughing at such a macho name for such a little dog. The boy and dog ran in circles around the room, the boy trying to catch the leash trailing behind the tiny dog. The yipping dog ran in front of Addie and she took the opportunity to step on the leash, ending the chase.

"Thank you for catching him. I dropped the leash and Spike ran off."

"You're welcome. Do you live around here?" He looked about the age of her kindergarteners. Surely, she figured, his mother was close. About that time she heard a woman frantically calling out on the sidewalk.

"Morgan! Morgan!"

"Uh-oh," he said as he edged toward the door, Spike following on the leash.

Addie stepped out onto the walk. "He's here. Spike got loose and ran in here and Morgan followed."

"Morgan, get yourself home and into the back yard with Spike. I'll be there shortly." The young woman approached Addie, shaking her head. "I hope he didn't get into anything in your shop. He was supposed to stay inside while I unloaded my car," she said, looking at Addie with worried eyes.

"He was no trouble at all. Spike ran in with Morgan close behind. They were only inside a minute."

"I don't want him to be a bother, though. Some people don't like children running around."

"I was a kindergarten teacher before I came here. I love children. They don't bother me at all." She pushed a stray curl out of her eyes. "I'm Addie Zappa. Madame, who used to have this shop, was my great-aunt."

"Hi. I'm Dani Washington, and I have the shop next door. I was very sorry for your auntee's passing. She was so good to me. I miss her."

"I never met her. In fact, I didn't even know she existed until she died and left this place to me. I've heard some very interesting things about Madame, though. The people in the neighborhood seem to think highly of her."

"Yes, she did good things for the people around here. My first week in town, I was looking for a place to open a shop, and also for an apartment. This place is just perfect for me. She was sitting out here on this bench and greeted me, and when JayMar came to show me the property Madame told him to treat me right, and he did."

She looked down and drew a circle on the sidewalk with her toe. "He's sniffing around now, with her gone." She looked up again. "You know about Madame practicing hoodoo, don't you?"

"Yes. People have told me about that. They seem to think I'm her replacement, but I have to admit I don't know a thing about hoodoo."

"I wish you did. I think that is what is keeping JayMar from hitting on me for real and from going up on the rent. He doesn't know whether Madame's power is still watching over me, or whether you can and would do what Madame could. I can't afford much more than what I'm paying, and I get the impression that I'll have to give in to him or he is going to go up on the rent. If I'm faced with sleeping with JayMar or moving, I'll move." Dani crossed her arms and looked despondently at the sidewalk.

Addie grinned. "There's nothing to keep him from believing I can do spells and stuff, is there? And if he believes it, and believes you are my friend, under my protection, he'll leave you alone, right?"

Dani smiled back. "Right. Most people were mighty afraid of crossing Madame, and from what I hear, you have some power of your own."

"What power? I can't do anything like that at all. I'm not sure I even believe in hoodoo. I'm really blown away by all this mystical stuff."

"People are saying that down at Simon's the first night you were in town you cured Mrs. Raynard of insomnia and found Sally Flournoy's lost ring. You have a reputation for magic whether you want it or not."

"Shoot! I had a small amethyst in my pocket, sort of like a worry stone. Amethyst helps control nervousness, and I was nervous that night, going down to Simon's Café to meet all those people, friends of Madame's, so I wore an amethyst necklace and put the stone in my pocket. When Mrs. Raynard asked me about something for insomnia I just took it out of my pocket and gave it to her. Amethyst helps several things, and insomnia is one of them. I told her to put it under her pillow at night, and to carry it with her during the day. I guess it must have helped."

"Well, there you go. You do magic with stones, whether you call it hoodoo or not, and you find lost things."

"Sally found her own lost ring. I told her to sit down in a quiet place with no noise or music or any distractions, to calm herself and after she had sat there a couple of minutes to ask her guardian spirit to show her where she left the ring. I told her not to beg, not to be upset, just to ask nicely to be shown. Then when she got up she should believe her spirit would show her, not to get anxious or in a hurry. It would show up in its own time."

"Sally is telling everybody you showed her how to find it. She picked up a pair of jeans she had worn a couple of days before and there it was, in the pocket."

"I may have shown her how to find it, but she found it herself."

"That's good enough!"

Addie wanted to get the subject off herself. "I've been wanting to come see what you have in your shop. I love unusual clothes. I wear vintage pieces a lot."

"Come over anytime. I have a lot of new old stuff to put out. I have been to several estate sales lately and I'm working through a lot of merchandise, repairing and cleaning before I put them out for sale. Come now, if you want."

"Thanks, but I have to finish cleaning the glass. The sign painter is coming this afternoon to paint on the front windows and I have to have them clean and dry."

"What are you going to sell in your shop?"

"Jewelry. I love designing and making one of a kind pieces, and I can only wear so much jewelry. I wanted a place to sell my designs before I moved here, so this is working out perfectly for me."

"Ooh, good. A jewelry store right next door is serendipity. I've always wanted to pair jewelry with the clothing I sell, either the vintage pieces I sell in their original design or the ones I remake, but I seldom find jewelry I can afford to buy and resell or pieces that match the clothing I have. Now I can send people over to your shop to get a necklace or bracelet to match."

"What do you mean by 'remake'?"

"I design clothing using vintage clothing as the base. Sometimes I put trims and beads on pieces; sometimes I use parts of several items to make one whole new garment. You'll have to come sometime and I'll show you."

"I'd love to, but I'd better get back to work now or I won't have dry windows when the sign painter comes." Both women started back toward their businesses.

Addie stopped and turned back. "I have an idea. I could make pieces to match your clothing, and you put them on the mannequins. If you sell something of mine, I'll pay you a commission. That way you won't have anything tied up in inventory for jewelry, and I'll make more selling in two places."

"You'd really do that? It sounds great. Let's get together on that later in the week. Now I've got to go take care of a boy who doesn't mind." Dani grinned while she went back inside her shop.

Maybe Spike's getting loose wasn't such a bad thing after all.

CHAPTER FOURTEEN

Evie wished she wasn't such a scaredy-cat, but in the months she had lived there she withdrew deeper and deeper into her own private world, only interacting with other people when she absolutely had to. When she realized she would have to get a local driver's license and car tags if she kept her car, she sold it.

Recently, she had only set foot out of the apartment complex when she had to go to the market. When it became absolutely necessary she would put on a scarf or hat and sunglasses and walk the two blocks to Coudart's Market, worrying the whole time about the possibility Ed might be lurking somewhere nearby and see her. Every couple of months, when she needed to go somewhere outside the neighborhood, she asked Parker if he would take her, and he graciously did so.

She stood on the gallery outside the French doors leading into her living room, trying to get up nerve to go down the stairs to the courtyard and join Addie where she sat at the bright blue table. Evie remembered the day the young black girl had come and painted the table and chairs for Madame. Evie had eavesdropped on their conversation, starved for contact with others, yet unable to reach out. Evidently the young woman had a shop next door, and Madame bought the paint and hired her to paint the outdoor furniture. Madame had supervised the operation while the little boy played on the bricks of the courtyard. He looked so sweet. She thought about the years before she married Ed. She missed teaching school and missed having youngsters in her care.

Madame and the girl, Dani, and the little boy, Morgan, had talked and laughed together, and when the job was done, Evie heard Madame tell Dani to take the rest of the blue paint and paint the facings around Dani's shop windows.

"Don't you want me to paint the facings around your windows, too, Madame?" the girl had asked.

"Non, merci. I do not wish mine to look better. I do not seek more customers. I have too many as it is."

At this moment, Madame's niece, Addie, sat in the shade of the tree, looking around the courtyard as if she were studying it, and Evie wanted very much to join her. She was nervous at first in Addie's living room while the electrician worked in her place, but after an hour or so, she felt completely at ease and wrote her articles.

At noon Addie had come into the living room from the bedroom where she was working, Evie wondered if the sense of security and protection she always felt when Madame was alive was still present because Addie had the same powers as Madame, or if the old lady's ghost really was haunting the place. One day soon after Addie arrived, Evie overheard two of the workmen talk about tools being moved and things appearing and disappearing from one day to the next while they worked in the empty apartment, which they kept locked. They decided it was a ghost, perhaps Madame's spirit lingering.

The sense of security hadn't extended to going down the stairs, where anyone standing at the gate could see her, and the thought of sitting out in the open, instead of being enclosed in an apartment — whether hers or Addie's — made Evie nervous.

Just do it, Evelyn. Just go! Don't think about it anymore or you'll never go down there. If you could endure Ed's torment all those years, if you could be brave enough to plan and run away, you can go down a flight of stairs and sit in the fresh air and visit with a perfectly nice woman. Don't be such a wimp!

Finally, she took a deep breath and moved along the balcony until she came to the area where the steps descended. Evie stopped and cautiously inched along, watching until she could see the gate that locked the courtyard away from the rest of the world. She held her breath as she checked to see if anyone was standing there, trying to see into the private area behind the shops. When she ascertained no one was watching, she quickly went down the steps and approached Addie.

"Good morning, Evie. It's such a beautiful morning, I thought I'd sit out here to have my morning coffee. Can I get you a cup?"

"No, thank you. I've been up so long I've already drank enough for the day."

"Then come and visit with me. I'm trying to decide about planting flowers in these beds. It seems a shame to have such a great courtyard, surrounded by planting areas, and not have plants and flowers everywhere, but I don't know much about what to plant where."

"Well, you need plants for sun to put over on that side," Evie said while she gestured. "It gets full sun all day. And then you need plants for shade for over there." She pointed at the flowerbed to the back. "What flowers do you like?"

By the time Evie thought about going back to her writing, she realized she had spent an hour or more visiting with Addie, talking about the pros and cons of various plants.

See, I can be sociable. I'm not a complete hermit.

"I'd better get back to my writing. I have a piece due in a few days I need to get finished."

"I know you don't get out much, but would you go with me to the nursery to buy plants and everything else I'm going to need to spruce up this courtyard? Please?"

Evie thought about it. "Maybe. I'll see if I have time later in the week."

Maybe I can go out in public again. I can't let myself become so frightened that I become a true recluse. Besides, Ed would never be in a garden shop.

It wasn't until she reached the door to her apartment that she realized she walked all the way across the courtyard and up the stairs without checking to see if Ed was at the gate.

CHAPTER FIFTEEN

JayMar looked at himself in the mirror. He looked pretty damned good, if he did say so himself. He thought it was important to give off the right vibe, to look like the man, the man who was in charge. He had an important job and had to look the part. As the representative of JMZ, Inc. he had a reputation to maintain, and looks were a part of it. He adjusted the chains around his neck.

Uh-huh, I look fly. He was ready to start his rounds of the rental property he managed for the man.

When he landed this job, he changed his name, just a little, from Jamar to JayMar. It didn't hurt for people to get the idea that he was the J and M in the company name. He never came right out and said he was, but people who met him since he took this job came away with that idea anyway. At least once a month he visited every rental property JMZ owned. He checked to see if everything was in good shape, arranged to have necessary repairs made, and reminded the tenant when the rent was due. Some people mailed the rent to the JMZ office, but others had to have it picked up in person or they never would pay. The ones who paid their money directly to JayMar did not know that the raises in rent they experienced didn't go to the company, but instead went into JayMar's pocket.

He thought about that sweet little thing who rented the shop and apartment above, the one next to Madame's shop. Uh-hum. He would like to see more of her, in more ways than one. When he first showed her the place, the old witch was sitting there outside the door and made it plain that the girl, Dani, was under her protection. It was not smart to anger Madame, not smart at all. He knew several people who had done something she didn't like, and he didn't want to have happen to him what happened to them.

One day his friend Darius had grabbed an apple down at the market. He just picked it up from the bin out front and went down the sidewalk eating it. Old Mr. Coudart hollered at him. "Come back, thief! Come back and pay for that apple."

Darius knew that Mr. Coudart couldn't do anything about it, and neither could the old woman standing there. Too bad Darius didn't notice the old woman was Madame. Within minutes of eating the apple he doubled over from terrible pains in his stomach. He threw up everything he ate for three days. When he felt a little better and went out and about again, the first person he saw was Madame.

"You will always get sick from eating stolen food. I have seen to it."

Darius lost weight because of the hex. He was a little chubby because of his habit of lifting candy or chips at the Quik-Mart, but after the apple incident he stopped doing that and slimmed up.

After a while Darius thought about what happened and decided there wasn't any such thing as a hex on stolen food, so a few months later the fool decided to test what Madame said. He went over to another part of town, where nobody knew him, ate a good meal at a café, then just stood and walked out without paying — dine and dash, it's called. He figured since he seldom went over there no one would ever see him and recognize him as the dude who took the café owner for a meal. Darius was lucky to make it home his stomach hurt so bad. This time he had the runs as well as throwing up, and it lasted for five days instead of three. He never tried to steal food again. In fact, he never stole anything at all again because he was afraid the curse Madame had put on him might work on everything.

JayMar knew the story was true because he knew Darius personally, but he knew lots of other stories about things Madame did, stories about people breaking out in a rash all over their body, losing all their money, or losing body parts. He even heard the story about Madame turning her husband into a dog, and he wasn't taking any chances. Madame might have put some spell over the fox renting the shop and apartment that lasted even after the witch's death.

Then there was that new woman to contend with, that Addie Zappa. The talk was she was Madame's niece, Madame's sister's granddaughter. Man, was that a surprise. JayMar noticed her the other day, sweeping off the sidewalk in front of the shop, and she sure didn't look like she was related to Madame.

Even so, he figured he'd better be careful. She might be as strong as Madame at casting spells and hexes and such. He sure didn't want to get a hex put on him. People in the neighborhood were buzzing about her arrival but JayMar couldn't get any firm idea whether she did hoodoo like Madame or not. He even talked with his brother, who was always in the thick of things, about what he heard, but there was not a lot of information out there yet. There were some stories about the new woman curing a couple of people and finding a lost ring.

Yes, it would be best to be very careful and not anger the new witch.

CHAPTER SIXTEEN

Dani stood in the window and moved the mannequin while Addie motioned from outside on the sidewalk. This was so much easier than when she tried to do this by herself. Running back and forth from inside to out and back again took a lot of time to get it just right. Addie was proving to be a good friend, and it was nice to have someone to talk to again. Since her grandmother died, going on a year ago now, she hadn't had anyone to visit with, woman-to-woman, friend-to-friend, until Addie came along.

"I think that is just perfect," Addie said, coming in the front door. "You go take a look."

Dani stepped out and surveyed the window. The mannequin was wearing a white tent dress that now had a band of brightly striped fabric about six inches from the hem, added by Dani. When she returned inside Addie was holding several necklaces over her hand.

"Which one of these, do you think?" she asked, holding one up to the dress and squinting, as though that would help her decide.

"They're all in the same colors. The oranges, yellows and greens in the necklaces are perfect with the band on the dress. You choose which one."

"Several of them, I think." Addie put the beads over the headless form, "That's what's in style right now. I'll put these three around her feet," she spread the other necklaces and giggled, "If she had feet, that is."

Dani only had two mannequins, one of them headless and legless, and thought she was very lucky to have those, although she was pleased with the wire form she used in the other window. Mannequins and forms were something that didn't turn up at estate sales or tag sales very often, and when they did they were frequently out of her budget. She and Addie were getting good at rigging up dowel sticks run through the arms of a garment and hanging them from the ceiling with monofilament line. They created some interesting displays that way.

"I ought to have the evening coat finished this afternoon, the one your aunt gave me, and maybe you could help me change out the other window. I have a red silk dress I am going to put on the form next to it."

"Ooh, I have some black and crystal pieces that will go with that, if you want them."

"I'd love to show them, but you have a jewelry shop yourself, Addie. You can't be putting all your work over here for me to sell, even if you do get most of the money from it."

"I have plenty to sell at my place. I'm focusing on gemstone jewelry at Zappa's. I'm concentrating on the powers different gemstones are supposed to bestow on people. Everyone is expecting Madame's niece to do hoodoo, and this is about as close as I can get."

"Do you mean like the amethyst you gave Mrs. Reynard?"

"Yes. Few people realize why jewels and gemstones became valuable to people."

"What do you mean? Don't they value them because they are pretty?"

"Yes, they're pretty. But they are much prettier now than they were thousands of years ago before men learned to cut them to make them sparkle. Even the jewels of a couple of hundred years ago are pretty dull looking compared to today's standards."

"So why did people value them back then?"

"Because they thought the gemstones had magic power. The amethyst I gave Mrs. Raynard, for example, is supposed to not only relieve insomnia, but also bring intuitive dreams, among other things. There is a long list of things amethyst helps."

"Do you believe in the magic power of gemstones?"

"To tell you the honest truth, I don't know. Sometimes I think it couldn't possibly be so, then something will happen to me, or maybe one of my friends, when we're wearing jewelry made with certain gemstones and I'll think, whoa. It's true. The stones work.

"The way I look at it is how does it hurt? It doesn't. Wearing a necklace or bracelet made of agate when I have to stand up and make a speech can't hurt me, and if that agate helps me be more eloquent, then so be it. If it is all in my imagination, that's okay, too."

"Hmm. Interesting. I'll have to reserve judgment until I read and see more."

"The jewelry I put over here in your shop is mostly glass, wood and plastic. That makes chic, au courant pieces in bright colors. I'm not against putting some gemstone pieces in your shop when that is what the dress calls for, but I'm not pushing the supposed mystic qualities of the stones over here like I do at my shop."

The two women walked outside where they stood admiring the windows. "I'm glad I had the painter do my windows the day he came to do yours," Dani said. "He gave me a really good deal since he already had his equipment out to do yours."

"He did a good job on both places. 'DANI'S — VINTAGE WITH A FLARE.' Now you look professional."

"Why did you only put 'ZAPPA'S' on your windows? Why not put ZAPPA'S JEWELRY?"

"Well, with all the talk about hoodoo and such, I wasn't sure if I wanted to limit myself to just jewelry. Not," she hurriedly added, "that I have any intention of practicing hoodoo, but I am learning about things like which color of candles to burn for certain times, like to bring things or push them away. This way it leaves it open."

Just then a tall African-American man dressed in black and wearing several bulky silver chains walked up to where they stood on the sidewalk.

"Good day, Miss Washington. You're certainly looking fine today."

"Thank you, JayMar. Have you met Miss Zappa, Madame's niece, yet?"

JayMar's smile disappeared. "Pleased to meet you, Miss Zappa. Sorry for your loss."

"Thank you, Mr. Davis. It is Davis, isn't it?"

"Yes ma'am, it's Davis, but you can call me JayMar, like your auntee did."

"JayMar it is.

"And you have your shop open, too, I see. Are you going into the same business as Madame?"

"Not precisely the same, but not altogether different, either." Let him figure it out.

"There's talk around the neighborhood about Madame's ghost still wandering around these parts. Have you met the haunt yet?"

Addie looked at Dani, whose mouth had dropped open. "I haven't personally seen the specter, but I've heard strange noises when no one is there to make them. The man who did some work for me heard them, too, and found things moved around. I guess I'll have to see to doing something to send her on her way. Although, it might not be a bad idea for my aunt to hang around the place so I can learn her particular spells. I imagine she is still looking over the neighborhood and its inhabitants, don't you?"

JayMar had an unhappy look on his face. "Yessum. I 'magine she is." He looked at Dani. "If everything is doin' all right at your place I'll be moseyin' on along."

"Yes, everything is just fine. Thank you, JayMar."

When he was out of earshot the two women broke into laughter, stumbling over to sit on the bench between the two shops.

"That ought to keep him in line for a while," giggled Dani. "But what is this about Madame's ghost?"

"The electrician who was here putting in more receptacles told everyone he met about hearing strange noises and having things in the vacant flat moved from one day to the next. Parker told me it's the subject of a lot of talk at Simon's Café. I would laugh it off except sometimes I hear noises, too, in the night, and I can't figure out what's making them. I went up into the vacant apartment, but there is no sign of anyone there, and no way anyone can get in with it locked up tight.

"I don't know what it is, but I don't believe in ghosts. I don't mind if JayMar believes in them, though. He can believe Madame is still around watching him. That'll keep him from bothering you."

Dani rose, saying, "It's time I got back to work. I want to get the new lining in the evening coat and get it in the window."

"I wish I could do something with all the clothing she left. There are some wonderful garments I put in storage. I couldn't wear but a couple of pieces. She was much smaller than I am and nothing much fits, but I have to wait until the year is up before I can dispose of any of it, according to Mr. Arceneau."

Dani retreated to her workroom. As she sewed she thought how happy she was to hear that Addie was planning on staying the year. By now everyone knew that she had to remain a full twelve months to get everything transferred to her name. Dani was glad her new friend planned to stay.

CHAPTER SEVENTEEN

People were treating Diane nicer these days. For that matter, Diane felt a differently about herself — better, more confident, like she wasn't such a geek. When she first moved to New Orleans and started to work she was very shy and had low self-esteem. Her friends told her that all the time. Recently, she had begun to think maybe she wasn't such a dweeb after all.

Thinking back on it, Diane decided it was about the time she started doing all the things Madame Badeaux set out for her to get more smiles and friendly greetings from people at work, men included. She started to feel prettier. She paid a lot of money for this transformation so Scott would find her attractive enough to ask her out on a date, and evidently it was working, just not on Scott. A couple of guys at the office started coming by her desk and flirting with her. One of the agents even asked her to have a drink with him after work, but she turned him down because she had to go listen to Scott.

Finally she came to the conclusion Scott needed a bigger push. He was still as friendly as ever, but her growing attractiveness (and she was sure it was growing by the way people at work were treating her) didn't bring him any closer to asking her for a date, so it was time to go back to the hoodoo shop and get some more help.

The place had changed a lot since the last time Diane was there. Yesenia and Jeanine told her that Madame Badeaux had died — passed is what they said — but her niece was there in the same place, the same shop. They weren't sure exactly what the niece did that was extraordinary, the talk was vague about that subject, but they knew she had special powers of some sort. Diane would just have to go find out. After all, Diane had received a guarantee of sorts from Madame, and it was up to the niece to honor the promise of a stronger spell if the ones Madame provided her didn't bring Scott to her.

Standing on the sidewalk in front of the shop, Diane saw the windows, which used to be so dusty she could barely see through them, were now sparkling clean and filled with jewelry. There were necklaces draped over black velvet stands and hanging from invisible thread from the ceiling. There were bracelets in silver and gold tones, some with colored stones, displayed, as well as earrings in various styles. The gold letters on the glass read ZAPPA'S: just that. There was no mention of jewelry and in Diane's mind that left the possibilities wide open. Through the open door she could see tiny rainbows flashing around the room as the wisp of a breeze moved the crystals in the chandelier. Taking a deep breath, she entered the shop.

"Good morning. May I help you?" said the woman behind the counter.

Surely this is not Madame's niece. Not this woman with the mass of strawberry blonde hair piled on top of her head and skin like gold burnished sunlight.

"Yes, I'm looking for Madame Badeaux's niece, the one who runs this shop now."

"I'm Addie Zappa and I am Madame's niece."

"You? But... er . . . but ..."

Addie smiled. "Yes, that's me, her great-niece. How can I help you?"

Diane took a deep breath. "Some time ago, I came to Madame for help. There is a man, a man I see often, who I would like to ask me out on a date. I see him almost every evening, and we are friendly, but he doesn't ask me out. Sometimes I feel like he sees me more as a little sister or just a friend, not date potential."

"Why don't you just ask him out instead of waiting on him to make the first move?"

"Oh, no. I couldn't do that." Diane reddened at the thought. Asking a man for a date was so far out of her comfort zone as to be impossible. "No, I want him to ask me out. I couldn't stand it if I asked him out and he refused." Her insides clinched at the very thought.

"Anyway, I came to Madame and she gave me several things to use and do — charms I guess, or spells or something. I paid her quite a lot of money for them,"

She frowned at the memory of just how much she had paid for something that didn't work the way she wanted.

"Anyway they did work, I guess, just not on Scott. That's his name, Scott. Men at my office have started asking me out, and they smile and flirt, but nothing has changed with this man I really want to go out with. He's as friendly as ever, but that's all. Madame said what she gave me was to make me more desirable to him, but if it didn't work to come back and she would give me something, a potion or something, to work on Scott. So that's what I'm here for. Madame guaranteed her, ah, work."

"Hmm. I see. The problem is, I can't do what Madame did. I don't know how. I don't have the training, I guess you would say."

"But the girls at the office are saying you have special talents, too, like Madame only different. Isn't there some way you can help me?"

"I know that rumors are flying around here, but they are greatly exaggerated, believe me. The few things I have done are nothing compared to what I have heard about Madame's feats."

"Didn't she leave anything that would tell you what to do? Books or notes or something?"

"Well," Addie paused and thought a minute, "yes, there are books, but I haven't studied them. A lot of it is in French, and I have forgotten most of my high school French."

"Maybe you could look in the books and figure out what she was going to give me. She seemed quite sure about what she was going to do. She said she would give me something to make him really look at me. 'We will concoct a potion to make him really see you' is what she said."

"I'll tell you what. I'll look through Madame's books and see what I can find, but I don't promise anything. In the meantime, let me give you this moonstone necklace. Moonstones are said to bring love and romance to the wearer."

Addie reached into the counter, where several necklaces were displayed behind the glass, and drew out a necklace of milky clear stones, pink pearls, pink stones, and glittering gems here and there.

"This one has moonstones in it. See? These clear white ones are moonstones. They are said to bring romance to you, as well as long life and happiness. The pearls help fight infection, and the pale pink stones are rose quartz. They do a lot of things. They help headaches, give inner peace, and stimulate the intellect and imagination. Rose quartz is called the love stone because it promotes love."

"Really? These stones do all that?"

"Well, some people believe they have power, some people don't. Why don't you wear it and let me know what happens? In the meantime I'll study my aunt's journals and see if I can figure out what she was planning on giving you. I'll get someone to help me with the French."

"Okay. I'll do that. I'll wear this every day and let you know if it works or not."

"Come back in about a week. That ought to give me time to find what she was going to do. If I'm able to, that is. What was it she said, again?"

"She said, 'We will concoct a potion to make him really see you.'"

"I'll go through all her books and see what I can find. You come back next week."

As Diane left she glanced back into the shop. She wondered what powers the other jewelry displayed on and in the counters had. She might explore the realm of magic stones further.

CHAPTER EIGHTEEN

Evie looked in the mirror while she adjusted the necklace to show above the tee shirt she wore. She left almost all her dresses behind when she ran, but Addie said jeans and a tee would be fine to wear to work. Evie couldn't believe she was really going to make this step, this very big step, of putting herself out in public again. Addie gave her courage. From the day the new landlady arrived, Evie started feeling braver, taking steps she thought before she could never take.

First, she spent the day in Addie's apartment while the electrician worked in hers. A couple of weeks later she went down into the courtyard and sat there talking with Addie as if she, Evie, were like anyone else. It was the first time since moving Evie had sat in the shade visiting with someone. Parker often sat there, as had Madame, but Evie usually stayed inside her apartment. If she ventured out, she'd scurried across the bricks, up the stairs and into her apartment before anyone saw her. She enjoyed the fellowship with Addie these days. It was so long since she had a conversation with another woman — with anyone, in fact — and it made her feel good, even if she was still nervous. She and Addie sat discussing plants for the flowerbeds surrounding the courtyard, as if Evie were like other people, not a fugitive.

That is how she thought of herself: a fugitive. Hiding lest she be found, and the longer she hid, the more she worried and the less she went anywhere in public. She saw this in herself but was powerless to overcome the fear that kept her indoors.

Addie persuaded Evie to accompany her to the nursery and help pick out the plants which gave the courtyard a facelift. Even sheltered with sunglasses and a floppy hat covering her dyed brown hair, she continually looked around, expecting Ed or some unknown private detective to pounce on her at any minute, as if either of them would be in a garden shop in New Orleans.

Evie loved gardening. Mixing peat, sand, and fertilizer with the soil and placing the seedlings where they would take advantage of the sun or shade gave her a feeling of accomplishment she had not experienced in some time. At first she tried to stay out of the line of sight from the gate, but soon she forgot and moved freely about the courtyard, eyeing the plantings they were doing and enjoying working with Addie.

Addie had even suggested Evie write an article about it for the web.

"You might as well make a little money from this day's work, since you didn't get any writing done today."

"You could do the same thing."

"I'll get back to writing after I get unpacked and the shop stocked and open. I'm sure I'll have plenty of things to write about by then. You go ahead and take this one."

So Evie did go back to her writing, but from that point she wasn't quite so reclusive. Many afternoons she came down to have a glass of tea or lemonade with Addie and Parker. They often asked her to come with them to Simon's Place for supper, but she wasn't that brave yet. She still clung to her fears, and imagined Ed walking into the café and seeing her sitting there, or maybe someone he hired to look for her. Not maybe, she knew for sure he would have done so. She shuddered at the thought of him finding her. He had a gun, and he might be furious enough to use it.

"You're mine," he used to say. "Don't forget it. You belong to me. You'll never leave me. Never." She shuddered at the memory.

She still lay awake at night sometimes, imagining him finding her and breaking into her apartment to kill her. Probably after beating and raping her. There were sounds in the night, sounds she perceived as someone trying to get in. She checked the locks repeatedly. Even when she knew every security device was secure, she would go back and check again. All the French doors in the flat were solid and secure and had double locks. Even if someone broke a pane out it would be impossible to get the door open. The window set high in the back wall of her bedroom opened onto the roof of the car shed in the back, and many nights she thought she heard someone on the roof. She would get up and check the iron grill covering the window and it was always secure. No one could get in that way. Even so, the next time she heard a noise in the night she would check it again, worried that maybe it had come loose, maybe Ed had found her.

The day would be a big accomplishment for Evie, if she could go through with it. Addie asked her if she could work a few hours in the shop. At first Evie declined, saying she couldn't do that. Addie didn't ask why not; she only sat there, sipping her iced tea, until finally Evie told her the whole story. She told her about the beatings and the verbal abuse, the accusations and hateful words flung at her every day. She told about being watched at everything she did, never trusted and never believed. She told Addie about the bruises carefully kept where clothing covered them so people wouldn't suspect the respected church member and prominent businessman of inflecting injury on his wife. She told about her flight from him and how she had tried to cover her tracks. But Ed was a persistent man. He would never let her go, and he had the money to hire people to track her. He was still looking; she knew he was.

Evie cried when she talked about her beloved son, and how after his death she felt as though she was free to run away and find safety in a new place. Instead she had found the anxiety of staying hidden from sight. She felt as though Ed would walk up and grab her and make her go back into bondage again.

When she was finished with her story she felt like a heavy weight had been lifted from her, like it had floated up into the sky. She was still cautious, but the big lump of fear that grew like a cancer in her chest started shrinking and was only a tiny portion of what it had been.

"We are here to help protect you," Addie said. "You wouldn't have to go with him, even if he did find you."

"You don't know Ed. If he couldn't kidnap me and take me back, he would kill me. He would find a way to do it. He might shoot me, or he might burn this place down. But if he knew I was here nothing would stop him."

"But you can't live the rest of your life this way, hiding, not having a life of your own. Aren't you miserable living like a hermit?"

"Yes, it's beginning to get to me. I'd noticed myself growing more reclusive until lately, until you moved here. I'll admit I need to start thinking about earning some money sooner or later. When I got here I had money. I had saved some, plus I had quite a bit from selling my SUV and buying a cheaper car. Then when I realized I would have to get a Louisiana driver's license and give my real name on my old license to get it, I sold the car. I can walk to everywhere from here and didn't have to give my real name to anyone."

"Wow. I never thought of that. It sounds complicated to disappear from an old life."

"It is. Months ago I sold the jewelry I brought with me. Ed always gave me nice jewelry to wear in front of other people. He wanted everyone to see what a good husband he was."

"Did you sell it to a jewelry store?"

"Yes. I had Parker drive me around to different stores one day. I went to several until I found one that gave me a pretty good price for it. They gave me about half of what they probably asked for it when they sold it. I've been living on what I make writing for the internet and using a little of the savings each month. It doesn't take much to live here. Madame didn't charge me much, and with all the utilities included I didn't have to put up deposits anywhere, so nothing is in my name."

"So how do you think he could find you?"

"I have no idea, but I know he won't give up. That's why I can't work in your shop. He might walk in and find me. Or if not him, somebody he has hired to find me."

Addie was quiet for a few minutes, then said, "So if you are thinking that you might need to go to work someday, what is the difference in working for me, now, or working for some stranger later on?"

Evie thought. "Nothing I guess. I'm just nervous about the whole idea."

"Let me think about it for a while and see if I can come up with an idea."

A few days later Addie brought her the necklace.

"You know I make jewelry, right? I've been doing it for several years now as a hobby. That's what I'm selling in the shop."

"This is really lovely, but I can't afford to buy jewelry right now, and I can't accept such an expensive gift."

"This is as much for me as it is for you. Let me explain."

Addie went on to tell Evie about how for thousands of years people have believed gemstones have power that can be imparted to people who wear the stones or keep them close at hand.

"That's how kings started wearing jewels in their crowns — to circle their head with the protection the stones gave them. Necklaces put the stones at the throat, broaches are placed near the heart, and belts, or girdles as they used to be called, were studded with gemstones to keep them close to the stomach and intestines."

"I thought people wore jewels for the bling, because they are pretty."

"Nowadays people do. But centuries ago gems didn't sparkle the way they do now. People didn't have the tools or knowledge to shape jewels into facets to catch the light and glitter. They were pretty, but not like today's jewels. No, they wore them for the power and healing the gems brought."

"Do you really believe that gems can do all that?"

"I don't know. I don't believe — but I don't disbelieve, either. I do know many, many people do believe and wear gemstones accordingly." Addie picked up the necklace from the table. "This necklace I made for you has several gemstones I selected to help with your problems. See these interesting stones in varying brown tones? Those are agate, and they are said to promote self-confidence and calm the mind. These little round shiny black ones are hematite. They give you courage. These pretty black ones are jet; they are said to protect you from violence. And this big one with the swirly brown patterns is sardonyx. It's for protection.

"I'd like for you to wear it and see if it helps you by relieving your uneasiness. You can think of it as being a test subject. You can report back to me any change in your anxiety — if you feel any calmer or less frightened."

Evie took the necklace from Addie and ran her fingers over the smooth coolness of the stones.

"Okay. I'll accept it and wear it. After all, what can it hurt?"

Addie leaned back in her chair with a smile. "That's just what I have always thought. It can't hurt, can it? And if it helps, then so much the better."

"Is this the kind of jewelry you are selling in your shop?"

"Yes, it is. People seem to expect something special from me as Madame's niece. Something mystic or magical. This is the closest I can come to magic. But I'm not going to guarantee anything. If you want to believe in this, fine. If you don't, that's fine, too. I'm only going by what the old legends say. It's up to each person to believe or not."

Addie stood up and moved toward the door. "It's about time for me to go open the shop. Would you think about one more thing for me?"

"Sure. I'll think about whatever, but I won't say I'll do anything."

"Think about working in the shop with me there with you. You could take care of the customers while I make jewelry. I could get a lot more done that way, instead of hopping up and down all the time to wait on someone."

"Well, I'm usually not nervous talking to people. At least I wasn't before I married Ed. But for many years I've had to watch what I said, both around him and other people, too." Evie took a sip of her tea. "And I don't know anything about these powers."

"Oh, I would type all that up and you could just look at it. I'm going to have signs posted with the information on them, so people can read and study them. And you would learn, over time." Addie leaned forward. "Maybe you would like to come sit behind the counter and observe a couple of days. See if you are okay with it."

Evie did that. She spent three days just sitting in a chair next to the door to the storeroom while Addie waited on customers and put together new necklaces, bracelets, and earrings. Finally, on the third day, while Addie was busy with a woman who was picking out several items for herself and for gifts, another couple came in. Without even thinking, Evie had hopped up and helped them. She had ended up selling a bracelet for the woman and a pendant on a leather strip for the man. It made her feel so good to have acted like a real, normal person, she grinned the rest of the day, whenever she thought about it.

Now she was going to work, actual paid work, for the first time in years. Addie tried to pay her for the other days, but Evie refused, saying she wouldn't take pay for sitting around keeping Addie company. She was going to work a few hours several days a week, and even though she was nervous over the thought that Ed might walk in the door, she still couldn't keep the smile off her face.

CHAPTER NINETEEN

Simon spooned crawfish etouffe over the grilled catfish filets and then checked the items on the take-out plates. Catfish ala Simon, boiled new potatoes in butter, sautéed spinach, mushrooms, onions and bell peppers, and French bread with garlic butter. He grabbed a big sack and carefully placed the plates in the bottom, then added smaller bowls of peach cobbler and Styrofoam cups of iced tea. After he carefully placed napkins and silverware inside the sack, he headed toward the door.

He handled his burden cautiously while he maneuvered his way out the door and called out to Estelle. "I'll be gone an hour or so. If you need me, call me on my cell phone and I can be back in a couple of minutes."

When Simon was gone, Leroy stuck his head out the swinging door into the kitchen. "The boss done got it bad. That little ol' girl's got him bringing her lunch."

"Don't blame it on her. He done thought of that all by hisself. She be playin' hard to get and he's trying to win her over. He done got it bad, awright."

Dani was in the window, arranging the display of jeans, when Simon arrived.

"And what's all this?"

"I thought you'd be getting hungry by now and with Morgan in school these days you prolly don't stop to fix something for yourself."

"That doesn't mean you have to take off from work and bring me food. I can take care of myself."

"I know you can take care of yourself, but I wanted to test out this recipe on someone who doesn't work for me. It's new and I want to know if it is good enough to put on the menu, or if I need to work on it some more. I know you'll tell me the truth."

He opened the sack and let the aromas fill the air. "Where do you want me to set this out? In the back room?"

120

Dani climbed out of the window. "I guess if you insist on feeding me, the back room is the best place. Let me go clear off a table." She preceded him through the door in the rear of the shop.

She gathered spools of thread, scraps of jeans, lace, and containers of beads and moved them to a desk in the corner. She grabbed a towel from the back of a chair and wiped the table clear of bits of thread and lint. Simon carefully placed the plates of food and glasses of tea, adding the silverware evenly placed on the napkins to the left of each plate.

"My oh my. You went all out didn't you? Real napkins instead of paper, and real silverware instead of plastic."

"I would have used real plates, but I couldn't figure out how to get the food down here on them without it spilling all over the sack."

"And why are you being so fancy?"

"I think food tastes better from a plate that isn't Styrofoam. Don't you?"

"Now that you mention it, yes, I do."

"And I want a true opinion of the food. It won't taste as good as it will in the café, on plates, but this is as good as I could do for now. Maybe next time I'll find a picnic basket and bring the right stuff."

"Next time! Who says there is going to be a next time?" Dani asked as she took a forkful of catfish and etouffe. "Mmm. This is delicious. What am I eating?"

"Catfish, lightly seasoned with my own seasoning mix, then grilled. When it is on the plate I top it with a big spoonful of my crawfish etouffe. I call it Catfish a la Simon. Like it?"

"Love it!" She ate from the other items on the plate. "And I love these grilled vegetables."

"Customers seem to like that dish. It's different from what most places serve."

They were silent while they ate. The bell on the front door jingled and Addie came in from the front room.

"Dani?" she called. "Oh, I'm sorry. I'm interrupting your lunch. I'm just bringing you these necklaces to display with the jeans in the window. I'll lay them here on the desk and go."

"No. That's okay. You don't have to go." Dani took a forkful of catfish and raised it toward Addie. "Here. Try this. It's a new dish

Simon's thinking about adding to the menu. Help me be a guinea pig. What do you think?"

"I think it's delicious. I'd get it in a New York minute."

"What's a New York minute?"

"I don't know. Quick, I guess. It's just something my mother used to say." Addie tore a paper towel off a roll sitting on top of the file cabinet and wiped her mouth. "Are you going to serve this tonight, Simon? If you are I'll come have some for supper."

"Now that you both like it, I will. I'll write it on the blackboard as tonight's special, and if it goes over well I'll add it to the permanent menu, since I always have catfish and etouffe on hand anyway."

"It looked like you have been busy today, Dani. Are you making lots of sales?" Addie said.

"These jeans I cut off and decorate with beads and lace are selling really well. I've sold ten pair this week already."

"I saw a lot of people coming in and out, so I thought you were doing a lot of business today."

"Don't remind me of the people coming in and out, or I'll get in a bad mood again, just when Simon's food got me out of it."

Simon was puzzled. "People coming into the shop put you in a bad mood?"

"Not usually. It was who came in today that like to have ruined my day."

"Who?" Addie and Simon asked at the same time.

"My aunt and uncle from Memphis. I thought I was rid of them forever, but they found me."

Simon and Addie looked at each other, frowning.

"I know, I know. I haven't talked about them. I don't want to even think about them." She sighed. "Aunt Janice is my mother's sister." She pushed the plate to one side and took a sip of the tea. "My mother disappeared when I was little, and I was raised by my grandmother. It was hard, let me tell you, to raise a child at her age on the little bit of money she made. Aunt Janice would come around and expect Grandma to slip her a few dollars. I had to watch out for my uncle. He tried to feel me up anytime he could catch me alone in a room, even when I was just a little girl. Grandma would yell at him and make him leave, but before long he would come back with Aunt Janice and it would start all over again. It was worse after I had Morgan. It was like since I had a child I must want it again. Finally, when Grandma died, I knew I would have to leave to get away from him or else I would do something to hurt him. So I packed up and left. Now they've tracked me down."

"How did they find you?" Addie asked.

"And why did they want to find you?" added Simon.

"Some friends of theirs from church were visiting relatives here in New Orleans when they saw the ad on those flyers we put out for the tourists." She looked at Addie, who nodded. They both invested in that advertising. "I used the same name for my business I used in Memphis, so they were pretty sure it was me. They went back home and showed it to Aunt Janice and Uncle Fred, and they high-tailed it down here to find me."

"Why?" said Simon and Addie at the same time.

"Money. They think I must be making it big since I can afford to advertise and they want a cut of the money."

"Why would they think they should have any part of what you make?" asked Addie.

"They are saying Grandma owed them money when she died, and she promised to pay it back, and she promised I would pay it out of her insurance when she passed. Grandma set aside some jewelry and a hundred dollars for them. That's all. And that's all they're going to get."

"So they left?" asked Simon.

"Only until tonight. There were so many customers coming in and out they finally left, but they said they would be back tonight after the shop closes. 'To talk,' they said. With customers in the store I couldn't say what I wanted to, but I wish they weren't coming back," Dani said, frowning.

Addie shivered. "I don't like this. I have a bad feeling about it. I'll be over here tonight from the time we close."

"I'll be here, too," said Simon. "Or else you can come down to the café and stay the evening."

"No, I need to be here and face them, or else they would keep on coming back until they could talk to me like they want to."

"Then I'll be here, too," Simon said angrily. "They aren't going to push you around."

"No, Simon, you need to take care of your business. I can handle them."

"I think he's right, Dani. Your uncle needs to know there is a man around close who will protect you. A big, strong man like Simon. He wouldn't dare try anything if he thought Simon would come after him."

"Yeah. I'll be on him like white on rice if he lays one finger on you. I'd purely love to have an excuse to beat him to a pulp. Acting that way toward any woman, especially his niece. Humph." Simon socked one fist into his other palm, imagining it was the evil uncle he was hitting.

"I'll try to dress like a hoodoo woman, whatever that's like. I'll be here, too. And I'll let him — them — believe I can do stuff to them if they don't leave you alone."

"AND, my dear friends, I'll accept your help. I could handle them, I'm sure, but having you here may stop it for once and all."

Addie turned to leave. "I've got to get back. Evie is doing better at working in the public eye, but she gets nervous if she is left by herself in the shop for very long, and I've been gone awhile." She shivered again. "I'm going to make you a necklace to wear every day until all this with your aunt and uncle is over:, something to keep you safe, like I made Evie."

Simon finished gathering the napkins and silverware to take back to his café. The thought of anyone hurting Dani made him angry and made his heart hurt.

No one, no one is going to hurt my woman.

He stopped and realized the words that had just run through his mind. His woman. That was the way he had started thinking about Dani, and he hoped she would soon begin to see him as her man.

CHAPTER TWENTY

Wearing her new necklace, Diane entered Le Chat Noir and approached the bar.

"Hi there, Diane. You want your usual?"

"Yes, thanks, Joe." Placing a couple of bills on the counter, she took her diet soda and wove her way through the crowd until she reached the baby grand piano where Scott was playing the final bars of "The Maple Leaf Rag." The customers broke into enthusiastic applause.

"Can't beat Scott Joplin, can you? Were you named after him?"

"Hi, Diane! I was wondering if you would be here tonight. It's time for my break. Would you like to join me?" He stood from the piano and moved to the small table nearby. "To answer your question, no, I was named after an uncle, not the composer." They had barely settled themselves when Joe placed a mug of beer in front of Scott.

"Here you go, Scott. Diane, you need a refill yet?"

"I'm fine, thanks, Joe."

The evening went like all their evenings did. It was filled with talk of music, composers, new styles of rap as compared to jazz and big band and music of the '40s, the Beatles influence and how rock and roll had changed the music scene.

It was the same the next night, and the one after, and the one after that. The next weekend was a repeat of the last. Diane listened to the first set, sat with Scott during his break, then left to be home early enough to get enough sleep to go to work the next morning. On Friday nights she stayed a little later, but it made no difference in the result. Still Scott made no move toward asking to see her outside Le Chat Noir.

Discouraged, Diane returned to the dark shop of potions and spells, where Addie was working at her jewelry table.

"I see by your face that the moonstone necklace didn't help you."

"No. He is as friendly as ever, but still he shows no interest in asking me out on a date. Did you find out what Madame was going to do to help me?"

"Yes, I think I did. I found a journal with what appeared to be recipes in it, except not the kind of recipes for food. She had a piece of paper stuck in between some pages. On it Madame had written some notes. They were in French, and, as I told you, I don't speak French, but I went online to translate them. At the top, the note said, 'To make the young man see the young lady,' and then there was a list of ingredients and instructions."

Excitedly, Diane looked at the papers on the countertop.

"And do you have all the necessary ingredients?"

"I do."

Addie took a small brown paper bag and put in a few leaves from one place and another. A pinch here, a pinch there. Finally, she lifted down a box of smooth blue stones and studied each stone until she found one that satisfied her and added it to the mix.

"You take these home and put them in a small pan. Fill it half-full with water and put it on the stove. Heat it just until it starts to bubble. Turn off the fire and let it sit overnight. The next morning, strain it through some silk cloth."

She reached into a basket and took out a tiny bottle. "Fill this bottle with the water you have prepared in this way." She added it to the sack of items. "When you are with him that evening, contrive to pour the contents into his drink. When he drinks the liquid, he will look at you and see you as you are. It may take a day or two for it to make its way into all of his body. I must warn you, however, that the note said it is a very powerful potion."

Addie picked up the piece of paper and read, " It said, 'He will see all that is real. He will see you as you are. If you are hateful or deceitful, he will see that. If you are selfish or arrogant, he will see that. He will see the true you. He will see that you love him and would be good for him. This is very powerful, so only use it if you are sure you want him to see you as you really are.' "

"Oh, yes. I'm sure." Diane took the sack and turned to the door. "Thank you for your help."

* * *

The next evening when Diane entered Le Chat Noir she patted her pocket to be sure the potion was where she could pull it out quickly. At the bar Joe greeted her. "A diet soda? Right?"

"Yes, Joe." She placed the bills on the counter. "Want me to take a fresh glass of water to Scott?"

"Sure. He's been singing a lot tonight and is probably ready for another glass." Joe poured a glass of Mountain Valley water and handed it to Diane. As soon as she was away from the bar she looked back and saw Joe talking to another customer. Setting the glasses on an empty table she took the bottle from her pocket and quickly poured its contents into Scott's water. She hoped it would not make the water taste funny, because she could not figure out how to pour it into the beer he usually drank during his break without him seeing her do it.

"Hi, Scott," she said as she approached the piano. "Joe sent over a fresh glass of water." She sat her diet soda on the table they used during his break, removed the almost empty glass from the piano, and replaced it with the magic potion.

"Thanks, Diane. I need that. I've been using my voice a lot tonight. One more song and I'll take a break." He picked up the glass and drank about half of it, then launched into Hoagie Carmichael's "Buttermilk Sky." When he sang the last notes he made his usual announcement.

"I'm going to take a short break, folks. Stick around and have another drink and I'll be back in a few minutes."

"Have you been enjoying this beautiful day, Diane? Or have you been stuck inside?"

"I enjoyed walking to work this morning, and walking home this evening, and back here. There sure are a lot of tourists out tonight, aren't there?"

"Diane. I want to ask you something, and it is okay if you want to say no. I want you to know I won't be mad or anything if you say no."

"What is it, Scott? You can ask me anything you want. If I can do it I will."

"Would you consider going to dinner with me some evening, maybe before I have to start playing, or on one of my days off? I was thinking of taking you to Chez Jacques, a few doors down from here, or maybe to Simon's Place. I eat at Simon's often. It's not fancy but they have very good food."

"Of course I'll have dinner with you, Scott." Her heart was filled with joy. All the work she put into the potions and spells to get him interested in her were finally paying off. He had just drunk half the glass of water with the potion in it and already it was working. Joe came over with Scott's glass of beer and when he left Diane asked Scott the question that was puzzling her. "Why would you think I would say no, Scott? I've been hoping you would ask me out."

"Lots of girls wouldn't want to go out with me, Diane. They don't want to go out with a blind man. I've known all along you are different from most girls, and I should have realized that my blindness doesn't bother you. Usually, women start treating me like I'm a little kid when they find out I can't see. You are an exception. You use the same tone of voice with me that you use with everyone else. You don't talk slower or louder as if I were retarded or deaf. You treat me like a regular guy. You are a beautiful person."

Diane sat in stunned silence. *Blind. How could I have not noticed that? Because it is dark in here. Because we only move from the piano to this table and back. Because we never talked about it — he never mentioned it.*

"I'm not beautiful. I'm a very plain girl," she said in a low voice.

"Oh yes, you are beautiful. It's not what I can't see that makes you beautiful, it is what you are like inside, and that comes through loud and clear, even to a blind man. People seem to think it is outward appearance that makes a person handsome or pretty, but in reality it is what they are like inside, and the way they act toward others. You are kind and helpful, cheerful and always optimistic. I've known you for several months now, and I've never heard you be rude to anyone, or down in the dumps, or critical of anyone. That's what makes a person beautiful. That's what is real, not appearances." Diane sat there in silence.

"And anyway, I asked Joe what you look like and he told me you are cute in the girl next door kind of way. He said you have pretty blue eyes and a terrific smile. Joe sees lots of women in this place, and if he says you are cute, I believe him."

They sat in silence for a couple of minutes. Finally Scott asked, "Do you want to back out? It's okay if you do. You probably haven't thought about what it would be like to go somewhere with a blind man."

"Oh, no, Scott. I don't want to back out. I'm looking forward to going out with you."

"I'm taking a few days off. My brother wants me to go to Biloxi with him for a week. When I get back we'll decide when to go to dinner together. That way, after you've thought about it, if the reality of going out with a blind man is too much for you, you can just tell me. I won't get mad. I promise." Diane agreed, but she knew she wouldn't back out.

Just because he's blind doesn't change the person he is, either.

* * *

Diane spent the next few days thinking about the shock of Scott's announcement. Had he not asked her out because he thought she would not want to be seen with him? His words about seeing her inner beauty convinced her that the potion worked. He couldn't see her physical self, but he saw her true self and liked what he saw, just as she liked him, whether he was blind or not.

The next weekend when she entered Le Chat Noir she was greeted by the sounds of a Dixieland group. She approached the bar and greeted Joe. "So Scott is still away with his brother, huh? When is he due back?"

"Diane, the most amazing thing has happened. Scott regained his sight! The doctors told he would never see again, but all of a sudden he's seeing as good as you or me. He gave notice. He won't be playing here anymore. Now that he has his sight, he said he was going to see what the whole world looked like. Scott's gone."

CHAPTER TWENTY-ONE

For the past few weeks Addie, Dani and Evie had met in Addie's kitchen each morning to share coffee or tea and talk before the shops opened. Addie had suggested it. She missed her friends back in Connecticut, and although she called them often, she needed the in-person support of other women. She felt a rapport with Dani and Evie, and enjoyed spending a few minutes at the start of each day with them.

Besides, she thought it would be a good idea to get Evie out of her apartment and into the company of other people even more. Already, Evie was more at ease, not looking nervously around like she was going to bolt back to the sanctuary of her apartment at any minute. After working in the shop for several weeks, she handled customers with grace and charm, and was very good at selling Addie's jewelry, pointing out the mystical attributes of the various stones.

Dani arrived with a plate of cinnamon rolls.

"I brought something to have with the coffee," she said, while she placed the plate in the center of the round oak table in Addie's kitchen. The aroma of the warm rolls wafted into the air.

"How do you have time to bake?" Addie asked.

"Not me. Simon brought a big box of them last evening. I can't eat them all, and Morgan doesn't need all the sugar. He's hyper enough as it is. I just warmed them up."

"Girl, that Simon is sure keeping you fed. He's all the time bringing you a plate of this or that," said Addie, while she placed plates in front of each person.

"Yes, he's courting you all right," Evie said.

Addie was glad to see Evie entering the conversation. The first couple of days the three met, Evie barely said a word, but now she was joining in, even teasing a little. Addie sensed the trauma of abuse, and then running away and hiding, had suppressed Evie's personality. The true Evie was beginning to shine through the fear.

"Well, I'm sure glad he's been around the last couple of weeks."

"Because of your aunt and uncle?" Addie took forks from a drawer and gave one to each person. "Are they still in town?"

"No, they left. Simon and Addie were at my place the first evening they came by, after the shop closed for the day," she explained to Evie. "I told them all about how my relatives wanted money from me, and how my uncle kept putting his hands on me, so I had to promise to call Simon if they showed up again." Dani stopped talking to take a bite. "But Simon shows up all the time, anyway, without waiting for me to call him."

"That's a good idea," Evie said. "I'll bet your uncle wouldn't dare try anything with Simon there."

"No, he wouldn't. It doesn't hurt that Simon is about six inches taller than my uncle, and he made it plain he would come after anyone who hurt me in any way. Addie, your appearance that first night put some fear in my aunt and uncle, too. They asked me if you could really put juju on people, and I told them to ask anyone in New Orleans about Madame Badeaux. I told them you are her niece and inherited all her property and power, and that you are my best friend in the world."

"Um-um. Simon can bring these cinnamon rolls anytime he wants. They are delicious," Addie said. She cut another bite with her fork. "Did you like my get-up for that evening?"

"He's hired more kitchen help, and one of the new cooks bakes these and is cooking the fried pies. I hate him taking so much time off from work to see about me, but he says it's fine, that he likes to get away from the café from time to time." Dani took sip of coffee. "And your get-up, as you called it, looked more like a fortune telling gypsy than anything."

"Likes to see you from time to time, is more like it." Evie grinned.

Addie placed her fork beside her plate, frowning. "I don't want to alarm you, but I have a funny feeling there is going to be more happening. You know how I told you things always happen in threes, and I get a feeling when more is coming?"

The other women nodded yes, their eyes widening.

"Dani, when you told me about your aunt and uncle showing up and hassling you, I got that feeling, and I still have it, even worse — like it wasn't over yet."

"Well, they came to see me more than three times while they were in town."

"I thought maybe that was what it was,, but the feeling hasn't gone away, even though they went back to Memphis. They have for sure left, haven't they?"

"Yes, they're gone. I'm sure. At least I think I'm sure."

"Then it's not them. It's something else that's going to happen. Maybe someone else unexpected showing up. Two someone elses, to make three."

Evie looked panicked, like she might bolt for the door at any second.

"Evie, I know I've been telling you Ed couldn't find you, and I've been happy to see the progress you've made getting out in public, but I know my premonitions always come true, so I think we'd better start taking precautions about you being caught alone."

"It wouldn't matter if I were alone or with you or someone else. If Ed finds me, he'll find a way to get me. If he can't carry me off, he'll kill me. I've told you before, he has guns, and he would shoot me. Or he might burn the place down. He'll do something bad if he finds me."

"Just because I have this feeling, and just because I think it has to do with surprise visits from people, doesn't mean he's going to find you. I just think we need to be cautious until the other two things happen, whatever they are." She picked up her fork and started to eat again. "I think I'll see what I can find about protection from harm."

"You mean, with your stones?" asked Dani.

"Yes, but other stuff, too. I'll look through Madame's journal to see if I can find something in there for protection. If I can translate it, that is."

Evie giggled. "You'd better do a better job than last time."

"What last time?" Dani stopped with the fork full of cinnamon roll in the air and looked questioningly at Addie. "I didn't know you had tried any of your aunt's spells."

"It was a potion."

"Tell," Dani said, looking at Addie.

"Well, there's this girl, Diane. She came to my aunt for help in attracting a man. Not just any man, but a particular man. Madame gave her something — spells, potions — I don't know what all, but they didn't work. He still didn't ask her out. Madame had guaranteed success, and said if what she gave Diane the first time didn't work, she should come back and Madame would give her something that would, quote — make the man really see you — unquote. Diane knew Madame had died, but she also heard Madame's successor was here, so she came to me for help. I gave her a moonstone necklace, but that didn't help. So I went to Madame's journal. There was a note stuck in the book. At the top was written, in French, 'to make the young man see the young lady.' My aunt left list of ingredients and instructions, copied it out of the book, really."

"Do you read French?" Dani asked.

"Not much. I studied it in high school, but it's been a few years. I looked up the words online to translate the ones I didn't know."

"So what happened? Was it a spell or charm or what?"

"It was a potion. And I gave her the ingredients and the instructions."

"So did it work?"

"Like a charm," said Evie.

"Too good," Addie said, marveling that Evie was joking around and wasn't so distraught over the thought of Ed appearing that she went and locked herself in her apartment again.

"How can it work too good?"

"It seems the young man was blind, but Diane didn't know it, and the potion made him regain his sight. He left, 'to see the world,' Diane said."

"Oh! You must be talking about the guy who played piano at Le Chat Noir! Simon told me about that. What was his name? Scott. Scott something."

Addie leaned back and stared at Dani, mouth open. "You've heard about this?"

"Yes, it's the talk of the neighborhood. Simon said Scott used to come in and eat there several time a week with his brother. The brother told him about Scott regaining his sight. 'A miracle' is what the brother called it."

"Well, what I want to know is why Diane hadn't figured out Scott was blind. It looks like it would have been obvious," Evie said.

"Diane said the club was very dimly lit, and Scott was always at the piano or at his table right next to the piano. She said he didn't look any different than anyone else." Addie took a sip of her coffee. "She came back and told me what happened. She's upset, but not at me. The potion did exactly what it was supposed to."

"Not really," said Evie. "It didn't make the young man see the young lady. He left before he could see her."

* * *

Martin took a sip of his coffee and looked at the papers laid out before him. What a mess, he thought. He had been all over New Orleans the past few days, and still had several more places to check out.

"Here you go. Chicken-fried steak with mashed potatoes, white gravy, and green beans," the waitress said as she slid the plate in front of him. "You need a refill on that coffee?"

"Yes, please," Martin answered while he gathered the papers into a stack.

She returned with the coffee carafe and a small basket.

"I brought you a biscuit and a piece of cornbread. That's butter over there," she said, pointing at a small bowl of cardboard containers. "Enjoy!"

Martin was tired of eating in restaurants, but he was tired of eating his own cooking, too. Although this meal wasn't half bad. He spent enough time married to think with fondness on home-cooked meals and miss them since he was single again.

It's not so much the food, as it is having someone to eat it with. Someone to share cooking, or help pick the restaurant, or discuss the food with. Somebody to be with.

When he finished eating, he pushed the plate aside and looked through the papers again. He had a few more places to check out, but the clues were all there. He was about ready to put them together. The confrontation was imminent.

Gathering up the documents, he put them back in his briefcase, tossed some bills on the table, and went back to work.

CHAPTER TWENTY-TWO

Simon stood, looking around at his kingdom, Simon's Place. Pride surged through him, filling him with a warm glow of pleasure and contentment. But not the kind of contentment that allowed him to stay where he was. His pride said, "I have accomplished what I had in mind five years ago, when I rented this building and started this café from scratch. Now, I'm ready for more."

He walked through the dining room, checking to be sure the black and white tile floor was spotless. It was all that remained of the '50s retro diner that had gone out of business before Simon rented the building. The previous tenant sold all the red vinyl booths and Formica tables to pay overdue bills. Simon, working with very little money, furnished the place with mismatched tables and chairs he had scrounged up from flea markets, rummage sales, his mother's attic, even a couple he found discarded on the side of the street. A buffet that had been his grandmother's now held silverware wrapped in spotless white napkins, sitting beside the pitchers that would be filled with tea and lemonade before customers arrived. It was the most elegant thing in the room. Behind it hung a large painting, a view of the Mississippi River, which once hung in his grandmother's dining room when she was alive. The mish-mash of furniture gave the place a certain homey feeling.

His family was supportive, but out of his hearing, they thought he would never make it. Sure, Simon could cook. His food was the best around. He had a touch with food that was almost magic. Anything he conjured up was a delight to the taste buds. Somehow, he knew just the right dash of this spice or that to make a pot perfect. But he had no money to speak of, only enough for a couple of months' rent and the barest of equipment. Not enough to make it in a competitive field like food service.

The last time he was at his mother's house, a couple of weeks ago, she hugged him and told him how proud she was of him. She lived on the other side of town, and only came to eat at Simon's Place occasionally. Simon pushed through the swinging 'in' door to the kitchen. Everything was meticulous in that room, too, scoured each evening by the young man he hired to be busboy, dishwasher and clean-up staff.

When he first opened the café, Simon was the only person working there. He couldn't afford to pay anyone. He would come in early and start a big pot of gumbo or jambalaya to simmering, and one of red beans and rice. Then he would start the dough for the fried pies, rolling and cutting the pastry, filling the rounds with apple or peach or chocolate, and crimping them closed with a fork before popping them into the hot grease. When everything was bubbling, and the pies were out of the hot oil, he opened the double front doors and let the aromas out into the street. That was all he served those first couple of months, gumbo, jambalaya, and red beans and rice, all served with homemade bread he bought from Amy Coudrant, who lived next door to his mother and was trying to raise two children without much help from a husband who drank up his salary.

Simon did all the jobs, back then, cook, waiter, busboy, and clean-up person. Whatever needed doing, he did it. As business got better, he hired a waitress, then another, and a cashier, assistant cook, and a busboy. Soon there were three of them cooking, so Simon could take time to go check on Dani whenever he felt like it.

He smiled at the thought of Dani.

Simon lived in the backroom at first, sleeping on a cot hidden behind the boxes and bins that eventually filled the storage space. Every couple of days he would go to his mother's house, take a shower and wash his clothes, buy more bread from Amy, and go back to his true home, the café. After a couple of months, Simon ventured up the stairs just inside the back door to see what kind of storage was up there. To his surprise, he found an apartment. Small and dusty, nevertheless it was better than a cot in the back room, so he spent his evenings cleaning and repairing the space, and soon it became a real, if shabby, home.

In the beginning, all the money he saved from his job as second cook at a hotel restaurant was used to by the things he needed, bare minimum, to open. He accumulated pots, pans, knives, silverware, napkins, plates, cups and saucers. He tried to plan for everything, but every time he turned around there was one more thing he needed before he opened. Salt and pepper shakers, sugar containers, glasses, an ice machine, all the little things that kept on costing after he had spent a small fortune on a commercial range and top-notch refrigerator. Before he had opened he had to borrow money from his mother to buy the food to cook for opening day.

From the beginning, though, people started coming to Simon's Place to eat. The first couple of days were slow, sure, but the word soon spread about how good the food was, and the neighborhood found it was much easier to let Simon cook than to do it themselves. They could sit and visit with their friends, and, as several women commented, "I don't have to heat up my apartment with all that cooking."

Simon tried to pay his mother back, but she said, "You keep the money and use it to expand your menu. You can pay me back in a year." So Simon added thick sandwiches of thinly sliced ham and excellent cheese, and muffalettas, those peculiarly New Orleans sandwiches stuffed with black olive mix; catfish with french fries and hushpuppies; chicken and dumplings; and to accompany anything, New Orleans soaked salad. After a while, he added pork chops, greens, dirty rice, and tourists learned about the good down home cooking at Simon's Place.

The business grew. Of course, looking back, Simon figured it didn't hurt that Madame Badeaux, the neighborhood purveyor of spells and potions, hexes and protection from hexes, hoodoo woman of great renown, ate at Simon's Place the first week it was open and proclaimed it "a superb establishment" and the food "the best I have ever eaten — rivaling the best known chefs. I taste magic in each bite." Any place that had Madame's blessing was bound to flourish.

Simon, satisfied everything was in order to start the day, turned his mind to the future. He wanted to rent the vacant store next door, knock the wall out, and make a more formal dining room in the new space. The problem was he couldn't get an answer from the rental agency that handled the shops in the building. They kept putting him off. Each time he called to see if they would agree, they gave him the runaround. They weren't the owner of the property, the agent said; they only handled the property for someone else. The company that owned it had property all over the city. The agent just couldn't get an answer about taking down walls and making one rental space out of two. He couldn't give an okay on altering the property without the owner's permission, and he couldn't get the permission.

"Are they trying to sell the building?" he asked, alarmed at the prospect of losing his present space.

"If they are, they haven't said anything about it to me," the rental agent answered. "They haven't sold any property in years, so I don't think that's it."

Simon thought about another aspect of this. "Is there apartment space above the vacant shop, like there is over mine?" he asked.

The agent checked his file. "Yes, there is."

"If they let me rent the next area and knock out the wall, can I do the same thing in the apartment above and make one big apartment?"

"You want me to ask the owners about that, too?"

"Yessir. Please."

"I'll get back to you when they let me know an answer, but I'm sure it'll be a while."

So Simon dreamed big and worried about what the delay meant. If he wanted his business to grow, it meant he needed more space, and if he couldn't get it here, it meant moving to someplace else. He didn't want to move. He liked it there. He liked the neighborhood, the people, and most of all, he liked being close to Dani and Morgan.

All his dreams included Dani and Morgan. Simon couldn't get through the day without seeing Dani several times. He'd had girlfriends before, but never had he felt like he did about Dani. He was so proud of what she was able to overcome in her life to get to where she was. Her creativeness and business sense and her perseverance to accomplish her goals awed him. She was a good woman, both honest and kind. She was everything he wanted in a…wife. He had avoided that word before. Wife. The word made him feel good. Settled. Like life was going in the right direction.

Simon spent his teenage years and early twenties knocking around from job to job and woman to woman. He graduated from high school with average grades, much to the dismay of his mother, who was a teacher and knew Simon was smart enough to do better. He rejected her suggestions of college in favor of cooking at one establishment or another, until he became disgusted at the poor management, poor working conditions, or slovenliness of a place and quit. He was never fired. His cooking talents became well known, and he could always get a job. He would have liked to work at one of the more famous New Orleans establishments, but the head chefs at most of them were like divas, and required secrecy agreements and non-competing clauses in loophole proof contracts, which Simon refused to sign.

He went from woman to woman with about the same speed as he went from job to job. Finally, when he had words with the last one, he packed up and left her apartment and moved back home to his mother's house. By that time he had the idea to start his own restaurant, and to do that he needed to save all the money he could. By living at home with his mother, even though he paid her rent, he could still save at a faster rate.

His grandmother was still alive then, and thought his plans were wonderful. "When I die, there will be something for you in my will," she told him. "I know you will do well. Your cooking is superb."

The money she left him became part of his startup money, and he thought of her whenever he looked at the buffet and painting, which had graced her dining room for as long as he could remember. One of the tables and four chairs in Simon's Place were from her kitchen. Waiting for him in the attic of his mother's house was her dining room table and eight chairs. It would go into the formal room he was planning next door, when and if word came he could knock down the wall.

He was impatient, though — ready to move on his plans — especially his plans for the apartment, which hadn't even occurred to him when he first started thinking about expanding. He had barely met Dani then. The first time he remembered seeing her was when Madame died and everyone came back to Simon's Place after the burial. After that, he guessed he was a goner and now the solution came to him.

Marriage. Living together in one place, one apartment, one house. If he could make a larger restaurant and increase his business, he could also make a bigger apartment upstairs, big enough for the three of them. Dani's business was also growing and her back room was packed full of her purchases. If they married and she moved in with Simon, she could use her apartment for storage and get more organized. Already she was using Evie several hours a week to wait on customers, so she could produce more clothing to sell. She was talking about hiring someone from the neighborhood to do some of the basic sewing. It was obvious she could sell more than she could make. Spending time hunting clothing at estate sales and waiting on customers took away from production time. Her business, like Simon's, was growing.

One Sunday Simon took Dani and Morgan to meet his mother. Later, when he thought about it, he realized Dani was the first woman he ever introduced to his mother, who was sitting on the sofa, looking through old photo albums when they arrived.

"Mama, I'd like you to meet Dani Washington and her son, Morgan. Dani, this is my mother, Maxine Bondurant."

"I'm so pleased to meet you, Mrs. Bondurant," Dani said as she extended her hand.

"Maxie, please. That's what everyone calls me. Maxie. I'm pleased to meet you, too. I've heard a lot about you. And about you, too," she said as she turned to Morgan. "I was just looking at pictures of Simon when he was a child. Would you like to see them?"

Dani and Morgan sat beside her and looked at pictures of Simon from birth through his teenage years.

"I wish I had pictures like this," she told Simon's mother. "I have a couple of snapshots of my grandmother, and a couple of my mother and her sister when they were children, but that's all."

"You don't have any of yourself, growing up?" his mother asked.

"No, ma'am. My mother was on drugs, you see, and left me with my grandmother when I was a little bitty thing, and Granny didn't have a camera, or money for pictures."

"So you don't have pictures of your parents and grandparents?"

"No. I wish I did. Simon can look at all these and know where he came from. I don't even know what my father looked like."

"Well, this is Simon's father and me, when we were in college. He was a big man, like Simon is." She ran her fingers over the picture. "He's been gone ten years, now. Cancer." She turned back to the front of the album. "This was his grandmother, my mother, when she was young and beautiful."

"Yes, she certainly was beautiful," Dani said, while she looked at the pictures of the young woman dressed in the fashions of the '40s. "I love the clothes she is wearing in these photos. I love old clothes from bygone times."

"Simon told me about your business. I think it's creative of you to turn the old fashions into new." She turned the page and pointed to another picture. "I think I still have this suit somewhere in the attic. Francine came from a wealthy family, and she dressed well. She was very glamorous. These are the only two pictures we have of Simon's grandfather." She pointed to a photo, obviously a professional portrait, of a handsome black man, and another snapshot of him standing beside a car. "He was tall. That's where Simon gets his height. He left for the war before he and Francine could be married, and he didn't even know she was pregnant with me when he left. He was killed in the South Pacific. She would never tell me his name."

"I don't know my father's name, either," Dani said in a low voice.

Maxie patted her on the knee. "I made it just fine without knowing my father, and it looks like you are doing the same." She closed the album and placed it on the coffee table. " I made a chocolate cake. Would you know anyone who would like a slice?" she asked while she rose from the sofa.

"Me! I'd like a piece," Morgan said while he danced around.

"Come in the kitchen, young man, and I'll cut you a big slice."

"Now I know where you got your cooking ability," said Dani, looking at Simon.

"Not from me," said Maxi. "He could always cook, even when he was just a boy. Everyone always raved about anything he cooks. He must have gotten it from his mystery grandfather, because my mother never cooked. We lived with my grandparents, and they always had someone to cook for us. I can make simple things, nothing fancy, and no Cajun dishes. Someone else has to do that. The gift isn't from my husband's side of the family, either."

Later, as they were leaving, Simon's mother pulled him aside and whispered in his ear. "This one's a winner, son. Take good care not to lose her."

"I will, Mama. I'll take very good care of both of them."

CHAPTER TWENTY-THREE

Simon and Dani's relationship was not without problems. The biggest was Dani's attitude. She was convinced she was damaged goods and would never be able to have a normal association with a man, never be able to enjoy sex, never be able to marry. She tried her best to run him off, to convince Simon she wasn't interested in him and never would be.

Simon tried to analyze why he was so determined to break down her barriers. Was it because she was playing hard to get? No, it wasn't that. Before, when a pretty girl didn't return his interest, he looked elsewhere. His buddies spouted that old cliché, "Women are like busses; wait five minutes and another one will come along," and it was true — if a man wasn't particular about which bus, or which woman, he caught.

There was something special about Dani, some spark that made her different. Sure, she was cute, pretty even, but not as much as some he'd known. It was her persistence to make something of herself, something uniquely her own. It reminded Simon of something deep in him, the knowing of one's own skills and talents and the fortitude and willpower to accomplish goals, something he recognized in himself.

Dani, on the other hand, was absolutely and positively certain of her talent for designing and redesigning clothing, and she fought her way through difficulties that would stop most people. He knew after he heard her story that she was someone who wouldn't give up, wouldn't quit.

He knew money was tight, so he started to bring more than they could eat. When he left he would tell her to put the rest upstairs in her refrigerator so Morgan could have it for a snack when he came home from school. Sometimes he would bring a plate of something just for Morgan.

"Put this back until Morgan's home from school. I want to know if he likes it."

"Why do you care if Morgan likes it?"

"'Cause he's a kid, that's why. I have kids come in with their folks, and I need to make stuff kids like too."

"You don't have no kids comin' in your place. Morgan is the only kid I've ever seen in there."

"You don't know everythin,' Miss Thing. I have plenty of kids comin' in when you aren't there. Ask Morgan what he thinks about this."

After a few weeks, Simon tried a couple of times to put his arms around her, even to kiss her, without success. That was when he finally heard the story of the gang rape that led to Morgan's existence.

She warned him. "I can't stand to be touched by a man. Not that I had any experience with that before, but I had the same dreams any young woman does. I looked forward to having a boyfriend, a lover, a husband someday. That night changed everything.

"For a long time, I got nervous when I was even in the presence of a man — young, old, it didn't matter. I finally got to where it didn't show, then to where I could be in a room with men without imagining them turning on me and raping me. But that's as far as I can heal.

"I'll never be able to be a lover, a wife. I'll never be able to show the kind of affection a man wants and deserves, so you might as well give up now. If that's what all this bringing me lunch is leading up to, you might as well forget it."

Simon thought about it for a long time. He was never to give up on what he wanted, and he was not going to give up on Dani. He decided he would take it slow and easy, see if he could get her more open to the idea she could have love like any woman, like all women deserved.

He started with something simple, his hand on her shoulder. He would get up from the table in the workroom where they shared lunch several times a week, and place his hand on her shoulder for a couple of seconds. He would retrieve the paper towels, or move something from the other end of the table. He had become quite inventive about planning reasons to pass behind Dani so he could briefly put his hand on her. After a couple of weeks, when she stopped tensing up at his touch, he started giving her shoulder a little squeeze. The first time was after she said something funny, and he had pressed a little while he laughed, then let up before she could react. From then on, sometimes when he put his hand on her, he did it again, not in a regular pattern. Not enough she would tell him not to touch her. Eventually it was just something Simon would do. For the next step he would grasp her arm, very briefly, and work on that until Dani was comfortable with his touch on the bare skin of her arm.

By the time Simon decided it was time for another step. He, Dani, and Morgan were beginning to go places together. One time it was window shopping at the mall, then the movies, the zoo, to hear jazz on the street corner. Simon's Place was closed on Sundays, and that became the day they did something special, like a family. Morgan was at the age when he didn't want to hold his mother's hand when they were in a crowd of people or crossing a street, and Dani would lose her temper with him, causing Morgan to sulk. Simon saw this as an opportunity to advance his agenda of familiarizing Dani to his touch.

"Morgan, we're all going to hold hands today. There's so many people here, we're liable to get separated," Simon said. "Here, hold my hand, and I'll hold your mama's hand, and we'll all stay together."

Morgan was happy to hold Simon's hand, and although Dani tried to work her way into holding Morgan's other hand, Simon was adroit at working it out differently, and Morgan helped by not wanting to hold to Dani when he had Simon's attention.

So it became the norm for Simon and Dani to hold hands when they were out and about, even when Morgan was running ahead of them, or stopping to look at something that caught his eye.

By the time Simon started to put his arm around her, the ice was cracking. Although she shrugged it off a couple of times, he didn't push it. He simply rested his wrist on her shoulder until that too became an accepted practice. Then his hand pulled her closer to him on occasion. He used the same method to get her used to his hand on the small of her back, which moved to her side, where he could pull her closer when the crowd was too near. He kept his little family together.

When her aunt and uncle discovered Dani's location, Simon was there with Addie, to show them Dani had friends and protectors who wouldn't let anyone take advantage of their friend. Simon made it plain he would use force, if necessary, to protect her. Addie, dressed in bizarre, gypsy-like clothing, hinted at horrible spells that could be brought forth on those who upset her friend. She told stories about her aunt, such as the time she turned her husband into a dog because he wasn't faithful to her. Addie let them know she was her aunt's replacement in the neighborhood — The New Witch — and alluded to horrific retribution to anyone who dared hurt one of her friends.

Simon didn't like seeing Dani upset, but one good thing came of it. When the unwelcome pair left, Dani threw herself into his arms, in tears. He held her close, stroking her back until she calmed herself. She drew back then, obviously embarrassed.

"I'm so sorry, Simon. I didn't mean to throw myself at you like that."

"Think nothin' of it. That's what friends are for."

Simon was cautious enough, and smart enough, not to push at that point, but he continued his handholding, arm touching, and shoulder squeezing. That's when he started to kiss her, just a light peck on the cheek, at first.

"Got to get back to work," he'd say, and give her a peck on the cheek or forehead and be gone before she could protest. After two weeks, he started to do it while she was standing, so he could put his hand at her waist and pull her ever so slightly closer to him when he bestowed the lightest of kisses on her face. Slowly, slowly, he pulled her closer each day. Somewhere along the line the kisses landed on her lips instead of her cheek.

At first, Dani put her hands on his chest and almost, but not quite, pushed. After a few days, she realized he was not going to pull her into an embrace, she only rested them there, and after a few more days, Simon could feel her returning the kiss. He always cut it off before she could become frightened of him.

Months later, the feathery kisses had turned to ardent ones, the loose embraces to passionate ones, and Dani, at long last, permitted — wanted — his hands not only on her shoulder and arm, but all over her.

Simon thought the time had come to disprove her theory that she could never enjoy sex, could never have a lover. He needed to convince her she was wrong about never having a husband.

By this time his mother had kept Morgan for the day a couple of times and Simon knew they were both happy with this arrangement.

Morgan enjoyed his time with the older woman and Maxie delighted in having a child in her home once again. He decided it was time to take his relationship with Dani to a new level, and he wanted it to be special — as special as her first time should have been.

"Mom, do you think you could keep Morgan all day Sunday and Sunday night, if I can set up something with Dani?" he phoned his mother to ask.

"Of course I can. I'd love to have him. Just let me know when you're bringing him over."

Timing is everything, Simon thought.

That evening, with Morgan asleep in the next room, Simon started his seduction with kisses — long, deep, powerful kisses that went on forever. His tongue drove in and out in the rhythm he hoped to repeat lower in their bodies. His hands pushed up under her shirt to find her breasts, the nipples already beaded hard, awaiting his touch. His large hands cupped her and his mouth abandoned hers in order to seek those nubs. He suckled through the cloth of her shirt, and she hurriedly grasped the hem, pulling the fabric up to allow him better access. He licked and tickled and kissed until she was half crazy. Then Simon pulled back and rearranged her blouse, covering what he had been so fervently adoring seconds before.

Dani looked at him with a strange expression and reached to pull him toward her.

"No, honey. I can't do this anymore. I want to be inside you so bad I can't stand it. I think about it all the time. I'm thinking about it when I wake up. I think about it while I work. I'm thinking about it when I go to sleep. I keep a permanent hard-on, thinking about you."

"We — we can go on. I'm not scared any more. I want you as much as you want me," Dani said, stroking his face.

"No, sweetheart. Not here. Not now. When we do it, it's going to be the first time for you."

"But Simon…"

"No buts. It will be the first time you make love, and it will be love. It won't be on a lumpy couch with Morgan asleep a few feet away."

146

Dani dropped her head and rested it on his chest. Simon placed his finger under her chin and raised her face until he could see her expression.

"Do you trust me?"

"Yes. Yes, I trust you. I wouldn't be here like this if I didn't."

"Then let me make plans. I want it to be special for you — something you will remember all of your life."

Tears came to her eyes, and Simon used his thumb to brush away the ones in the corner.

"I want you to pack a bag. Dress for a casual day, but take a dress — something for dining at a fine establishment, fancier than my place. Bring everything you need for spending the night. I'll pick you up Sunday morning about eleven."

"But what about Morgan?"

"My mother is going to keep him overnight. I've already cleared it with her."

"It sounds like you've been planning this a while."

"Longer than you know, darlin.'"

"What if…if I can't go through with it?"

"Could you have gone through with it five minutes ago?"

"Yes."

"That's nothing like what you're going to feel Sunday. You'll want to go through with it — I guar-on-tee."

* * *

Both Simon and Dani were nervous while they waited for the coming weekend. Simon visited Dani in her shop when it was open and sneaked in a kiss when no one else was around. Each evening he went back to his place after Morgan was in bed. It was the only way he could be sure he wouldn't preempt the plans he had made. He made sure he wasn't alone with Dani except briefly in the shop. There and in front of Morgan he only gave her short unpassionate kisses.

Finally Sunday arrived.

"Morgan, calm down," Dani said for the third time in as many minutes, as the active boy ran by her to the bedroom window yet again, peering out to see if he could spot Simon.

"When is Simon coming? Is it ten yet?"

"It is one minute later than it was the last time you asked me. Simon will be here when he gets here." Dani was as excited about the upcoming day and evening as Morgan was, but she was determined not to let it show.

"I'll get to sleep in Simon's old room," he told Dani. "And Miss Maxie and me's gonna make a cake. There he is! There's Simon's car!" he yelled already racing toward the door.

"Come back here and carry your bag," Dani said, handing him the canvas backpack.

Following along behind, Dani held her own bag behind her, hoping Morgan wouldn't see it and ask her where she was going to be spending the night. For one thing, she didn't know, and for another she didn't want to tell Morgan she was spending it with Simon. It wasn't that she was ashamed, exactly, but she didn't want her son asking a lot of questions she couldn't answer.

By the time they reached the front door to the shop Simon had the trunk of his car open .

"I'm ready, Simon! Here's my bag."

"I can see that. Here, let's put it back here. You go on and get in the back seat." He smiled at Dani and reached for her bag.

"Hi," he said softly to Dani.

"Hi." She couldn't think of another word to say and thought she was lucky to even be able to utter that one word.

Conversation wasn't necessary on the way to Maxie's house, since Morgan kept a non-stop commentary going. Simon would ask him a question and then keep quiet as Morgan went into details about something Spike had done, or what he and Miss Maxie were going to do.

Finally, with Morgan safely deposited with Simon's mother, they were alone.

"Nervous?" Simon asked.

"Yes, definitely."

"I want you to know right now that you can stop what we are doing at any time. You are not committed to doing anything you don't want to do. There'll be no pressure from me to continue with something you aren't comfortable with. Understood?"

Dani nodded, unable to speak. Her throat felt like it was filled with sobs, but she didn't know why. *I want this, truly I do, but I hope I don't freeze up on him. Simon doesn't deserve that.*

"First, let's go check into the hotel and leave our bags. Then we have some sightseeing to do," he said as he started the car and pulled out into the street in front of his mother's house.

"Sightseeing?" Dani asked. She hadn't expected sightseeing.

"Yep. I want to show you more of New Orleans than you've seen so far. First, though, while we're in the neighborhood, I want to show you where I grew up."

He drove by the high school he had attended and the big old house where his grandmother had lived. He told stories of pranks he and his buddies pulled, stories he wouldn't tell in front of Morgan. He drove by a park and pointed out where he first kissed a girl, under the spreading limbs of an old oak tree draped in Spanish Moss.

"You've sure had a lot of practice since then."

"Now how do you know that?"

"Because you're so good at it."

They both laughed. Simon was glad to see her becoming more at ease than.

"Oh my," she said when they pulled into the drive in front of a luxurious hotel and a valet approached the car. "Are you sure you can afford this fancy place?"

"Nothing but the best for my lady." He turned to pat her leg and said, "Don't worry about expenses. Simon's Place is doing really well and I can afford it. Besides, this is a special day."

He told the valet he would be leaving again shortly then escorted Dani into the lobby of the hotel. She found it hard not to gape at the place. There were beautifully patterned marble floors and comfortable chairs arranged in conversation groups. Orchid plants sat on the tables that were scattered throughout the lobby. Several stories high, sunlight beamed through the glass ceiling, setting twinkles of light dancing around the room. Music came from some unseen source.

Simon approached the front desk. "My name is Simon Bondurant and I have a reservation," he told the woman behind the elaborate counter.

With the checking in completed, Simon picked up their bags and took Dani by the arm. When they were in the elevator and out of earshot of anyone else, Dani let her excitement bubble over.

"Look, Simon. The elevator has one side glass! You can see down to the lobby as we go up!"

"Sure 'nuff can."

Upon reaching their floor and exiting the elevator Dani's attention was caught by the carpeting.

"It feels like we are sinking down into this carpet, and look at the pattern. Isn't it pretty?"

Opening the door to their room, Simon ushered her in.

"Oh, Simon! I've never even been in a hotel before. I've only seen them on TV. This is wonderful!" She looked around the room, drinking in the luxurious surroundings. "Look at how high the ceiling is. This is prettier than any of those decorating shows I watch. I would never think to put up black and white striped wallpaper. And this bed…" she paused and patted the white duvet on the white wrought iron bed. That's when she remembered what this was all about and she started to feel nervous again.

"Yes. This is real pretty all right. But I have plans for the afternoon. Let's hang up our clothes so they won't be wrinkled and get out of here."

"We're leaving?"

"For a few hours. We'll be back," he said as he hung a shirt and trousers in the closet. "I'll just pop in here for a minute," he said as he went in the bathroom. He didn't really need to go, but he thought he'd give Dani a chance to unpack without him watching. She was so fidgety he didn't want to add to her nerves. He thought unpacking in front of him might be embarrassing. It's the first time she's every spent the night with a man, he kept reminding himself.

When it was Dani's turn she freshened her makeup — which she seldom wore — and checked to see that her hair was presentable. When she returned to the bedroom she was over her nervousness, enthralled with the lush bathroom.

"Simon, did you notice the walls in the bathroom? The ceramic tiles are black and white striped to match the bedroom walls. And the towel rack is heated so you always have a warm towel!"

"Yeah, it's really somethin,' isn't it? Are you ready to go?"

She picked up her purse and started toward the door. "All ready."

* * *

By the time they returned to the hotel late in the afternoon, Simon was hungry and ready to sit down for a real meal. Although they had snacked along the way, he was a big man and needed more than a kabob, ice cream, and sodas to keep going.

They had visited Mardi Gras World, the museum and storage where pieces and parts of Mardi Gras parade paraphernalia were displayed. The beauty of St. Louis cathedral had awed them both. They were entertained by the Ghost Tour, but having known Madame and living with the possibility of her ghost still lingering, some of the spookiness was lost.

"I'm starving," Simon said. "Let's go change clothes and go to dinner. I have reservations at a top restaurant."

"You own a top restaurant."

Simon smiled. "Yes, but not as well-known as this one, at least not yet."

"The food won't be any better than what you serve."

"Maybe, but I want to check them out. I want to see what they're serving and how they're serving it."

An hour later they dined in quiet elegance, attended to by a tuxedo clad waiter.

"This place may be fancier, but I swear the food is no better than what you cook," Dani said.

"Thank you for the compliment," Simon said. "I must admit I like the casual atmosphere of Simon's Place better than this high-toned establishment. Still, I always wanted to eat here and now I have."

When they left they walked hand in hand down the street, following the sound of music issuing from bars and music venues along the way. They went in one place and had a drink, listening to the jazz that drew in locals and tourists alike. When the band took a break, the trumpet player stepped from the platform.

"Simon! Man, I haven't seen you in forever. Where you cookin' now?"

"I've got my own restaurant, Simon's Place." Simon handed him a business card that he pulled from his shirt pocket. "Come see me sometime and I'll give you a bowl of gumbo on the house."

"You know it!" The man slipped into the crowd and made his way to backstage.

Simon and Dani listened to jazz on the street corner, then made their way to where the mellow sounds of slow dance music spilled out onto the sidewalk. Entering, they found a small table and ordered a glass of wine.

Simon extended his hand to Dani. "Will you dance with me?"

"I can't dance."

"I'll teach you."

"I've never danced. Ever. There was never room for it in my life."

"There's room now. With this kind of music, it's just swaying to the music, that's all."

"I guess I could do that. Maybe."

Simon led her to the small dance floor and turned toward her. He took her arms and placed them around his neck. He put his arms around her and pulled her toward him until their bodies touched.

"Simon! This is too close!"

"Nah," he spoke softly in her ear. "Everybody is dancing this close."

She looked around and saw he was telling the truth. Every couple on the dance floor was cheek-to-cheek and body-to-body. The music began to seep into her, immersing her in rhythm and melody. She rested her head on Simon's chest and let her feet move as they would. She thought she was doing as well as anyone else there. This wasn't the kind of dancing where you needed to learn steps.

After a couple of songs they weren't so much dancing as standing still and swaying to the music. Dani felt Simon's erection pressing against her, and she imagined doing this in private, without any clothing between them.

"Let's go," Simon whispered, and turning, he led her toward the door.

* * *

Dani stood in the bathroom, summoning up the courage to face Simon while she was wearing the filmy nightgown. She splurged at a lingerie shop on a brand new gown of pale apricot silk. She wanted to wear something new for this first time, as Simon called it.

It would be the first time for her. Nothing existed before this night. This was the first time she would ever make love, and the occasion demanded something special, not something that had been worn by someone else, like the rest of her clothes. The symbolism did not escape her.

Entering the bedroom, she found Simon already in bed, the sheet pulled up to his waist.

"You are so beautiful," he said. "Stand there and let me look at you. That peachy color makes you glow. You should wear that color more often."

Dani stood there debating whether to climb into bed beside him when he held out his hand.

"Join me here, babe. I have to admit I messed up. I forgot to pack any pajamas. I don't even own pajamas, but I should have bought some for tonight. I didn't think it would be cool for me to show myself right off. I didn't want to scare you."

She climbed onto the tall bed beside him and leaned back into the big puffy pillows. Simon turned toward her and gently urged her onto her side facing him. He kissed her softly on her forehead and cheeks, ending with a small kiss on the lips.

"What was your favorite part of the day?" he asked, drawing back to look at her.

"Hmm. I had lots of favorites."

He kissed her again, a bit more firmly this time. "So name one," he said after he drew back again.

"The Mardi Gras museum was fun," she answered, having a difficult time thinking as Simon gathered her closer and bare skin connected.

"Yes. What else?" he asked, in between the kisses he was depositing behind her ear and on her neck.

"Well, umm, the dancing. I liked the dancing."

"Me too." He leaned her back into the pillow and covered her breasts with kisses.

When he stopped and raised his lips back to hers, he tried to convey all the passion and love he could, plunging his tongue deep into her mouth. As she held his head with her arms wrapped around him, he let his fingers check to see if she was ready for him. Her legs automatically opened to allow him access and he turned and positioned himself over her.

"I love you," he said as he slipped inside her.

CHAPTER TWENTY-FOUR

Parker picked up the flowers and headed toward her door.

I should have gotten the roses. No, these are better. Addie is more a mixed bouquet kind of girl. She's eclectic. Yeah, that's the word, eclectic. Roses are more formal, and she definitely isn't a formal person. But roses are more important. They show you are serious. Maybe I should have bought roses.

Parker only became a ditherer lately. He put this off as long as he could stand it. Tonight might start a wonderful romance. It might be the beginning of the rest of his life. Or it might be the end of several months of a growing friendship. Either way, he had to make a move. He couldn't continue to dither about Addie. Their kisses had been growing more passionate each day, but the conversation remained light. They talked about the neighborhood, the city, and the country. They talked about the world. They talked about movies and books and their childhoods. But they definitely didn't talk about their relationship. Never had Parker gone this long, being this close to a woman, hugging, kissing, but not ending up in bed.

A person would think something's wrong with me.

But this thing he had with Addie, this friendship, this relationship that wasn't a full-blown relationship, was so good, so important to him, that he didn't want to mess it up. *So what's the worst thing that could happen? If we start sleeping together, and it doesn't work out, my living here will be very awkward and I might have to move. But if I don't make a move, I can't stand living this close, anyway. If someone else moves in on her, I couldn't take it, especially if I hadn't even tried. If I dilly-dally around and lose her to another guy, it'll be my own fault.*

Standing with his hand on the door, he rethought the same things that had been going over and over in his mind. *Hyatt, get a move on. Do it and get it over with. Whatever happens, it can't be worse than this indecision.* The last time he was this nervous was Junior High School. *Make a move. Either she accepts or she rejects. If she rejects, move on. There are more fish in the sea,* as his brother always said, until he fell in love and got married.

Parker turned the knob, then stopped again. Maybe that was the difference. He was falling in love with Addie. It wasn't simply lust, it was love. It was important. Maybe the most important thing in his life, and he didn't want to mess it up.

He picked up a flashlight from the table by the front door. The power had been going off and on ever since he got home from work, and he might need it before the evening was over. He didn't know if Addie had flashlights and candles or not. Although the power was on right that minute, it might go off again.

He opened the door and slipped out onto the gallery. The rain had let up a little. Earlier it had been coming down in torrents, and the weather report said it was supposed to rain for two more days. The wind was pretty heavy, too. He supposed that was the problem with the power. Parker took the long way around, staying under the cover of the gallery instead of cutting across the courtyard.

Addie opened her door as soon as he knocked.

"Come on in. Are you wet? Oh, are those for me?"

"Yes, they're for you, and I'm not wet."

"The stew is ready, if you're ready to eat. I thought a good, hearty stew sounded just right on a rainy evening like this." Addie led the way into the kitchen.

The round oak table was set with placemats and heavy silver. Candles flickered in the center of the table, as well as here and there around the kitchen.

"I have candles burning all over the place. The power's been going off all afternoon, so I just leave them burning. Thank heavens the stove is gas, or we wouldn't have any supper."

She moved to fill large bowls from the big pot on the stove.

"Can I help you with that?"

"Yes. Take this bowl and I'll bring the other. The bread is already on the table, and the wine, it's there, too."

Just as they took their places, the lights went out again.

"That makes it feel cozy," Addie said.

"Yes, a romantic dinner by candlelight." Parker smiled at her.

After they'd eaten, and the dishes were rinsed and put in the dishwasher, they went into the living room.

"No TV tonight, I'm afraid, but I have a battery powered radio. Maybe we can get some music on it." Addie soon had a station playing soft and easy songs.

When she turned to Parker, he took her in his arms.

"May I have this dance?"

Swaying to the music, they soon stopped making any effort at dance steps and stood there entwined, kissing. Parker pressed her closer to him, running his hands up and down her back. Finally, Addie took his face between her hands, looked deeply into his eyes, and said, "It's time."

Taking him by the hand, she took a candle from a nearby table and led him into the bedroom.

She started to pull her sweater over her head, but Parker stopped her.

"I've dreamed of doing this for so long. Please let me," he said as he gathered the fabric in his hands and lifted it over her head. "My God. You are more beautiful than I imagined."

He was surprised she wasn't wearing a bra. Placing his hands over her breasts, he allowed the puckered nubs to peek out between his fingers. Bending, he suckled each of them in turn, producing a moan of pleasure from Addie.

"My turn," she said after a minute. When he stood straight she unbuttoned his shirt and pushed it back over his arms until it fell to the floor. She put her arms around him and pressed her breasts against his chest. "I've been wondering what this would feel like," she said.

"So, what does it feel like?"

"Wonderful!"

She broke away from him, took his hand and led him toward the bed, stopping only to let him remove her skirt and his own jeans before climbing up onto the cool sheets.

* * *

Afterward, while they lay among the tangled sheets, her head on his shoulder, his arm around her, holding her close, he asked, "When you said, 'It's time,' what did you mean? I know you meant it's time for us to finally make love, but when you looked at me like that, and said those words, I had the feeling you meant more."

"Haven't you had the feeling, all this time, that this was inevitable? That it was going to happen — us going to bed together — but the time wasn't right? I thought that was why you were holding back."

"I held back because I thought if this — this thing between us — didn't work out I would lose both a very good friend and a place to live. I was uncertain. For the first time in my life I didn't know whether to go ahead or not."

"That was because it just wasn't the right time yet. I've known for a long time this was coming, and tonight was the right time."

"I'm sure glad, because I was going crazy," Parker said and kissed her.

At that moment, there was a loud thump from overhead and they both jumped at the noise. Parker sat up in bed and looked at the ceiling.

"That must have been the vacuum cleaner," Addie said, gathering the sheet around her.

Parker looked at her quizzically, "The vacuum cleaner?"

"Yes. I was dusting and vacuuming the upstairs apartment today. With all the rain, I didn't even open the shop. There weren't any customers out and about. I was cleaning the bedroom above this room when the power went out. I left the vacuum sitting in the middle of the floor so I could finish when the power came back on, but I never got back to it. I guess it got overbalanced and fell over."

"I thought I heard footsteps after the thump, but it's hard to tell with it raining so hard."

Parker lay back down and gathered Addie in his arms. "There's more important things to think about right now," he said and kissed her.

CHAPTER TWENTY-FIVE

Addie opened the shop late. She couldn't help but smile and hum to herself while she dusted the tops of the counters and straightened the necklaces on their velvet stands. The last few weeks had been filled with happiness. The shop filled her days and Parker filled her nights. Things couldn't be going better. Even the frequent rainy days and the premonitions of something bad coming to pass couldn't dampen her spirits.

She told Evie not to come in first thing. Even though it had stopped raining, at least for a while, and the sun peeked out, she might not have any customers that day. Evie was going to come down and check later.

She tried to string a necklace of rose quartz, moonstone, light green jade and pearls, but she couldn't keep her mind on the task. She mostly thought about Parker and the previous night. She could remember his hands while they stroked her skin, his lips while they caressed her body. She left the beads, wandered around the shop, touched this and that, and found herself standing and staring, unseeing, at nothing.

She tried to analyze the sparks that flew around inside her head and heart. Love, that was one of them. She loved Parker. The friendship and affection had been growing since the day they met, and now it had burst into an open flame.

Get a grip. Don't go gaga! Stay calm and don't be moonstruck. Even though I believe in a lot of stuff most people would say is weird, I have plenty of commonsense. And this isn't my first romance.

But in her heart, she knew this was serious, not just an affair.

She was standing behind the counter, admonishing herself, when a man strolled in the door, and the tingle that had been with her since Dani's encounter with her aunt and uncle revved up a notch. It felt like walking across a carpet in the wintertime with the built up static electricity discharging when this man walked in.

He wasn't a tall man, probably less than six feet, and he had sandy colored hair mixed with some gray. He was in casual clothes

— khakis and a red polo shirt. Addie's customers were usually women or couples, not men alone. She wondered if he might be looking for Madame, looking for a potion or spell from her successor. Maybe Evie was right and it was somebody looking for her, although Addie didn't have that feeling of foreboding that usually accompanied something bad about to happen.

"May I help you?" *Might as well find out right now what he wants and why I'm tingling.*

"I was in the neighborhood, and I saw the name on the window — Zappa. That's not a common name."

"No — no it's not."

"It's my name, too, and whenever I see it, I try to meet another Zappa."

"I'm Addie Zappa," Her tingling increased tenfold.

"Are you from New Orleans? I've been in and out of the city over the years and have never run into another Zappa here, other than my brother. He lived here until he passed away recently. He never mentioned knowing any other person with our name."

"I've just lived here a few months. I moved here from Connecticut when my great-aunt died and left me this property."

"What a coincidence. I've recently moved here from Baton Rouge. My brother and I owned property together in both cities, and since he died I've moved here so I can oversee everything in New Orleans.

"I lived in Connecticut for about two years, over twenty-five years ago." He held out his hand to Addie. "Martin Zappa is my name. I'm glad to meet another Zappa."

The sparks could have flown off Addie, like a sparkler on the Fourth of July. "Martin? You are Martin Zappa?" She couldn't shake his hand or they might both explode. She backed up and leaned on the tall stool that sat behind the counter.

"Yes, I am. Is something wrong?" Martin Zappa dropped his hand and stared at Addie.

"My father's name was Martin Zappa. He left my mother before I was born."

Martin grew still. "And what is your mother's name?"

"Carol. Her name was Carol Henson Zappa."

"My God." He reached out to grip the counter with both hands.

Addie stood staring at the stranger. Finally, pulling her wits together, she rounded the end of the counter and went to the front door and closed it, flipping the sign to CLOSED.

"I think we'd better talk about this. Come into the kitchen," *Said the spider to the fly,* she thought as she went to the door into the back room. "It's through here." *He left my mother over twenty-five years ago and hasn't been heard from since. It's time I found out why my father never acknowledged me all these years.*

When she reached the kitchen and turned to look at him, Martin Zappa looked so white and drawn, she feared he would collapse.

"Here, sit down. I know this is a shock." Her heart softened just a little. This could be her father, after all. Maybe he was. Maybe he wasn't, either. Whoever this Martin Zappa was, she didn't want him to keel over in her kitchen.

Addie opened the refrigerator and took out the pitcher of lemonade. Some sugar was what they both needed. Wasn't that what they said about shock? Get your sugar level up? She filled two glasses with ice from the refrigerator door and placed them on the table, then took a package of cookies from the cupboard.

Sitting herself across the table from Martin Zappa, she took a sip, then, steeling herself for what she was about to find out.

"So. Are you my father?"

He wrapped his hands around the glass and looked directly into her eyes. "I don't know, but it looks like it's possible."

"Tell me why you think so."

"I'm Martin Lewis Zappa, and I was married to Carol Henson for just over a year. We lived in Greenview, Connecticut, about twenty-six years ago."

"Why did you split up?"

" We were very happy until my brother, James, wanted me to move to Louisiana and help him manage the family property. I was — am — originally from south Louisiana, and our father had extensive holdings in Baton Rouge, Lafayette, and New Orleans, which he and James managed. I never got along very well with my father, so I was pursuing another career. I ended up in Connecticut, where I met Carol, fell in love, and we married."

"What went wrong?"

"Everything was great until my father died. When that happened, James felt like he couldn't take care of our holdings in both cities, and he asked me to come back and live in Baton Rouge and take part of the work burden from him.

"I thought I had no choice but to help my brother maintain the family income, which supported not only my brother, but my mother, who was still living then. At the time, I didn't know about the trust my father set aside for me. He always thought I would return home and we would reconcile."

Martin stopped and took a drink of the lemonade.

" I never dreamed Carol would refuse to come with me. It's not like I didn't talk it over with her, and explain how important it was for me to help in the family business. And at first, she seemed happy with the idea of moving down here, excited, even. But her mother wasn't. And you probably know how your grandmother can be."

"No, actually I don't. She died a couple of months before I was born."

"Died? Adelaide died after I left? If I'd known, I would have come back and tried to get Carol to come with me." He looked down and drew a circle in the water ring left by the glass. "Is Carol still alive?"

"No, she died five, almost six, years ago. She never remarried. It was just the two of us. Since I never knew my grandmother, why don't you tell me about her?"

"Well, at first, when Carol introduced us, Adelaide seemed to like me fine. She was as friendly as can be until I mentioned that I was from south Louisiana, that my parents lived in New Orleans. Then she turned to ice, and started trying to get Carol to break up with me. I couldn't do anything right in her eyes. Carol and I finally eloped. We came back two days later already married and there was nothing Adelaide could do about it, since Carol was of age. Then, when this came up about moving down here, Adelaide really threw a fit. And she won. She persuaded Carol to refuse to come with me.

"I thought sure when I left, Carol would follow me. I called a few times, but Carol had moved back home with her mother, and Adelaide always answered the telephone and said Carol didn't want to talk to me. I finally stopped calling. I got the divorce papers in the mail a few months later.

"But I didn't know about you. I didn't know Carol was pregnant when I left. I swear by all that's holy, if I knew I had a child, nothing would have kept me from you." Tears filled his eyes. "I can't believe I have such a beautiful daughter."

Tears filled Addie's eyes too, and she swiped them with the back of her hand. *I lost having a father because of my grandmother's denial of her past and my mother's weakness in standing up to her.*

"Did you never marry again? Do you have other children?" Addie thought how odd it would be to find out she had brothers and sisters.

"I married again, after a few years, but we didn't have any children. She had a son from a previous marriage, and I raised him like he was my own. He's a doctor now, here in New Orleans. Sylvie couldn't have more children."

"So I have a stepmother and a stepbrother? That seems so weird."

"Sylvie died four years ago of cancer."

"I'm sorry." She didn't know what else to say. She stood and moved toward Martin, who rose and embraced her.

"I always wondered what my daddy looked like. I always wanted a daddy, like the other girls," Addie said, her voice tremulous.

"Well, you've got one now, honey. I hate I missed your growing up. You are going to have to tell me everything about yourself."

"Ahem," came the sound from the French doors leading out onto the courtyard. "I just came by to see if you needed me to work today," Evie said.

"Oh, Evie. You'll never guess," Addie said, taking Martin by the hand. "This is my father, Martin Zappa. And Martin, this is Evie White."

Martin extended his hand to Evie. "I am so pleased to meet a friend of my newly found daughter."

"Newly found?"

"Yes, come sit down and I'll tell you," Addie motioned her friend toward a chair. "It's some story, all right," she said as she fixed her friend a glass.

"I saw the name Zappa on the front window and came in to meet another Zappa."

"And who he found was his daughter," Addie said.

"Who I never even knew existed."

"I'll leave and let you two visit. Do you want me to open the shop for you?"

"No, let's leave it closed today."

"Okay. I'll see you later. It was nice to meet you, Martin."

He rose to his feet as she left. "She seems like a nice woman. Does she live close by? I notice her walking across the courtyard."

"Yes. She lives in the upstairs apartment across the way."

"Tell me how you came to be running a shop in New Orleans," Martin said as he sat down again.

"It's the funniest thing. My mother always told me my grandmother was an orphan who met my grandfather in New Orleans, where she lived, and they married and she went home with him to Connecticut. She said Adelaide had no living family."

"Yes. That's what she told me, too."

"A few months ago, I got a phone call from a lawyer, who said my great-aunt, Adelaide's sister, had died and I was her only heir. I inherited the shop and these four apartments. The one condition is that I live here a year.

"So, Adelaide turned her back on her sister and denied having any family. I wonder why?"

"I've been puzzling over that, too, and I think the reason was Aunt Clotilde and what she was — what she did."

"What do you mean by what she was and what she did?"

Addie took a deep breath. "The shop you entered this morning, the one where I sell jewelry, was a hoodoo shop. Aunt Clotilde — people around here called her Madame — sold spells and protection from hexes, and she made love potions and all sorts of things like that. Some people called her a witch, and now they call me the new witch. I think Adelaide was ashamed of all the hoodoo stuff, and wanted to forget all about it when she married and moved."

"My, oh my! I've heard of Madame, but I never met her. I think perhaps my brother had, but I don't know any details. I take it you aren't into anything like that? Or are you, since people call you the new witch?"

"Not really, but maybe just a little. I do believe in some things most people don't. I believe there are a lot of things in the universe we don't understand."

"I'm with you about that. So you sell jewelry in the shop now, instead of hoodoo spells?"

"I sell jewelry I make myself, using gemstones, which some people believe have power. And I am slowly learning a little bit

163

about what Madame did. I'm studying the different colors and kinds of candles now, and what to burn to get different results. I don't say I believe, but I don't exactly disbelieve, either."

"Your mother and your grandmother never did anything like that, but they did speak about spirits guiding them, and they didn't believe in coincidence. They believed things that happen are connected in some way."

"Like things happening in threes?"

"Exactly! I remember Carol and I were walking down Main Street, window-shopping, and in the window of an antique shop sat a big, black cat. We stopped to look, and the cat rubbed up against the window in front of Carol. On the way home we stopped at a farmer's produce stand, and there was a black cat asleep in a chair. Carol said, "You watch, there will be another black cat show up." That evening, after supper, we went for a walk around the block, and a boy was sitting by the sidewalk with a box of kittens and a sign saying FREE KITTENS. There was one black one, and it struggled over the side of the box and went right to Carol. Of course we had to adopt it. We called it…"

"Trey! I remember Trey. We had him until he was an old cat. I was about twelve when he died. I cried and cried, I missed him so much."

Martin excused himself to answer his chiming cell phone.

After a few moments, he said, "I'm sorry, but I have to get back to the office. Something has come up I need to tend to. May I take you to supper tonight? I don't want to miss any more time away from my beautiful daughter."

"I have a date for dinner tonight, but I would love for you to join us. There is someone I want you to meet, and I want him to meet you, too."

"Ah, yes. A young man, I presume? I didn't get around to asking you if you are married or engaged."

"Neither one. But he is special to me, and I want the two of you to meet."

"I would love to join you."

"Do you know where Simon's Place is? We eat there quite often, and were planning to go there tonight."

"It's around here somewhere, isn't it?"

"Yes, about a block and a half down." Addie pointed the direction.

They set the time to meet, and Martin left, after giving Addie a hug and a kiss on the cheek.

CHAPTER TWENTY-SIX

Dani paced from one side of the room to the other, pausing to straighten a display she had already rearranged three times that morning. Returning to stand behind the counter and stare out the front window at the almost deserted sidewalk, she finally allowed the panic that had been nibbling at the edge of her consciousness to get a grip on her thoughts.

She had been trying so hard to succeed, to give Morgan a better life. Her ambition, her dreams and hopes, had been put on hold for so many years, and now, just when she thought she was at last building something substantial, it threatened to come tumbling down around her.

She walked to the front door and turned the sign to say CLOSED. She doubted she would lose a sale because the sky was once again covered with rain clouds.

Going into the back room, she stood looking at all she had collected.

I sure couldn't get all this in my car. And where would I move it to? Boxes and racks held clothing in transition from bargain finds to one of a kind designer outfits. Equipment and supplies filled every available space.

The stairs, which started on the back wall, turned and led upstairs to the two rooms that were home for Dani and Morgan. "Cozy" is what she called them. One room held a small but adequate kitchen plus a table and chairs, a couch and an easy chair. The other room held the double bed she and Morgan shared, and a dresser. The small bathroom was clean, which was what mattered.

Downstairs in her workroom, a washer and dryer were lined up against the stairs, next to the door leading into the tiny washroom under the steps. Madame was responsible for the addition of those much-needed appliances. When she had found out Dani was avoiding harsh commercial washers and dryers by hand washing the clothing she found at the estate and rummage sales that supplied her, Madame approached JayMar.

"Jamar," Madame never called him the JayMar he preferred, "you will put in the connections for a washer and dryer for Mademoiselle Dani, oui? It is something she needs, you understand? And you will not charge her for this, *n'est pas?* And the things I know about you will stay our secret? That is best, is it not?"

Of course he'd agreed. No one ever went against Madame's wishes. As soon as the connections were installed, Mrs. Molyneux, who owned the bakery in the next block, came by to offer Dani her old, but serviceable, washer and dryer. To her surprise, Mrs. Molyneux had won the drawing for a new washer and dryer at the grand opening of a new appliance store in the shopping center across town. It was a surprise because Mrs. Molyneux didn't remember registering for the drawing. More of Madame's magic was at work, Dani supposed. But Madame had been gone for months now, and things were bound to change.

Dani walked around the room, running her fingers over the pieces and parts that formed her dream, her business, her income, her life. Other than Morgan, her design business was the only thing that meant anything to her. *Except Simon.* Simon was now just as important. What would it mean to their relationship if she had to move away from this neighborhood?

A table against the right far wall held painting supplies, used to paint on jeans and jackets. Shelves to the left held cutting and sewing supplies, and a large table in the middle of the room served to lay out works in progress. Her sewing machine and embroidery machine stood against the front wall.

I should have saved my money instead of buying an expensive embroidery machine, she thought. When she saw it at the estate sale, read the instruction book, and saw the samples piled on the table beside it, she yearned to buy it.

"My mother only had it a couple of months before she fell ill, and she didn't use it anymore," the woman running the sale said. "It's the top of the line machine, and it's just like new."

Dani had gone home without it. It stayed in her thoughts, though, all that day, and the next. Finally, on the last day scheduled for the sale, she went to an ATM and withdrew half of the asking price, which was most of what she had in the bank, and went back to the sale. Addie kept telling her to have faith, that some things were meant to be, so Dani offered half of the asking price and went home with an almost new embroidery machine.

Although she was making back that money, a little each month, she might wish she had the cash if she had to find another place or come up with more rent — a lot more rent.

Dani sighed and moved to look out the door into the back yard. Small, yes, but it allowed a safe outdoor space for Morgan and Spike to play, close by so Dani could keep an eye on them. She kept a padlock on the gate that led to her parking space in the alley behind, so no one could come in that way. The brick walls of the buildings on either side sheltered the small yard, and the tall boards of the back fence kept prying eyes from seeing the boy and his dog romping in the enclosure. She wondered how she would ever find another place that offered shop, workroom, apartment, and yard, for what she was paying. She couldn't. So she would have to come up with whatever figure it took to stay here.

What if she couldn't do that? What if the new rent was so high it was impossible? If she had to move, they would have to leave this neighborhood, which seemed so much more like home than the place in Memphis where she grew up. The people here were like family to her, especially Addie.

Quickly, Dani went back through the storeroom and shop. Going out the front door, she pulled the key from her pocket and locked the front door. Next door, she found the entry to Addie's jewelry store unlocked, which meant Addie was close by, even if she wasn't in the shop. Addie gave her a key to the shop and one to the wrought iron gate at the end of the brick path next to the shop, just in case Dani needed in at any time. But this time, the shop was unlocked and she cut through the backroom and entered Addie's kitchen to find Addie and Evie sitting at the kitchen table.

"That's so wonderful. I just can't believe it," Evie was saying. "It's like a fairy tale come true."

"I'm glad something good has happened to someone," Dani said, "because my life is going down the tubes."

"Oh, no. Your aunt and uncle again?" asked Addie.

"No, even worse. I could handle my uncle, even if I had to ask for Simon's help. This is something no one can do anything about."

"Tell," said Evie.

"This morning, a man came into the shop. He said he represented the company that owns the property, and he came by to inspect the property and talk about the rent."

"You mean, someone besides JayMar?" asked Addie.

"Yes, not JayMar. Another man, a white man, older. I didn't catch his name. He had all these papers, and he kept looking at them as he went through the rooms. I think he was comparing what was on the papers to what was there. I told him I painted every wall in the place myself, that it was old and dirty when I moved in, and he made a note about that."

"That's good," Evie said.

"Yes, but when he saw the washer and dryer in the workroom he kept studying the papers and finally he said, 'Those aren't listed on the inventory.' And I told him they were mine. So he asked if the connections were there when I moved in, and I told him they were put in later. He asked if I paid to have them put in, and I said no, I hadn't, JayMar had them installed, and he made another note."

Addie placed a glass of lemonade in front of her, and pushed the plate of cookies closer. Dani took a sip and continued.

"He looked upstairs, and asked about the furniture in the apartment. I told him it was all there when I moved in except the mattress, which I replaced, and the TV. When he was all through looking around, he asked me how much rent I was paying, and I told him."

She stopped and put her hands over her face, willing the tears not to fall. Addie reached over and put her hand on Dani's arm. Taking her hands down, Dani continued.

"He said I was paying half the rent that the previous tenant had paid, but JayMar, except he called him Jamar, was turning in the full amount due. Then he asked me why JayMar would do that."

"You mean JayMar, or Jamar, or whatever his name is, was making up the difference in what was owed?" Evie asked.

"Seems like it. He asked me what I was doing for JayMar to do that, and I said 'not a damn thing, but it's not for his lack of trying,' " and with those words, the tears started trickling down her cheeks. "I try so hard to be a good person, to have good morals, and people accuse me of things anyway. Just like my uncle accused me of being fast and easy because I was raped." Sobs threatened to break into her words. "And where does it get me? Nowhere, that's where.

Accused and found guilty, that's where. And maybe without a home, that's where."

Both Addie and Evie put their arms around her. When the tears had slowed they went back to their chairs, each holding one of Dani's hands.

"He didn't tell you to get out, did he?" asked Evie.

"No, he didn't, but I can't afford to pay twice the rent I'm paying now. No way can I afford that much right now. When I first came to New Orleans, I looked all over for an apartment and a shop. This is the only place I found with both together, and the only place I could afford."

"I imagine that Madame had something to do with the rent being so cheap," Addie said.

"Maybe. I heard her say something to JayMar one time about keeping his secrets, so I imagine he was doing it to keep her quiet about something. But I'm surprised he has kept on doing it. He has come around, hinting he wants to be 'better friends' with me, and I've told him no way is that going to happen. I never thought about him putting his own money up to pay part of my rent. I just thought his name, JayMar, was the J and M in the company name, and he could do what he wanted, since it was his company. I can't imagine him being so scared of what Madame could tell that he would pay part of my rent."

"And keep on doing it after Madame's death," Evie said.

"That's probably because of Addie being here. Everyone in the neighborhood thinks she can do magic things, like Madame did. Simon says they don't think she's as powerful as Madame, but she's younger, and her power will grow. She's not as scary as Madame was, but no one is taking any chances with her."

Addie sat still, her eyes growing wider.

"Me? They're scared of me?"

"Yep, they sure are. You know people call you the new witch, don't you?

"Yes, I knew that. I just never thought of anyone being scared of me."

"I'm scared, but not of you. What am I going to do? I can't afford twice the rent."

"That'll never happen. If your rent gets doubled and you can't afford to stay where you are, I have the perfect apartment for you," Addie said, looking smug.

"Where?"

"Right up there," she said, pointing at the ceiling. "The upstairs apartment. It's been vacant all these months since I moved in. I've been real hesitant about finding someone to rent it. It just didn't feel right, somehow. I found a note in Madame's secretary that said the apartment was to be kept vacant until the spirits sent someone who needed it, so I guess that must be you. It's real big, as big as mine plus another bedroom and bath above my shop and storeroom."

"Wow. That is big! I knew there is an apartment up there, but I never thought about it. How much rent would you charge?"

"Let's think about that part later. Right now, you don't even know if you are going to have to move or not. If you do, I don't know what we could do about a shop, but there ought to be plenty of room upstairs for storage and a workroom. And Morgan and Spike would have the courtyard to play in."

"Oh, Addie, that takes a lot of worry off my mind. At least we would have a place to live. Maybe I can find a place to rent for a shop somewhere close by."

"Let's go upstairs and look." Addie got to her feet, rummaged in a drawer for a key, and started out the French doors.

As they went up the stairs at the back of the courtyard, Addie said, "You know people in the neighborhood say the apartment is haunted, don't you? Will that scare you or Morgan?"

"I've never given much thought to ghosts, whether I believe in them or not, but if it is, it's bound to be Madame's ghost, and she would never hurt us. So no, I wouldn't be frightened."

"I sometimes think I hear noises coming from up there," Evie said. "I used to imagine it was Ed, coming to get me, but no one has tried to get into my apartment, and I think if it was Ed, he wouldn't be messing around in the next apartment, he would confront me in some way. Now I know it's just my imagination, or the wind, or something."

"How did the rumors about a ghost get started?" Dani asked.

"When I had a workman here redoing the electricity, he said someone moved tools and things he left up there, and he told people it must be a ghost. I think he just forgot where he laid stuff down."

171

Addie unlocked the big wooden door with her key, and they all entered a large living room. It was furnished with painted pieces and a big pine sideboard, unlike the more formal furniture in the other apartments. There was a large pine table surrounded by mismatched chairs in various colors and styles. There were no paintings on the walls, such as those in the other three apartments.

"This is nice!" said Dani. "Much more casual than your place, Addie. I wouldn't be worried about Morgan scratching up anything, and there aren't any knick-knacks to get broken."

"Parker told me Madame said this apartment was originally occupied by a couple of servants when she and her brother and sister moved here from the big house. They lost all their money in the stock market crash, you know. My great-grandfather was in the cotton market, and when he and my great-grandmother died, the big house had to be sold. They were able to hold onto this building, and each child had their own apartment. A couple of servants moved with them, but eventually moved on and this apartment was rented out. Madame was very picky about who she rented to, only to those the spirits told her to rent to."

She turned to a door on the right. "Come see this bedroom. It's right above mine."

They entered a room furnished much like the living room, with a combination of pine and painted furniture, dressed with durable, if faded, fabric.

"This looks like something right out of the pages of a country home magazine," Evie said.

"It's wonderful!" said Dani.

Addie pointed out the bathroom

"That big claw-foot bathtub is just like mine," Evie said as they peeked into the white-tiled room.

"It's so clean," Dani said. "I love all this white tile. It's about ten times bigger than what I have now."

"Now, let's go see the kitchen and the other bedroom."

They went back through the living room and into the kitchen. It, too, had the green painted cabinets that looked like they were from the 1930s. The appliances weren't as new as the ones in Addie's apartment, but they were clean and serviceable. From there the women entered a short hall with a bathroom and a closet opening off it, then into a large bedroom overlooking the street.

"Wow! This is cool! The trees along the street make it seem like you are in a tree house," Dani said.

"You could make one or the other of the bedrooms into a workroom. Either one of them is big enough to share with Morgan," Evie said.

"Yes, I could. I could even put another bed in for Morgan. He moves around so much when he's asleep I get woke up all night long. We'd probably sleep in this one, since the other bedroom is closer to the stairs and it would be easier to carry stuff in and out."

Addie stood staring at the bed. "You know, I come up here once a month to dust and vacuum. I leave everything neat and straight, but I swear that bed looks like someone slept in it and didn't make it back straight."

They all looked at the bed.

"Someone didn't smooth out the wrinkles," Evie said.

"Hmm. A ghost that sleeps in a bed," Dani said.

"I check the doors every time I'm up here, and I keep the key in the kitchen drawer, so I don't know how anyone could get in here."

They went back into the kitchen and Addie checked the doors leading out onto the gallery. "Locked up tight."

"I'll go check the ones in the other bedroom."

Addie and Evie went into the living room and found the French doors locked as well.

Something caught Evie's eye. She stooped and reached under the dining table.

"Those are all locked up, too," Dani said, as she returned from the bedroom. "What's that?" she asked Evie.

Straightening out the paper, Evie showed them. "It's a wrapper from the Burger Shack. Unless your ghost eats hamburgers, I'd say you have a real, live person staying up here,"

CHAPTER TWENTY-SEVEN

Parker had been thinking about Addie all day. Nothing unusual in that. He thought about her every day at the office. His belongings stayed at his apartment, but he spent almost every night at her place, returning to his own flat in time to shower and change for work.

The project that occupied the last few weeks was finally completed, and he was able to take off work over an hour early. He planned to surprise Addie and perhaps she would be able to take a little time out for some loving.

He went to the shop first, but it was locked and the closed sign was showing, so he entered the courtyard, using his key at the gate. He knocked at her front door, and when she didn't answer, he found it unlocked and went in. Checking first in the kitchen and storeroom, he went into the bedroom. Hearing the sound of splashing water, Parker proceeded to the bathroom door, where he stood watching a nymph, his nymph, piling bubbles onto her shoulders while she reclined in the big, white tub.

Finally she sat up and rinsed the white foam from her arms and body, allowing him a view of her pink tipped breasts and slim body. She stood and stepped out onto the soft rug by the tub, reaching for the thick, white towel hanging on the chair standing nearby.

"Don't cover up all that beauty. I've been thinking about it all day."

"Parker!" she yelled as she clutched the towel to her. "What are you doing here?"

"I finished the job early. I thought you'd be glad to see me."

"I am. You just surprised me, that's all."

He approached and took the towel she was trying to wrap around her body.

"We have some time before our reservation at Simon's. I have an idea of how we can spend it." He took her hand and pulled her into the bedroom.

"Parker, I have some exciting news."

"Later," he said, then covered her lips with his. "You can tell me later." He lifted her onto the bed, pausing only long enough to strip off his clothes before joining her.

* * *

As they drowsed on the tumbled covers, Addie remembered what she had to tell him.

"Parker, my father came to see me today. He found me. That is, he wasn't looking for me, because he didn't know I existed, but he found me."

"I thought you didn't know anything about your father."

"I didn't. He saw the name on the shop window, Zappa's, and he came in to meet another Zappa. And he found me."

"How did you figure out he's your father?" Parker leaned on one elbow, fascinated.

She explained how he knew all about his mother, grandmother and Connecticut.

"What a story! I guess you're both happy to find each other."

"I'll say. He seems like a good man. I invited him to have supper with us at Simon's tonight so you could meet each other."

Parker swung his legs off the bed and reached for his clothes.

"I'd better call Simon and change our table to a larger one. As busy as his place has become, we won't have a table unless I call."

"I already took care of it."

Parker slipped on his trousers and shirt and sat on the chair to put on his shoes when he spotted the picture leaned up against the wall.

"Where did you find that? I wondered what had become of it."

"Francois batted his ball behind the armoire and couldn't get to it. I was trying to fish it out and found it was caught on the frame of the picture. I had a time getting it out. Who is it? Do you know? She's certainly beautiful."

Parker looked at her, a funny expression on his face.

"What? Do you know who it is?"

"It's your aunt. It's Madame when she was young."

"But — but that's a black woman."

"Yes. Madame was black."

Addie sat, staring at the portrait. Finally, she turned back to Parker.

"Why didn't you tell me?"

"Tell you what? That Madame was black? I thought you knew."

175

"How could I know?"

"Didn't that attorney who handled the estate tell you?"

"No, why didn't you tell me?"

"And what would I have said. 'Pardon me, Addie, but do you know you are part black?'"

"Well, you could have said something."

"At first, when you first got here, I wondered if you knew, but then I forgot about it."

"Why would you wonder about something like that?"

"Well, Madame told me the story about her sister, your grandmother, being very fair-skinned, and passing for white. She met your grandfather at the hotel where she worked, and went back to Connecticut with him. She told him she was an orphan with no family."

"And you knew this story all the time and didn't tell me?"

" I did. I told you that story."

"But you didn't tell me Adelaide let her husband think she was white"

"It didn't come up in conversation," Parker said.

"How do you know all this?"

"Madame told me the story a couple of months before she died."

"And you didn't think it was important enough to tell me?"

"It's just that the more I got to know you, you became not Madame's heir, but Addie, your own self. Like I said, I thought you already knew, and it didn't seem important."

"I would think the person closest to me would tell me something so important."

"Why is it so important? Does it change who you are? No! Does it change the way you think about yourself? It shouldn't!"

Addie was silent.

"There are lots of biracial people around here. Creoles, by nature of their heritage, have some black ancestors. It's nothing special in this neighborhood."

Parker glanced at his watch.

"You'd better get dressed. I'll be back to pick you up for supper in half an hour."

He left by way of the French doors leading from the bedroom out onto the gallery. Reaching his own apartment on the other side of the courtyard, he went to shower. Instead of thinking about Addie, he couldn't get it out of his head that he'd done something wrong, as if he had told a lie. But he hadn't. Told a lie, that is. Maybe he should have said something, but that wasn't something one can just come out and say or work into a conversation. He told the truth that he'd forgotten all about it. She was just Addie to him, not Madame's niece, not 'the new witch,' not his landlady, just Addie, his Addie

CHAPTER TWENTY-EIGHT

After Parker left, Addie stood looking at the portrait. The woman in it was certainly beautiful, no question. And there was something Addie couldn't quite put her finger on, perhaps the shape of her face, which looked like the photos she had seen of her grandmother. Of course, her grandmother was fair skinned, looking more like she had a light suntan, and had masses of curly blond hair, just as Addie did, and her mother before her. This woman, Clotilde, was darker, and her black hair tumbled in loose curls down one shoulder. Her dark eyes looked as though they held many mysteries. Addie thought Madame would have been a formidable woman to face in person. No one would be able to keep secrets from her.

Addie shivered, then she realized she was naked. She returned to the bathtub, and drawing more hot water into the tub, she sank into its warmth to wash away the scent of sex. There was no time to spend thinking over the startling discovery. She needed to get dressed to be ready to go to Simon's Place with Parker to meet her father.

Back in the bedroom, she held up the dress she planned to wear. She wanted the dress from the moment she'd seen Dani working on it in her shop. Dani had bought a cocktail dress from the 1950s, with a full skirt made with many layers of chiffon and tulle. The original bodice was sweat-stained under the arms, and had been made of silk taffeta adorned with sequins, which had turned dark with age. Dani carefully removed the skirt and sewed a new top, a simple design with narrow straps. Then she paired it with a long-sleeved lace jacket in the same shade of light blue. The skirt that came with the jacket had impossible to remove stains, so it was trashed. New buttons on the jacket completed the combination. Dani said the whole thing reminded her of the outfits Rosemary Clooney and Vera Ellen wore in the movie Holiday Inn. Addie bought the DVD and watched for the scene where they wore her dress. It wasn't the same, of course, but it did remind her of the one Dani was making. Both were light blue and lacey and full-skirted.

As soon as Addie could try it on, she did, and from that moment on it was her dress. She knew from the first glimpse, with Addie's kind of knowing, she was going to have it, so she asked Dani how much she was going to ask for it. Then, when she bought it, Dani couldn't go down on the price because Addie was a friend, like she suspected Dani did when Addie bought something from her. Dani argued, of course.

"But I always give friends discounts."

"Nope! No discount on this dress. It's worth full price. It's worth more than you're asking."

So there Addie stood, holding the fabulous dress, which she saved for a special occasion. This occasion. Meeting her father for dinner for the first time and introducing him to Parker was special, indeed.

When she was dressed, she picked up the jewelry she made especially to go with this dress. The necklace, bracelet, and earrings were made of Blue Lace agate, Lapis Lazuli, and Sodalite. As she put them on, she thought of the special properties those stones imbued.

Blue Lace agate was a calming stone, with cooling and soothing energy. She certainly needed that, and it was said to neutralize anger. That couldn't hurt, since she was angry with Parker earlier for not telling her Madame was black.

The Lapis Lazuli was said to help the wearer acquire wisdom and see the truth. Another trait she needed that night, to see and use wisdom and truth with Parker and her father. It was said to cut through superficialities and find the inner truth.

Sodalite was said to guide the wearer toward logical and rational thought, and to widen perspectives, so maybe she would see more clearly why Parker had not told her about Madame, and why her father had never come back to try to persuade her mother to move to Louisiana. Together, perhaps the three kinds of stones would help her through the evening in peace and calmness.

When she was ready to go, she sat down on the edge of the bed once more and stared at the portrait of the beautiful woman who saw to it that Addie was there, in New Orleans.

"So you're my aunt. My Great-aunt Clotilde," Addie said aloud. *The same blood that ran in your veins, and in my grandmother's, is in me. I'm your heir, in more ways than just inheriting your property. These things I sense, the things I know without understanding how, does that ability come from you, too? And my grandmother, did she leave here because she didn't want to be black? Or because she was running from the gift of mysticism, or magic, or whatever it is?*

Addie rose and paced back and forth in front of the picture, finally standing before it again.

Being your heir is a greater responsibility than I ever imagined it could be. You helped these people, protected them from harm, urged them to do right. If you expect me to do that, too, you'll have to be around to help me.

A breeze fluttered her skirts and moved her curls, and Addie smelled the scent of roses in the room.

Addie smiled. *I guess that means you're here, and you're going to show me the way. I'll never be as good as you, but I'll try.*

She went to the small table by the bed and turned on the lamp. Going to the French doors to the gallery, she turned back to the portrait one last time.

Thank you, Aunt Clotilde. Thank you for bringing me here.

CHAPTER TWENTY-NINE

Parker ran a comb through his still damp hair, checking his appearance in the mirror one last time before leaving to meet Addie in the courtyard, as was their custom. He frowned at his reflection. *You may have screwed up big-time. Why didn't you bring up the subject of Madame being black before she found out on her own? It wasn't a secret, so why didn't you make sure she knew?*

He went out into the courtyard and took his usual chair at the table under the tree. *Because after the first day or two, I never thought of it again. Madame was Madame and Addie is Addie, each of them individuals.* Even though Addie was Madame's niece, Parker never thought of her that way. He never thought of her as black or white. To him, she was a unique person, not anyone but Addie. The color of skin of her ancestors has nothing to do with who she was.

He sighed and put his head back, looking at the leaves above him. *I have to make her understand I wasn't deliberately hiding anything. It just wasn't important to me. But I should have known it would matter to her. I should have made sure she knew.*

The door leading from Addie's bedroom out onto the gallery opened and she floated out into the courtyard. Parker stood and watched her come toward him, looking, as she often did, like she just stepped out of a movie from fifty years before. Even the people in the neighborhood, the ones Addie met at Simon's Place or at the market, talked about her appearance, about how she looked like she came from a different era. It added to the mystical quality surrounding her. Some people said she was someone who came back from decades previously — a spirit instead of a real person.

He stood and walked toward her.

"I'm sorry if I hurt you."

"It was such a shock. The way I thought about myself all my life — it was changed. Like I'm somebody completely different somehow, but still the same, too."

"You look beautiful tonight."

"Thank you."

"You know, everyone in the neighborhood, everyone knew Madame, and no one has commented on the differences or likenesses between your appearance, or on your skin color."

"No. No they haven't."

"It's because skin color doesn't matter. They accept you as her successor, even though you're white."

"I know they call me the new witch."

"They know you are her niece because the people who have lived here for generations have passed down the story of how Adelaide went away to live as a white person. It was no surprise to them to see you, to see the color of your skin. They thought, like I did, that somehow you already knew all this — all the story."

"But I didn't," Addie said as tears came to her eyes. "I didn't know any of it. No one told me anything."

"Then I'll be glad to tell you all that I know — all that Madame related to me. But if we are going to be on time to meet your father, we'd better be going now."

"Yes. Perhaps you'd better tell both of us. After all, it concerns him, too."

"Maybe I ought to tell you who some of the people think you are," Parker said as he tucked Addie's arm through his.

She glanced up at him, surprised. "Maybe you ought to!"

"Some think you are Madame who has come back in the body of a movie star from fifty years ago," he said with a grin while they strolled toward the gate.

"You're kidding, right?"

"No, not at all. The rumor is going around that at the moment of death, Madame's spirit swooshed around and somehow found the body of some beautiful actress from the middle of the century, and Madame made it young again, and that's who you are, a young, beautiful Madame come again in new form. In other words, the new witch."

The sound of Addie's laughter filled the courtyard while Parker opened the gate and they stepped out onto the sidewalk.

CHAPTER THIRTY

Martin wasn't an "if only" kind of man. "If only" didn't do a bit of good to anyone. What happened, happened. What was, was. Still, sitting with his newfound daughter and her young man, listening to Parker tell them about Madame and her family, about the plantation owner and his slave mistress, and the little boy who grew up to be a wealthy man who lost everything in the Great Depression, and about that man's children — Clotilde, Adelaide, Jean-Paul — he couldn't help but think how different things might have been — "if only".

"If only" Adelaide had not wanted to escape her roots, her black family, the specter of magic and mysticism hoodoo had thrown over her, it would have been an entirely different story. He would never have met Carol because there would have been no Carol, at least not the Carol he met and loved. There would have been no Addie, sitting across the table from him that night. He wouldn't have the charming young woman for a daughter.

"If only" he had gone back to see Carol in the months after he moved back to Louisiana, to make one more attempt to get her to come with him. He would have known she was pregnant, and he would have been a father to Addie for the last twenty-five years, instead of missing those years of her life. He wouldn't have missed her baby smiles, her first steps, her childhood years of growth and discovery.

Once, about a year after he and Carol divorced, he thought seriously about going to see her, to see if she regretted not moving with him, and to see if she still had any feelings for him. He still loved her, and would have gladly remarried her, if only she would reconsider and come with him. "If only" didn't do any good. He hadn't followed through, and what he lost, he lost.

That night, as he sat and listened to Parker and looked at the daughter who reminded him so much of his beloved Carol, he concentrated on the good things that happened, especially the fact that he had business in the neighborhood that morning and saw her name on the shop window. The "what ifs" could work the other way, too. What if he had come by months earlier, before Madame died? He wouldn't have made this important connection. What if he hadn't noticed the name on the shop? What if he hadn't taken the time to go into the shop to make the acquaintance of someone with the same name as his?

Addie said she believed that if someone had faith, everything works out for the best in the long run, that spirits would guide people the way they ought to go.

"Your mother thought that way, too. I remember her saying that very thing, many times. Although I regret what I lost not being in your life growing up, I can't say my life hasn't been good, even without you and Carol. I know I'm probably not saying this right, but…"

"You're saying it fine. I wish I had known you, too, but my life with Mom was good too, and just look at how things have turned out. Me, in New Orleans, running my own jewelry shop, with lots of new friends…" She put her hand on Parker's, "very good friends, who I would never have met if the spirits hadn't sent me this way. So I know what you mean."

"Listening to Parker tell about Adelaide's background, and Madame's, I'm finally beginning to understand Adelaide's actions." Martin mused. "Obviously she didn't want anyone to find out about who she was and where she came from. She told her husband she was an orphan with no family. She was friendly toward me for months, until the evening we talked about me being from New Orleans. That was too close, and she started turning Carol against me. I don't know exactly what she told Carol to keep her from moving back here with me, but whatever it was, it worked."

Addie said. "My grandmother must have been terrified all her secrets would come to light, and she couldn't let that happen."

"She was a pleasant person until she turned against me, but after that time, we didn't get along at all."

"I'll admit, it was a shock, moving here and learning about my great-aunt and her spells and potions, and hearing all the stories about her. But I've always had these strange 'knowings.' It's hard to explain what I mean, but I just know when something is going to happen, and if it is something good or bad. So now that I know about Madame, it's funny, but I don't feel like I'm so strange any more. It's more of a family thing, something I inherited, like Madame did.

"It was even more of a shock today, finding out that I'm black…or biracial. I was upset at Parker for a while, for not telling me, until I calmed down and thought about it." Addie felt the necklace at her throat, thankful it had helped her remain calm. "Everyone around me knew it, and no one said a thing. I don't know what that means."

"It means everyone sees you for who you are, a charming, kind, beautiful, woman, like I've been telling you," said Parker.

"You inherited yours looks from your mother," Martin said. "You look very much like she did when we married. Do you have pictures of yourself growing up? I'd like to see them, if you do."

"I do, but they're in storage back in Greenview. I'll call my friend and have her send them."

"I want to hear more about your life growing up. I want to see a lot more of you."

"How about coming for supper tomorrow night at my place?" Addie asked.

"I would love to, but I have to be out of town for a few days. I have to go to Lafayette to attend to business, and I don't know how long I'll be gone."

"Do you have something to write on? I'll give you my phone number and you can call when you return. We'll set up a date, okay?"

Martin took a pen from his shirt pocket and wrote Addie's number on a paper napkin.

"Here, let me give you one of my business cards." He reached in his pocket and took out a cardholder. "If you need me, for anything, anything at all, just call. I'm ready to be a dad."

Addie looked at the card. "JMZ Enterprises? You're the man from JMZ Enterprises?"

CHAPTER THIRTY-ONE

It had been a busy evening for Simon. Addie had called during the afternoon to tell him to reserve a table for three, instead of the usual two, for dinner.

"I'm bringing my father, Simon!" she had told him in an excited voice. "Be sure you drop by our table and meet him."

Simon had never thought about who Addie's father might be. Everyone in the neighborhood knew Addie's mother and grandmother were dead, but a father had never been mentioned.

Simon told Estelle, who manned the register, and Estelle told Angie Coudart when she came over from the hardware store to pick up some fried pies for a mid-afternoon snack for her and her dad. From there the news spread like the proverbial wildfire, and by six o'clock, the time Addie and Parker usually came to eat, the place was packed. Everyone wanted to see the man.

When Addie and Parker came in, Simon showed them to a table near the back wall. It gave them a little more privacy than one out in the middle of the room, but he was sure they would be interrupted several times in the course of the meal, as usual. Not only did people want a good look at Addie's father, but no meal at Simon's Place ever went by without one or two requests for help directed at Addie. Simon had tried to get folks to let her alone while she was eating, but it didn't always help, and as soon as she finished her last bite and put down her fork, there was somebody at her elbow with a problem.

When the stranger came in and stood at the door looking around, Simon greeted him.

"Good evening, sir. Are you Mr. Zappa?"

"Yes, I am. I'm joining my daughter, Addie, and another party for dinner."

"We've been expecting you. This way, please."

Simon had led him to the table where Addie and Parker waited. He hung around long enough to hear the introductions.

"Parker Hyatt, sir. I'm pleased to meet Addie's father."

"Martin Zappa," said the stranger. "I'm pleased to meet you, too. But I'm overjoyed to have met my daughter earlier today."

By this time, Simon had already heard the story from Dani, about how a man saw the name Zappa on the window of Addie's shop and came in and introduced himself. That man turned out to be Addie's father, whom she had never met.

"This is our friend, Simon, who owns this place and serves the best food in New Orleans," Addie said.

Simon shook hands with the man, taking measure of him as he did. Addie, after all, was a neighborhood treasure, and they made sure to protect and shelter their own. Simon would keep an eye on anyone who claimed to be her father. He, among others, would see to it she didn't get hurt, just in case this man was a hustler of some sort. But then again, he would hate to be a hustler who tried to take advantage of any relation of Madame's. If Addie had even a small portion of the power Madame had, retribution would be powerful and painful, indeed.

The handshake was firm and dry, and Martin Zappa looked him in the eye as he repeated his name.

"Martin Zappa. I'm happy to meet any friend of Addie's, and I'm looking forward to sampling your cuisine."

"I'm pleased to meet you, too, Mr. Zappa. We think highly of Addie in this neighborhood. Very highly," he said as he tightened his grip slightly, so the Martin Zappa would get the idea.

Simon left then, so they could study the menus, and Rosie stepped up to take their drink orders.

"What's he like?" Estelle asked as he went back to the register, after pausing at several tables to speak to customers, two of whom had asked the same question.

" I only just met him, Estelle."

"Yes, but what did you think?"

"He seemed okay to me," Simon said. He left to seat two tourists who stood at the door looking around for a table.

When he returned to the register, Rosie came by on her way to put the order ticket in the kitchen window.

"He ordered your special catfish with extra etouffe. He say he like etouffe."

"That be a good sign," said Estelle.

Simon waylaid three people who wanted to go ask Addie about a problem, telling them to wait and let her visit with her father uninterrupted. When Rosie came by again, after having delivered their meals and refilled their drinks and asked twice if there was anything else she could do for them and not being able to think of any other reason to hang around their table, she reported her latest findings.

"When he left, he didn't know her mother was in the family way, so he didn't even know Addie existed. Addie's mama wouldn't move back here to Louisiana with him. Her mama, that Adelaide what was Madame's sister, tol' her bad things to keep her there."

Simon, who had heard the whole story from Dani, could have told them all that, but he had kept the information to himself. He figured if Addie wanted it told, she would tell it herself, which evidently she was doing.

Rosie wasn't the only one who was spreading every word said at the table. The customers who were sitting close by were listening to the story with fascination, and passing it along to those who couldn't hear so well. Old Mr. Pettit turned his hearing aid up as high as it would go, and it kept squealing, drawing angry glares from the people around him.

When the meal ended, Mrs. Bayard slipped by Simon's watchful eye and approached Addie, to request something to help her nephew, Ronald, who had a job interview coming up.

"Come by the shop tomorrow, Mrs. Bayard, and I'll give you a piece of aquamarine for him to carry. That's just the thing for job interviews."

Simon took Mrs. Bayard by the arm and led her away just when Addie was about to introduce her father. If that started everyone in the place would come by to shake hands with the man. When he took the old lady back to her table, he walked around and glared and shook his head at everyone in the place, except the tourists.

"Leave Addie alone," he mouthed quietly, and several people who had planned to approach her sank back in their seats.

Finally, Simon decided he shouldn't treat them any differently than he did his other customers, and he always checked to see if his customers were satisfied, so he addressed the newcomer.

"I hope you found everything to your satisfaction."

"It was excellent, excellent. I don't think I've ever had better etouffe. I'm sure I'll be a regular customer from now on," he replied. "I want to try some of your other dishes."

"I'm glad you enjoyed it," said Simon. "I'm looking forward to seeing you again.

He continued his way around the room, greeting the tourists who were eating there for the first time and cautioning the locals to let Addie enjoy her meal in peace.

The next time he was near the table where Parker, Addie and her father say, he heard her say, "JMZ Enterprises? You're the man from JMZ Enterprises?"

CHAPTER THIRTY-TWO

"Your father is the man who came to see me yesterday? He owns JMZ Enterprises?" Dani asked.

"Yes. J was for his father, John, then for my uncle James, and now it's for James's son Jasper. M is for Martin, and Z is for Zappa. JMZ Enterprises. It was never for JayMar. He just wanted people to think it was."

"Did he say anything to you about raising my rent? Or did you even mention you know me?"

"Sure I did. I told him you are my friend and you are worried about what he said about you not paying the full amount of rent. I told him you didn't know anything about JayMar putting money in for you."

"What did he say?"

"He said JayMar, or Jamar, as he calls him, raised the rent on lots of people, but he kept the extra for himself. James was sick for the last couple of years, and didn't pay a lot of attention to what was going on. You are the only one paying less, and Jamar was making up the difference. I told him about Madame, and how she told Jamar he'd better give you a good deal or she would tell Jamar's secret. Now we know what the secret was — skimming money. Jamar was paying the rest of your rent out of what he was skimming off the other people."

"Oh, Lord. Now I know I'm going to have to move."

"Not necessarily. He said when he walked into your place yesterday, he was expecting to find a dump. He said they have continually had problems keeping that shop rented. It has never been rented so long at a time, and especially by someone who is paying every month on time."

"Yessum. That I do. That ought to count for something."

"It does. He said before you rented it the occupants only stayed three or four months, then moved out after tearing everything up. He was very impressed with how well you are keeping the place. He has photos of the way it was before, and he knows you are the one who has made the improvements."

"Impressed enough to let me stay without raising the rent?"

"I don't know about that, but he said he would rather have a good renter in there at less rent than to have it vacant part of the time and have to pay for repairs every time someone moves out."

"You don't know how relieved that makes me feel."

"I thought Simon would have told you all this. He was standing right there when my father handed me his card and I found out about JMZ."

"He told me that part, but then he had to go tend to business and didn't hear the rest — the part about my rent and all."

"We can talk about that next week when my father comes to dinner. He had to go to Lafayette on business, but when he gets back I want to have a little dinner party for him, and I want you and Simon, Evie, and Parker to come. And Morgan, of course."

"Did I hear my name?" Evie said. She came into the kitchen through the French doors onto the gallery.

"Yes, you did. I'd like to have you come to a little dinner party I'm going to have next week so my friends can meet my father and my father can meet my friends."

"Oh, no, Addie. I don't think I'm ready for a party, even if I have been working a little bit in your shop and Dani's."

"It won't be a real party. Just dinner for you, Parker, Dani, Simon and Morgan and my dad. No strangers, I promise."

"I guess that will be all right. I don't get nervous being around all of you."

"You know it's time you started saying 'y'all,' don't you?"

"I've learned to like gumbo and muffalettas. Isn't that enough?" Evie laughed.

Dani stood and took her coffee cup to the sink.

"I'd better go open my shop. It's a beautiful day and I have feeling I'm going to have lots of customers today."

"Are you starting to have feelings about things, too?" Addie said.

"Not the kind you do, for sure. And what about your premonition? The things happening in threes thing. Was your father showing up part of it?"

"Yes, I think it was. But there's something else, or I should say someone else, coming. I starting having that tingling sensation yesterday when he walked in, and I knew, even before I knew he was my father, that he had something to do with three people showing up. I still have the same feeling, sort of, but whatever, or whoever, else is going to show up has bad vibes. He, or she, is bad, or bringing bad news, or bad luck, or something dreadful with them."

Evie shuddered. "I think it has something to do with Ed finding me."

"I think you might be right. I need to go through Madame's journal and see if I can find some spells for protection."

Dani started toward the door.

"Thank you so much for talking to your father about me. Maybe, just maybe, we can stay where we are and not have to move." She stopped and turned back toward Addie. "You know, Morgan had the oddest attitude about moving over here to the apartment over yours. I was preparing him for it, in case we had to make the change, and he acted reluctant about moving to that flat."

Addie frowned. "Did he say why?"

"No. He just said he didn't think it was a good idea. When I questioned him, he would only shrug and say 'No. Don't move there.' I have no idea why he would say that, since I know he loves being around you and Evie."

"I may ask him, sometime. For now you can stay put."

Dani returned to her shop, wondering about Morgan's reluctance to live at Addie's.

CHAPTER THIRTY-THREE

Addie spent her days studying Madame's journals, often asking someone in the neighborhood to translate a word or two. She didn't have much luck with that, since she didn't want to show anyone the old book after what Parker told her about Madame keeping it secret. She tried to pronounce the words as well as she could, but they didn't always sound like anything recognizable. Copying down the words didn't work, either. Most of the neighborhood inhabitants grew up with parents and grandparents speaking Cajun French as well as English, but reading anything but English was another matter.

The feeling of foreboding grew each day. She ought to be happy. She knew she should be, and for the most part, she was. But there was something bad coming and she knew it, and it was her job to forestall it, soften it, turn it aside — whatever she could do. It was her job. She knew and understood that now.

She found Madame's instructions about candles, written in English, thank heavens, and set about placing candles in the shop, in every room in her flat, every room in Evie's and Parker's flats, in Dani's shop and apartment. Every place had a group of candles arranged on the mirrors she found in the shop cabinets. She put a mix of blue, gold, and white candles, all listed in Madame's notes as having protective qualities. After some thought, she added a short black candle in the front of each group. Black, Madame said, turned the evil back on the person bringing it.

She gave instructions to each of her friends.

"Keep the candles lit in the room you are in all the time. Be careful not to go off and leave them burning unattended. We don't want to catch anything on fire. If one burns low, come back to me for a replacement. I have plenty. Madame kept a good stock of candles, and I haven't put any out to sell yet. Maybe I will, though, since I'm studying up on them."

One day she kept the shop closed and went shopping. She so seldom left the neighborhood, having everything she needed close at hand, she had to ask Parker where she might find some decorating shops or antique stores. It was late afternoon before she found what she needed, a pair of Fu dogs to place by the front door of the shop. They were so heavy she parked in front and waited for Parker to get home from work to unload them for her.

"My gosh, these weigh a ton! How did you get them in your car?"

"The man at the antique shop loaded them for me," Addie said as Parker struggled across the sidewalk. "No, the other side. The male goes on the other side."

"They look alike to me. How do you know this is the male?"

"Because he has a ball in his mouth. The male always has a ball in its mouth and the female doesn't"

"Huh."

"It took all day to find the right pair."

"They look nice," Parker said when he settled the female Fu dog into place, "but I get the idea they are for more than just decoration."

"They are supposed to make anyone who has evil intentions uncomfortable in my place."

Parker turned and looked at her, not knowing what to say to her pronouncement.

"I figure, the way I'm feeling about something bad coming, it can't hurt to have some extra help. Besides, a couple of weeks ago, a sweet-looking old lady shoplifted a bracelet, and I've lost a pair of earrings or two. Maybe the Fu dogs will deter my losses."

"Maybe," was all Parker said.

Martin was delayed by his business in Lafayette and it was over a week before he returned to New Orleans. Addie planned her dinner party for that evening. Parker helped her move the long table from the upstairs apartment down to her living room, and she rounded up enough chairs from all her rooms to seat everyone. She rummaged in drawers and found various cloths and scarves, which she placed overlapping in a bohemian fashion to cover the table. Beautiful old dishes were carefully hand washed and arranged and rearranged on the table until Addie achieved the look she wanted. She talked to Mr. Coudart at the market about having plenty of flowers on hand that day. He usually had a flower stand on the sidewalk in front of his store, but Addie wanted nothing left to chance.

She thought a long time about what food to serve. Simon would be there, and no one could beat Simon's cooking, especially Cajun dishes. So Addie wouldn't even try. She decided she would offer her guests her specialty from when she lived in Greenview: spaghetti with meatballs, salad, and garlic bread. She refused Simon's offer of help, saying he was hurting her feelings, trying to make her think she couldn't cook.

"Now, you know I don't mean that," he told her. "I just like to cook. I get great pleasure from preparing food for people."

"And I thank you for the offer, too, Simon, but it's important for me to cook for my father."

"I understand. How about I bring dessert?"

"Okay, I'll give on that. You can bring dessert."

"How about bread pudding with a choice of lemon sauce or whiskey sauce?"

"Perfect!"

The event was a success. Everyone ate and talked, and ate and talked some more. The stories about Madame were told once again, in case someone missed hearing one. Martin, who hadn't heard any of them, was fascinated.

"And this was Adelaide's sister? That's as unlike Adelaide as you can imagine."

Then the story had to be repeated about Adelaide meeting and leaving with Gregory Henson, moving to Connecticut, and how everyone thought she was never heard from again, but in reality she was writing her sister from time to time, and how the attorney found Addie, by the postmarks on the letter, which Madame had saved all those years.

At last, everyone seemed to have eaten enough, and talked enough, and they all helped Addie clear and clean up. While she was gathering the glasses to take to the kitchen, she felt a tug on her skirt. Looking down, she saw Morgan, studying her with a serious expression on his face.

"Miss Addie, can I talk to you? Private?"

"Sure, Morgan. Do you want to come into my bedroom to talk?"

"Uh-huh. I mean, yes ma'am."

Addie led the way, sitting down in her slipper chair and pulling up a footstool for Morgan.

"Can I help you with something, Morgan?"

"Mama says you are makin' stuff so as to keep any bad person from coming to hurt any of us."

"You don't have to worry about that. Your mother will keep you safe. And besides your mother, you have me, and Parker, and Simon to help keep you safe. No one or nothing is going to hurt you."

"Well, I'm not worried. But when you fix the stuff, would it work on other folks, too? I mean folks that you don't know?"

"Do you mean, can people other than us use the protection?"

"Yessum. That's what I mean."

"Sure. It'll work for anyone. If it works at all, that is. I'm kind of new to all this. I'm not experienced at making protection stuff, like Madame was. I'm just learning."

"Could you make some extra? So I could give some to someone else?"

"Who needs it, Morgan?"

Morgan was silent, looking down at his fingers twisting and twining together.

"Is someone you know in danger? Does someone need help? You can tell me. Maybe we can help him or her."

There was no answer.

"Okay, then. I'll make extra and give you some for your friend."

Morgan bounced up and wrapped his arms around Addie neck.

"Thank you, Miss Addie! Thank you!"

CHAPTER THIRTY-FOUR

For the past month, since he met the daughter he never knew existed, Martin couldn't stop thinking about the time he spent with Carol. Since the divorce, that part of his life was pushed into the background of his consciousness. Reminded by Addie's presence, he started to remember all sorts of things. Like how Carol believed in all sorts of omens, both good and bad. He used to tease her about it, about believing 'old wives' tales, but she insisted they were signs of things to come. Her mother had told her so.

He now knew those ideas reached farther back than he ever imagined. Adelaide may have wanted to escape New Orleans, escape the fact of her race, and escape the influence of hoodoo, but obviously she clung to at least some of those beliefs and passed them on to her daughter. Adelaide's granddaughter, his daughter, Addie, not only believed in signs and omens but in spells, potions, and what she called juju.

Martin visited Addie several times since the evening he'd had dinner with her. He took her to his office, to introduce her and show her off to his employees. They lunched together at a famous New Orleans restaurant, and she and Parker joined him in dining at various establishments on several occasions. Tonight he was again joining Addie and Parker for an evening out. He liked — really liked — Addie and liked being with her. She was kind, charming, talented, and had a sense of humor like his.

He liked her friends, too. Parker was courteous and treated Addie with respect, the way a man ought to treat a lady. Martin had the impression there was a serious relationship developing between them. He enjoyed talking computers and new technology with Parker, as well as football and the Dallas Cowboys.

Martin spoke to Addie's friend, Dani, and assured her there would be no change in her rental status for a long time. He was pleased to have the shop and apartment rented to someone who was steady, reliable, paid the rent on time, and kept the place in good repair. He figured he was making as much on the place at a lower rent than he would if the rent was higher and it was only rented part of the time. Besides, he was still cleaning up Jamar's messes and had plenty to deal with. Dani could rest easy.

Martin admired what Dani had done with her life. Addie didn't go into details, but said Dani had a rough time before moving to New Orleans. Her business was thriving in a small fashion and growing as time went by. Martin felt good about helping a fledgling entrepreneur stay afloat while the company grew. Time enough to talk about a higher rent in a year or so.

Martin was especially interested in Addie's friend, Evie. She was a mystery and Martin was fascinated with mysteries. Addie didn't say much about Evie's background, saying it was Evie's story to tell. He knew she was reclusive but not shy. She talked and laughed with him and seemed to be good friends with Addie, Parker, Dani, and Simon, but she didn't leave the quad of apartments and Addie's shop, and for the last few days, she no longer went to the shop.

"Addie doesn't think it's a good idea for me to go there right now," she told him, and he wondered why Addie told her that. He guessed it had to do with the concerns Addie had right now about something bad headed their way.

Martin asked Evie out, on a date he guessed he would call it. He and Addie and Parker planned to eat supper at Simon's Place that night, and then go to Le Chat Noir to listen to some jazz. Martin had asked Evie if she would join them, make it a foursome.

"Oh, no, thank you. I don't go anywhere like that," she said.

"It's a respectable place. Tourists and home people go there. Parker and Addie go there to have a drink and listen to the music. You can just have a soda if you don't drink."

"It's not that. I'm sure it's a very nice place. Parker and Addie go there all the time. I just don't go out."

"Even to Simon's?"

"Even to Simon's."

He wanted to ask her why, but thought it might sound nosy, so he held his tongue, but he was curious, extremely curious, to know why this attractive woman was so reclusive. Her personality didn't seem in keeping with someone who hid from the world. He was also curious about Addie's recent preparations, if they could be called that. The evening he came back from Lafayette and had dinner with her and her friends, there was a pretty arrangement in the center of the table, made of brightly colored flowers surrounding candles.

During the evening there were several references to candles by members of the dinner party, and finally he asked.

"What's the deal with candles?"

"These candles, and the ones in our shops and apartments, were chosen for their colors. White, blue, and gold candles offer protection, according to Madame's notes. And the black one in the front of each arrangement turns any evil back on the one bringing it. I made arrangements of candles on mirrors for everyone, to keep them safe."

"Why do you need protection? Is someone after you? Because if there is, I can do something about it. I can hire a bodyguard, or something."

"No, it's nothing like, that, at least I don't think so. I don't know for sure who or what is coming, but as time goes by the feeling gets stronger, and I know someone bad is on their way."

Martin didn't know what to say. Seeing the expression on his face, Addie continued.

"All my life, I've known things, like when something good was going to happen, or something bad. I know, for example, that there is no such thing as coincidence — that things happen for a reason, and it's up to us to figure out the reason. And things happen in threes.

"First, Dani's aunt and uncle from Memphis tracked her down and came to New Orleans to hassle her. When I heard about it, I got that tingle that told me it was the first thing in a set of three. Three unexpected visitors showing up, maybe, or three relatives, or something.

"Then you showed up, and you were the second person of the three. And that was a good thing, a very good thing, for you to show up."

"How do you know I'm a good thing? Maybe I'm a bad person, coming to take advantage of you?"

"Because I feel all smiley inside. I know you are a good thing. I can tell. But there is something bad coming. I can feel it. It's like a black cloud hovering somewhere, coming closer and closer. So it's important I do everything I can to keep everyone safe."

Martin wondered why she had looked pointedly at Evie when she said that, like she thought Evie might be the person in danger. Later, when Evie had commented about Addie not thinking it was a good idea for her to come in the shop right now, he was sure he was right.

Over the next few days, Addie did more to protect not only Evie but also all the people around by handing our various types of amulets. She didn't know for certain who was in danger, and said everyone should keep the amulets with them at all times. Whatever it was, it was getting closer.

She began with simple necklaces and pendants of Tiger's Eye, and others of quartz crystal, and hung them from strips of leather or suede. "Wear them even at night when you are asleep."

Martin protested. "I've just now arrived, and you've had this feeling since before I came. I'm probably not involved in whatever is going to happen."

That sounds like I believe all this hoodoo stuff. No wonder old Adelaide wanted to keep away. It'll make you crazy.

"I don't know. It could be the evil is following you. You wear this, if for nothing more than to make your daughter happy."

So, of course, he did.

The next time he dropped by to visit with Addie, she gave him a little bag.

"Keep this in your pocket every day. Put it under your pillow at night. Usually people wear them on a string around their neck, but I thought that might be pushing it too far."

"Definitely. What's in it?" he asked, sniffing at the bag. If it smelled he'd throw it away when he left, so she wouldn't know what he did. To his surprise, however, it had a mild, pleasant odor.

"Bay leaves and caraway seeds. I found out about its power from reading Madame's notes. Don't worry, it doesn't smell bad."

The night he was supposed to meet Addie and Parker to eat at Simon's Place, then go on to Le Chat Noir. He checked himself in the mirror before leaving. The Tiger's Eye necklace looked just right, very young and with it. Or cool. Or fly. Or whatever young people were saying these days.

He thought he would go a little bit early and sit in the courtyard at Addie's. Evie was often there so maybe he could visit with her, even though she wouldn't go out with him.

CHAPTER THIRTY-FIVE

Evie surprised herself. She marveled at how calm she felt as Addie became more anxious by the day. It was over a year since she came to Madame's place, and she was certain that Ed would show up. It wasn't that she was no longer afraid — she was — definitely afraid — but she could handle it, handle the fear and not let it paralyze her or make her stay in her flat with the curtains drawn and the doors locked and bolted.

It must be because friends surrounded her. *I've never had friends like this before*. Before moving here she was never close to anyone from fear she would let it slip about Ed's abuse. She could talk and joke with Addie and Dani and tell them anything. She didn't have all that misery bottled up inside, and it made her feel so much lighter and freer. *Yes, I'm afraid, but my fear doesn't rule me now.*

Evie checked her appearance in a mirror, smoothing her lustrous brown hair. Adding a touch of lipstick and a mist of perfume, she walked out onto the gallery and down the stairs, after checking to be sure there was no one watching at the gate. Even if she wasn't acting like a scared rabbit any longer, she still needed to be cautious.

She knew Parker, Addie, and Martin were going to supper at Simon's and afterwards to listen to jazz. Martin asked her to go with them, but since she was certain it was Ed who was coming, she couldn't go. Better to be a little cautious and keep the Tiger's Eye necklace, the quartz crystal necklace, and the bag of herbs on her at all times. The candles were burning whenever Evie was in her apartment. Addie had replaced all the different colors for her twice.

Evie spent the day on the computer, writing articles and submitting them to be published on the web. Some days she worked a few hours for Addie, and occasionally for Dani. Her income was slowly growing. Some months she made enough money she didn't have to take any out of her stash. Maybe it wouldn't be long before she could start putting some back. There wasn't anything she needed to spend money on, nothing she didn't have. She paid rent and bought food. That was the extent of her spending.

She was thinking about having all her friends to dinner some evening. Addie had everyone to her flat for dinner from time to time, and Evie enjoyed the camaraderie they shared. She would like to play hostess to the group. That was something she not even consider when she was with Ed because no matter how good the food, how creative and beautiful the settings and home, or how much the guests proclaimed their enjoyment, Ed criticized her without mercy, which often led to a beating. She tried to please Ed, but she had eventually realized there was nothing she could do to please him, no matter how hard she tried.

A TV show said that people like Ed weren't happy with themselves. They always fell short, but they couldn't admit that they were to blame, so they laid it off on someone else. Whatever went wrong was always someone else's fault. Evie didn't know if Ed, deep down, was unhappy with himself, but she sure knew when he was unhappy with her. When she was so sore and in such pain she could hardly walk or sit or sleep made that clear.

That part of her life was over, and she was determined it would never happen again.

With these thoughts in her head, she sat in the courtyard when Martin unlocked the gate. Evie flinched; she couldn't help it, the habit was too strong.

"It's just me. I didn't mean to alarm you."

"That's okay. I was deep in thought. Come and have a seat."

"Thank you, I will. I came a little early because I enjoy sitting out here visiting with you while I wait for Addie and Parker. I hoped you would be here."

Evie said nothing. She couldn't think of anything to say.

"I hope I didn't embarrass you."

"No. Well, maybe a little. I like visiting with you, too."

"Perhaps someday you will be able to go out with me. On a date. Or with us. As a group, I mean."

The words seemed stuck in his mouth, and Evie thought he sounded sweet and shy.

"Maybe," she said, and took a deep breath. *Addie and Parker, Dani and Simon, they now know my story. Why not get it over with and tell Martin? That way he'll know it's not him I'm rejecting.*

"First of all, you need to know that I'm married."

She told him all of it. About Ed and the beatings. About saving up money for years. About Billy, his life and his death. Martin didn't say anything, but at that point he reached over and took her hand, sitting there holding it while she told the rest. She told about the planning of her escape, making sure she did everything right, as right as she could, about running, and setting false trails as best she could. And finally, she told about ending up in New Orleans, the city she had chosen from the internet. She told him about going into Simon's Place to eat, and meeting Madame, who offered her a safe place to land, all furnished with everything she needed.

"I thank God that I was sitting in Simon's Place when Madame came in to eat. I have always thought of that occurrence as a coincidence, but Addie says there's no such thing as a coincidence, that it is something that was meant to be. God, or Fate, or whatever you want to call it, is directing your life, but it is up to you to take advantage of opportunities. I could have turned down this apartment, for example, choosing some other path."

"I've thought about Addie's theory of no coincidences. And I've thought about being in this neighborhood, checking on the building Dani is renting, and seeing the name on the shop window. Everything timing just right for me to walk in and meet the daughter I didn't know I had. Was that coincidence? Or was it Fate?"

"We'll never know for sure. We can only believe what we believe. And Addie believes something really bad is headed our way. I'm can't help thinking she's right.

"She won't say, but I know she thinks it's Ed. I told her, and I tell you, he will stop at nothing to find me. And when he does, he'll take me back with him or kill me; also, he won't hesitate to hurt anyone who gets in his way."

"You can be sure we won't let him do either one."

"I don't want you to feel sorry for me. I only told you so you'll know why I don't go out. Ed could be watching. Or he could have hired people to find me. I've changed my appearance, but I'm sure it wouldn't fool a professional."

"And that's the reason you make your living writing on the internet. Under a pen name, I assume?"

"Yes. I never use my real name. I've tried to stay out of sight, although Addie talked me into helping in her shop from time to time, and I also work some in Dani's shop. Doing that has helped me a lot. I can never thank them enough.

"But now, Addie said to stay out of sight and not come in the shop at all. So I know she thinks Ed is close."

"Hi, folks. Sorry to keep you waiting, Martin. I have to work a bit later these days, getting ready to install a big new system at a company over in Slidell," Parker said as he came out into the courtyard.

Martin released Evie's hand and stood to shake hands with Parker.

"That's okay. Evie and I were visiting. The time passed quickly. I came a little early, myself."

When Addie joined the group, she went to Evie and wrapped her arms around her, pulling her close. She closed her eyes, trying to mentally place a protecting aura around the woman.

"You'll be okay here by yourself?"

"Sure, I will. You all go and have fun."

Evie went up the stairs to the upper gallery and turned back to look at the gate.

Someday, I'll be able to join them. Someday I'll be free enough to leave this place without fear.

CHAPTER THIRTY-SIX

Dani had a jillion things on her mind and wasn't able to concentrate on any one thing long enough to follow through and get the job done. Such excitement! Good things, bad things, everything demanded her attention.

Morgan came in from school and stood patting his mother on the leg.

"Mama. Mama. Mama."

"Hold on a minute, Morgan. Can't you see I'm in a tizzy?"

He stopped patting and thought a few seconds, frowning.

"What's a tizzy?"

"That's a word Grandma used to say. Don't you remember? When someone was all excited over things and needed to calm down. She used to say it to you all the time."

"Oh." He thought a minute. "Yeah, I 'member her saying that. She'd say 'Morgan, settle down. You're all in a tizzy.' "

Dani was glad Morgan had some memories of his great-grandmother. Although she knew they were fading away the older he got, she hoped he kept some close to his heart as long as he lived.

"So what do you need, sweet boy?"

"Mama, I need to ask you something."

"You can ask me anything, Morgan. You know that." She sat down in one of the chairs in the showroom and put her arm around him.

"What do you do when a friend is in trouble?"

"It depends, sugar. Did your friend do something bad? Is he in trouble with his parents, or the school, or the police?"

Morgan shook his head, looking at the floor the whole time.

"Can you tell me what it is?"

Another shake of the head.

"Then I guess the only thing I can think of is to just be his friend, someone he can talk to."

"Okay, Mama." He paused and then continued. "I'm his friend. He can talk to me." He went off to the backyard to play with his dog.

That evening, after she tucked Morgan in bed and kissed his forehead, Dani went back downstairs to straighten the workroom. She was so excited over the day's happenings she couldn't have gone to sleep if she'd tried. She'd told Simon all about it when he came to see her after the supper rush at the café.

"Simon, this woman came in today, and she is the wardrobe person for that movie they're shooting on the plantation right out of town."

"Huh. What'd she want? She buy something"?

"A whole lot.' The movie is set back in the 1950s and '60s, and she needed a lot of clothes for the actors to wear. She bought a bunch of dresses and hats and stuff, and she said she'd probably be back for more."

"That's good for business."

"It sure is. It was several hundred dollars' worth today, and she said she'd spread the word that this is a good shop to find period clothes. She liked my original designs using vintage clothing. She said sometimes they wanted clothes that are like mine — unique she said — for movies."

Dani continued straightening up the mess she made earlier going through the boxes of clothing not yet ready to sell. She needed to have more stock out to show the movie lady when she came back. The clothes in the boxes needed to be washed or dry-cleaned and checked carefully for repairs. The pieces that were going to be disassembled and remade into something different went into a different box.

Dani also needed to dig out some of the jeans she'd bought at rummage sales and wash them. It was Thursday, so that meant day after tomorrow her newest employee was coming to paint on them.

A month ago, on a whim, she bought a pair of jeans having paint splashes on them. They were only a quarter, because of the paint, and she wanted to experiment with them. After washing and drying them, she stuffed the legs with newspaper, so the paint wouldn't bleed through, and artfully applied more paint. The original paint was pink, so Dani added different shades of pink and purple, making streaks and curlicues in a pattern that looked intentional. When the paint dried she ironed them to set the color, added a few beads in the same colors, and voila — a new style.

She'd put jeans in the window, knowing the teenage girls always came by after school to check for something new. They sold the first day. Two days later, three girls came in the shop. One was wore the pair Dani fashioned, and her friend wore a pair with yellow and orange paint streaks, splotches, and vines, plus some tiny splatters.

"Look, Ms Washington. Look at the jeans I painted," said the girl, twirling around. "My mom was mad at me for getting paint on my jeans, but now I have some really cool ones, and she isn't mad anymore."

"My mother won't let me paint my jeans," said the third girl. She says I'll mess them up. Do you have any more like that to sell?"

"No, not right now. But I may do some more, if you girls like them."

"We do!" they all said at the same time.

"And so do the other girls in class. They all want to know where we got them, but we wouldn't tell them. We wanted first chance at any more you had."

So Dani painted two more pair. But her painting skills were over shadowed by Amy, the girl who had done her own yellow and orange pair. She returned a few days later with a pink design of her own. Dani thought the twists and turns Amy put down the side of her jeans were much better than anything she could paint herself.

"Amy, would you be interested in a job here?"

"Me? A job? Here?"

"Yes, you. You could come in a couple of hours on Saturdays, if you want, and paint jeans for me. I'll pay you for each pair you paint, and you use my paint."

"Oh…I'd love that."

"Be here Saturday about half past nine and I'll show you where to paint. Did you use fabric paint on yours? Or mix fabric medium in with your paint?"

"No. Was I supposed to?"

"Yes. What you did may wash out when you launder them."

"Oh, I never thought about that."

"Well, iron them with a hot iron. That will help. And if it does wash out, you can use my paint to go over the designs."

Amy left bubbling with excitement over her new job, and Dani was happy to get new and different stock for her shop.

Later, when she settled into bed beside the sleeping Morgan, she thought back over the day, a connection with the movie industry which brought added sales; Morgan worrying about a friend in some kind of secret trouble; Addie checking on everyone to be sure they had their candles burning, their necklace of Tiger's Eye or quartz crystal around their neck, and their bag of bay leaves and coriander seeds in their pocket.

As she drifted off to sleep, her hand under her pillow grasping the bag of spices, it occurred to her she hadn't seen Morgan's necklaces or juju bag the last few days. Her last thought was to remind herself to ask him about it tomorrow.

CHAPTER THIRTY-SEVEN

Smiling, Maxie opened the scrapbook and slipped the last two pictures into the corner brackets. Morgan would enjoy having his very own book full of pictures to take home with him. She still didn't quite understand why it was so important to him to look at the family pictures every time he came to her house. Dani said it was probably because he had so few pictures of his own family.

Each time he came it was the same thing.

"This is Simon when he was my age?"

"Yes, that is Simon when he was six, almost seven."

"And he had lost his front tooth, just like me?"

"Yes, just like you. And it grew back in, just like yours will."

Morgan turns the page and says, "And this picture is his daddy, right?"

Maxie fears the day he asks about his own daddy, but she guesses Dani has already covered that subject. Simon told her all about Dani's past, and with all Maxie's experience with children, having taught hundreds if not thousands, in her life, she didn't have any idea what to say to Morgan about his lack of a father.

"I don't have a daddy."

Maxi remained silent, relaxing when he dropped the subject and moved on to the next picture.

"And this is Simon's grandmother."

"Yes. That was my mother. Her name was Francine."

"And this was his grandfather. He died in a war, right?"

"Right."

"And Simon never got to meet him."

"That's right. He died before I was born."

"I knew my grandmother," he said, proud of the one ancestor he was sure of, besides his mother. "I have a picture of her." The next time he came to visit he brought two pictures, one of an elderly woman standing on the porch of a white house, the other of a little girl standing beside the woman, at the same house.

"See? This is my grandmother, and here she is with my mother when she was a little girl."

Maxie had left room in the back of the book for those pictures to be added.

Simon brought Dani and Morgan to see her a couple of times a month, and Morgan looked through the photo album each time, as if assuring himself those people were still there, in the book, and were still Simon's parents and grandparents.

The next day Maxie was going to watch Morgan while Simon and Dani had some time alone. He was a delight to have and made her realize how much she missed having children around. When she retired, she thought she would be happy to leave kids behind, at the school, and not worry about them and their problems anymore. To her surprise, she found she missed them. She volunteered at the At Risk Children's Center and that helped, but still she missed children around her.

Her heart broke when she saw the children who came there and heard their stories. There were kids whose parents stayed drunk or high, kids who never knew when a parent would be home or when they would eat. Children who were so worried about safety and food and parents fighting they couldn't concentrate to do their homework or even listen and understand what was going on in school. Maxie mothered them all. Any child who would halfway behave was welcome in the center after school and on Saturdays.

It wasn't enough, she knew. So many of the children needed a new home, new parents, and new life. The city and the state didn't have enough foster homes as it was, and foster homes and group homes were filled with children who had no parents at all, children who had been deserted or whose parents were in jail. It seemed like children with a bad parent had no place to turn.

Maxie sighed. No use thinking about that. She needed to check her pantry.

When Morgan came to visit, there were certain activities that were sure to please him. The first thing he did was to find her big cat, Grizabella, to pet and talk to, telling her about his week, and asking about hers. She would purr, which he said was her way of talking to him. At first, he laughed about her name, which was difficult for him to pronounce, so Maxie told him the cat's nickname was Grizzy, and he could call her that. Sometimes he did, but he also practiced saying Grizabella until he had it right. Well, almost right, anyway. Maxie thought the next time "Cats" came to town, she would take him to see it, to see the inspiration for Grizzy's name. She was looking forward to introducing him to the theatre.

Morgan brought Grizzy toys on occasion. He saved up the coins Dani gave him for helping clean up her workroom to buy a catnip mouse. Another time he tied some scraps of fabric together in a knot on the end of a long string, which he pulled around for Grizzy to chase. He and the big, gray feline were best of friends. Maxie enjoyed watching them play.

The big photo album was another one of Morgan's amusements when he came to visit. While Maxie, Simon, and Dani talked, Morgan would sit on a footstool in front of the coffee table and look at the pictures of Simon growing up and of Simon's family over the years. It fascinated him to see the progression of life, Simon as a baby, Simon as a toddler, Simon in a play in the sixth grade, Simon graduating from high school. When Maxie thought on it, she realized he had never been around a real family, never seen the progression of life and growing up. He never heard the stories of family, what they did and how they grew. Dani didn't talk about her mother, didn't know her father, and although her grandmother was much loved, she was gone now. Morgan only mentioned his aunt and uncle one time, to say they were mean. So the photo album held his attention for long periods of time, and the pictures of Simon's parents, and grandparents, all in one place mesmerized him.

The other subject that always interested Morgan was cookies. Maxie smiled at the thought, and went to see if she had all the ingredients to make chocolate chip, his favorite. Tomorrow, when he spent the afternoon with her, they would make cookies together. He wanted to know if Simon cooked when he was a little boy, and when Maxie said yes, Morgan showed interest in cooking himself.

So they would make cookies, look at Morgan's very own book of photos, for him to take home, and she would read to him. She loved reading to children, and Morgan took pleasure in settling back on her lap and hearing about the adventures of Toad, Mole and Rat. Maxie thought she needed to go to the bookstore and buy some beginning-to-read books for him. Dani didn't have money for extras right now.

She sang while she surveyed her pantry. She was so happy. Simon confided to her that he was going to propose to Dani. As she checked to see if she had enough chocolate chips, she hummed "Happy Days are Here Again."

CHAPTER THIRTY-EIGHT

Although the sun shinned brightly, Addie felt like the atmosphere was filled with a dark seething miasma, threatening to choke her with fear and hate. Never before had she felt anything like it. In the past, she had feeling of unease when something bad was going to happen, but never to this extent. Each day that went by, the air felt thicker and more malevolent, until Addie thought she would fall to the floor under the weight of it. Sometimes she woke in the night with a start, heart pounding. In the daytime, she started to imagine a stranger around every corner, waiting to attack. If she hadn't been so sure of her gift, she would have thought she was going crazy. She knew she was not crazy and that something bad was on its way.

She wondered if she oppressive weight came from true evil being near, or if somehow living in Madame's house and reading her journals made her overreact to approaching problems. Whatever it was, she couldn't take much more of it. It had been building for weeks, since not long before Dani's grasping aunt and uncle showed up to try to wring money out of her.

The thing was, she felt certain it had something to do with a set of three occurrences, and if the common thing was three unexpected visits from people, then her father's appearance was number two, and if all three were bad things, that made Martin suspect. Addie didn't get any bad vibes from Martin, though. Indeed, she had accepted him into her life as her father, the only living family she had. If there was something wrong with his interest, if he had ulterior motives for his friendship, Addie thought she would sense it. In the past, it didn't take long for her to start getting that knowing feeling about people who were covering up something, whether it was actions, intentions, or personality. If Martin was deceitful about who he was or what he was like, she would already know.

Dear God, please guide me through this safely. I don't think I can take much more without breaking into tears or hiding in bed all the time. Please, God, give me assurance that I have protected those around me sufficiently for what is coming.

She went into the shop and opened the front door wide to allow the sun-warmed air to enter. She turned the sign to OPEN and started lighting the candles. Circles of mirror held groups of white, gold, blue, and black candles every few feet along the counters. The small black candles in the groups had burned down to nubs, so she rummaged in the baskets in the storeroom to find more. Her supply was depleted from keeping the groups of candles burning, not only for herself but also for Dani and Evie. Gathering three large black pillar candles, she returning to the shop and placed them among the already burning tapers. They stood out in the midst of the slimmer candles, but they were the last of the black candles.

By late morning, she had sold necklaces and bracelets for both adornment and mystical power. It was hard to keep smiling and chatting with the customers with the pall hanging over her.

"Hiya, kiddo. How's your day going?" Martin said as he entered the shop. "Beautiful day, isn't it? Having lots of customers?"

"Hi to you. Plenty of customers, but I haven't really noticed the day."

"Are you still feeling something bad is going to happen?"

"Big time. I can't take this much longer. Even if it's bad, I wish it would come on and get it over with."

"Good morning, Miss Addie," said the woman who leaned on her cane as she entered. "Mighty fine day, isn't it?"

"Good morning, Mrs. Lanier. How are you this morning? Is your rheumatism any better?"

"It sho-nuff is. That pretty yellow stone you gave me, that amber, I carries it with me all the time, in my pocket, and at night it goes under my pillow. That ol' rheumatiz be better, uh-huh."

"How can I help you today, Mrs. Lanier?"

"Wellum —"

A tall, gray-haired man with military bearing strode into the shop, nearly knocking down the old lady. Addie literally had to grasp the edge of the counter to hold herself upright, so strong were the sensations of malice that rolled off him. She thought for a moment she could actually see hatred come from him in waves, like an electric current.

"I'm here to find my wife and take her back home," he said in a drill sergeant voice.

"Y — y-our wife?"

"She's going by the name of Carol Farmer. I have traced her to this address, so there's no use denying she's here. I know she is."

"But I —"

"Don't try to hide her. She stole from me and ran away. I traced the name her internet address back to this place. I know the woman calling herself Carol Farmer is here and I demand to see her."

"You're looking at her. I'm Carol Farmer. Sort of."

"You're lying!"

Mrs. Lanier gasped and made the sign of the cross.

"Now, look here —" Martin said. He moved toward the man.

Addie put up her hand to stop him. "It's okay, Dad. I'll handle it."

"No, I'm not lying. Why do you think someone calling herself Carol Farmer is your wife, and why do you think she is here?"

"She stole from me and ran away when it became obvious I was going to find out what she had done. I spent months tracing false trails until I hired a private investigator to help find her."

"I repeat, why do you think she's here?"

"My wife went to our local library often, and when she was there she used the same computer each time to go online and do research. I bought the computer from the library and turned it over to a specialist in computer forensics. He found over a period of many months she kept researching two subjects, New Orleans and writing for online sites."

"I'm in New Orleans and I write for online sites. That doesn't make me your wife."

"A couple of months ago, he found frequent articles posted to the web under the name Carol Farmer. Carol is her middle name, and Farmer was her maiden name. The stupid bitch couldn't even make up a better alias than that. The computer specialist traced the postings back to the Internet Service Provider, and the ISP, under threat of legal proceedings, said the messages came from this address.

"The piddling stuff she posts is about subjects my wife has knowledge in, like gardening and teaching small children. She was a teacher before we married. And," he gave a chuckle, "she gave herself away when she wrote about being newly arrived in New Orleans.

"So the game is up. Tell me where she is," he said as he stepped forward.

"I'm telling you the truth. I'm Carol Farmer." It took everything Addie had not to take a step back, away from the evil she felt rolling off the man in waves. "My full, true name is Adelaide Carol Zappa. Adelaide for my grandmother, Carol for my mother, and Zappa," she loosened her grip on the counter long enough to motion toward her father, "is, of course, for my father. I write articles that I place on various sites on the internet. Before I inherited this shop from my great-aunt several months ago, I was a teacher in Connecticut. I have written and posted a great many pieces about small children and teaching, even before I moved here. I have also written about being new to New Orleans. When I started posting on the web, I decided to use a pen name, so I use Carol for my mother, and for my last name I use an Americanized version of Zappa, which is the Italian word for a person who uses a hoe to farm, in other words, a farmer."

"I don't believe you."

"My daughter is telling you the truth, mister," said Martin, "and I don't appreciate you calling my daughter a liar." leaned against the shelves, hands stuck in the pockets of his jacket.

"Here, let me get my laptop," Addie said as she let go of her support and went to the end of the counter where the computer sat. "See? I'll open this file. Here are the articles I've posted. See this? 'How to Teach Your Child Numbers,' 'Fun A-B-C Games for Kindergartners,' 'Make Word Cards for Beginning Readers,'" Addie pointed down the line of titles. "There are more than a hundred pieces I've written and the name of the sites where I have posted them. And in this file," she clicked on another folder, "here are the ones about moving to New Orleans."

"My private detective talked to people in the neighborhood. They said a blond woman moved here over a year ago."

"Well, it hasn't been a year yet, but they're talking about me, I'm sure. I'm the only blond newcomer around here."

The stranger's complexion turned from the red flush it had been to a pasty gray that matched his gray suit and tie. He stood silent, reading the list of article titles, then turned and strode toward the door.

"I may have wasted a year chasing the wrong clue, but I'll find the bitch, see if I don't. And when I find her, she'll pay — she'll pay big time."

When he exited, Martin rushed toward the door.

"No! No, Dad! Don't close the door!" Addie yelled as she reached under the counter for the bowl she had placed in readiness. Grabbing a broom leaning against the wall, she went to where the man had stood and sprinkled the salt that filled the bowl all along where the man had walked, repeating the words, "John over John. John over John," until she reached the door. There she threw more out onto the sidewalk, saying, "Don't come back".

Addie then took a broom and swept the floor until every grain was outside on the sidewalk, and then she went out and swept it all off the sidewalk into the street. Entering her shop again, she turned back to the door and spit once to the right and once to the left.

"There, that ought to keep him from ever coming back, if I followed Madame's instructions correctly."

She turned to Mrs. Lanier, who had stood muttering *"Mon Dieux, Mon Dieux,"* and making the sign of the cross throughout the whole ordeal.

"Maybe you'd better go now, Mrs. Lanier. I need to rest. I'll help you later."

The woman scurried out the door as best she could and Addie closed and locked it, turning the sign to say CLOSED. She turned toward Martin, who gathered her into his arms just as she burst into tears.

"There, now. He's gone. He got into that silver Cadillac parked across the street and took off so fast he almost hit another car coming up the street. The idiot followed the wrong trail."

"But that's just it, Dad. He followed the wrong trail to the right place. That was Evie's husband. If she'd been in the shop when he got here, he would have found her." She sobbed and buried her face in Martin's shoulder.

"But he didn't find her." Martin led her through the shop, workroom, and kitchen. When they reached the living room, he eased her onto the fainting couch. Taking an afghan from the back, he spread it over her.

"Do you have any liquor in the place?"

"Just wine. It's in the kitchen."

He returned with a bottle and two glasses.

"Here, drink this."

Addie sat up and took a sip.

"I can't get over it. He followed the clues to me, not to Evie. If I hadn't moved here, he wouldn't have come. He wasn't following her at all. What if she had been in the shop? I almost led him to her."

"He didn't see her, didn't find her, and you got rid of him. He won't come back because he thinks all the clues led to you, not to Evie." Martin stopped to take a sip of wine. "Well, one good thing came out of this."

"What?"

"You called me Dad."

CHAPTER THIRTY-NINE

Parker was hot and short-tempered by the time he arrived home that evening. He had been working on the north side of Lake Pontchartrain all week, setting up a new computer system for a corporation and training the people who would use it. It was hard to concentrate on what he was supposed to do because he was so worried about Addie's frame of mind.

He didn't know whether to believe she could tell when trouble was coming or whether it was some wild flight of imagination plaguing her, but whatever it was kept her at first concerned, then edgy, and now panicky. She couldn't eat, couldn't sit still, and she woke in the middle of the night worrying about who or what was coming. She apologized for waking him, and told him he could go sleep in his own apartment so she wouldn't disturb him, but he wouldn't leave her, not when she was so upset. Besides, he wanted to be close to her to protect her from any danger, in case it wasn't her imagination running wild.

It started with a comment about something bad coming their way. In the past weeks, the tension increased in her until she was a nervous wreck. By that morning when Parker left for work, she was pacing and saying, "It's going to be bad, whatever it is. And it's close. Very close."

Parker was anxious to get home so he could hold her and soothe her and tell her everything was going to be all right. He loved Addie, and hated seeing her so fearful, especially over some unknown mysterious event that might or might not happen. Addie, of course, had no doubts about it occurring. The only questions in her mind were when and how bad.

When he finished his work early, he felt a sense of relief because he could get home and try to keep Addie's fears in check. Unfortunately, things didn't work out the way he hoped. There was a terrible wreck on the highway into New Orleans and traffic was held up for over two hours, until the police, ambulances, fire trucks, and wreckers could clear away the remains, and a cleanup crew sweep the debris from the highway. Cars and trucks were backed up for miles as they got caught in the traffic snarl with no opportunity to exit on a side road. By the time Parker got home, he was later than usual, hot, tired, and disgusted.

Addie's shop was closed, he noticed, which time-wise wasn't out of the ordinary, but the street was busy with tourists, and she usually stayed open late when there were so many potential customers around. Using his key, he opened the gate and entered the courtyard. Going first to her flat, he entered, calling out, "Honey, I'm home." There was no answer.

She's probably over at Dani's, he thought, and pulled out his cell phone. He pushed speed- dial for her number, but after several rings it went to voice mail. He went to his apartment, took a quick shower and dressed in shorts and a tee shirt. Thinking she might be with her father, he hunted until he found Martin's business card with his cell phone number jotted on the back and called.

When Martin answered, he said, briefly, "We're all in Evie's apartment. You need to come here."

The tone of Martin's voice left no doubt that something had happened, and Parker flew up the stairs to the flat located over his. Evie, Addie, Martin, Dani and Morgan were there. The adults were at one end of the living room, while Morgan was watching cartoons on the TV at the other end.

"We're trying to stay calm, and keep our voices low, so as not to upset Morgan," Addie said.

She went on to tell him about what happened that day, with comments from Martin. "It was my trail he followed — my articles posted on the web led him to me. If I hadn't been here he probably wouldn't have come. He was led here by my email address," she said, voice quivering.

"If you had never moved here he would have found her some other way, and then you wouldn't have been there to protect her," Parker said, gently rubbing her back.

"I didn't think of it that way."

"You are always saying how there is no such thing as coincidence. Well, this is proof of what you preach. This worked out just like it was supposed to. You moved here where Evie is, the evidence he thought was leading him to his wife led him to you, and you were able to turn him away with proof that you are the person he thought was his wife. See, everything is in order," Parker said, squeezing her hand in his.

Evie said to Addie, "I'm so thankful you were here; if not, I'd probably be dead by now. Do you think he's gone for good? Do you have any feelings about that at all?"

"For an hour or so afterwards, I still had that same horrible feeling inside, but I guess it was just my nerves on edge from the confrontation, because after a while it went away.

They couldn't decide how safe Evie might be. Was Ed gone for good, convinced Evelyn was not in New Orleans?

"So how do you feel about it, Addie?" Dani asked. "After all, it has been your gut feeling all along that the danger was coming closer and closer. We all certainly believe in your feelings now. What are the spirits telling you?

"Right after he left, the wickedness was still around. But I performed everything Madame's notes said to do, and I started feeling much better. I wouldn't say all those feelings are completely gone, but I don't think we are in any danger.

"That being said, common sense tells me Evie doesn't need to take any chances right now, like going out where people can see her. I think I'll figure out more as time goes on."

"I'll tell you what," Martin said. "Food will make everything look better. The only thing Addie and I had for lunch was wine. How about I call down to Simon's Place and see if I can buy a big pot of gumbo, or some sandwiches. I'll go get them and bring them back here. Is that okay with everyone?"

"Sandwiches would be easier to carry," Parker said. "I'll go with you and help."

Parker called down to Simon's Place and ordered a dozen sandwiches and a dozen fried pies to go.

"You must think we've been going without food for a week, the way you ordered," Dani said.

"I'm hungry," Morgan said. "When are we gonna eat?"

"Martin and I are going to walk down to Simon's to get our supper and bring it back here. Want to come with us?"

On the way to the restaurant, when Morgan was running a few feet in front of them, Martin said to Parker, "She wasn't in any danger. I had a pistol in my jacket pocket pointed at him the whole time. If he'd made a move, he was a dead man."

"I have to admit something. I can't get over the fact that Addie knew something like this was going to happen. Some way, somehow, she knew danger was on the way. I've never believed in this hoodoo stuff. Even when I heard the stories about Madame. Now, I don't know what to think."

"I'm with you, buddy. My daughter is making a believer out of me."

When they returned to Evie's apartment with sacks of food, Dani asked Parker, "Did you get a chance to tell Simon what happened today?"

"We didn't have to. Mrs. Lanier is being wined and dined for her firsthand account of the new witch in action, saving the neighborhood from the forces of evil with her spells. She'll eat out for a month on that story. Simon said he was upset at first, until he found out everyone is safe and Dani and Morgan were nowhere near the action. He says he'll be down to see you when he closes tonight. They're busy tonight, thanks to Mrs. Lanier."

Later that night, as he held Addie in his arms, Parker asked, "You seem so much more relaxed tonight, now that this happened. Or maybe it's the glasses of wine you drank. Are you going to be able to sleep tonight?"

"I hope so. It's not the same thing, not fear like it has been, but I'm still all wired after today."

"I know just the thing, the perfect thing to relax you and put you to sleep," he said as he gathered her close and kissed her.

CHAPTER FORTY

Martin hardly slept that night. His mind replayed the scene in Addie's shop, and all the things that could have happened ran like a movie through his head. What if the man, this Ed person, had gotten violent? Could he have used the gun in his pocket? *Yes, I would have shot him if he had made a move to hurt Addie. The same for Evie. I would have used it to stop him from taking her away.*

The morning before he laughed at himself when he put the small revolver in his pocket. He wasn't the kind of man to carry a gun — not that kind of man at all — and he had to laugh at the idea of a gun in his pocket, like he was a character in a movie. Well, he wasn't laughing now.

Addie's premonitions, which once amused, were a long way from being funny now. Oh, he thought she believed what she said about danger coming, evil coming, a bad person coming — he just thought she had a good imagination.

No longer. From now on he would listen to every premonition she had, no matter how out there it was. Somehow she knew things. He had no idea how, but she did.

When he finally fell asleep he tossed for much of the night until he decided to get up and get an early start on the day. He put coffee on and clicked on the TV to get the weather report before leaving. He'd go by the office first, before going by to check on Addie and Evie. They might be sleeping late, if they had as much trouble falling asleep as he had.

He was pouring his first cup of coffee as the news came on. He listened intently, then turned off the coffeemaker, grabbed his jacket, and left.

* * *

Evie sat on the sofa in her apartment, Martin beside her, while Addie paced the length of the room, softly crying.

"I can't believe it. I can't believe Ed is dead," Evie said for the fifth time in as many minutes.

"You can believe it. They wouldn't have released the name on TV if they weren't sure of the name." Martin patted her arm.

"And I killed him!" Addie said.

"No, you did not kill him," Martin said forcefully. "The accident wasn't even his fault. It was the drunk driver who plowed into an eighteen-wheeler who caused the accident. That's whose fault it was. Ed was only one of the people in the wrong place at the wrong time. The news broadcast said there were ten vehicles involved in one way or another."

"But the black candles, they turn evil back onto the person who is evil. That's what really killed him. And I put out black candles — big ones."

"If Ed hadn't been intent on doing evil to begin with, there would have been no evil to turn back."

"Please don't blame yourself," Evie said. "You were only trying to protect me and everyone else around here. Ed's actions, his black heart, killed him, if it really was evil turned back."

"Maybe. At least he wasn't the cause of the accident," Addie sniffed. "If he'd caused it, I don't know if I could stand the guilt over all those people getting hurt."

"And that is very fortunate. If he had caused it, his estate might get sued for damages by every person who was injured in the wreck," Martin said. He handed a box of tissues to Addie.

"His estate! I hadn't thought about that. Do I need to do something about that?" Evie asked.

"Does he have any other relatives besides you?"

"No. His parents are dead, and his only sibling, a sister, died several years ago from cancer. I'm the only person left." At that tears began to roll down her cheeks. "How can I go back and face all the people we knew — the neighbors and the people in our church? Ed was a deacon and everyone thought very highly of him. Everyone will know I ran off and left him, and I'm sure he has told terrible things about me," Evie said as she wiped her eyes. "Terrible things that people will believe because he was such an upstanding member of the community."

"Only because they didn't know what kind of a person he really was," Addie said.

"But I can't face them. I just can't."

"I think the wisest idea is to contact a lawyer about all this. We don't know if Ed has legally divorced you or not, or if he has a will."

"I hadn't thought about that. Yes, that would be the thing to do, I guess."

"I could see if Mr. Arceneau would check into it for you, if you want." Addie, her crying over, stood in front of Evie.

"Yes. I'd appreciate it. I've never had to take care of business of any kind. Ed always handled everything. I'm feeling — oh, I don't know what I'm feeling right now. Relief that I don't have to be afraid of Ed any more, guilt that I feel that way, regret that our marriage wasn't a good one, overwhelmed with the idea I have to face all this, sadness that my life has come to this."

"You have nothing to feel guilty about," Martin said, taking her hand. "You did nothing wrong. You ran to save your life. You took nothing but what belonged to you, the car, jewelry, and your clothes. If you hadn't run, you might not be alive today."

"My head says that's true."

"It is true. You'll come to believe it. You deserve to have a happy life, after all you've been through."

Dani rushed through the open French doors from the gallery.

"Here y'all are. When I couldn't find anyone at Addie's, I thought you must be up here. What's wrong? Has something else happened? Did your husband come back?" she said to Evie.

"My husband is dead." Evie started crying again.

"What? How?'

"After he left here yesterday he was in a bad wreck. Some drunk driver ran into a big truck, causing a pileup of cars, and Ed was killed," Addie said.

Martin said, "Addie thinks she's to blame because of the black candles. We've been telling her she was only protecting and what she did was better than what I was ready to do."

"What were you going to do?" three voices asked together.

"I had a gun in my pocket. If he had made a move toward hurting anyone I would have shot him. Your method," he said, turning toward Addie, "was much better."

"Oh. Yes. Yes, I guess it was, for sure."

"Addie, can you call Mr. Arceneau today and ask him if he will help me with everything?"

"Sure thing. I'll call him right now."

"Explain everything so he'll know if he can help me, or wants to help me."

"I will. I'll tell him about yesterday, too."

"It'll be easier than me telling it. I'd just break down and cry."
Evie reached for another tissue.

Dani followed as Addie left saying she needed to open her shop.
With the sidewalks were full of people, she didn't want to miss any
sales.

"Do you want me to go to the attorney's office with you?"
Martin asked. "I don't want to intrude on your private matters, but
I'll be glad to go with you for support, if you want."

"Would you? I think I'd feel much better if you were with me.
My mind is going every which way, and you would be calm enough
to ask questions and help me understand things."

She paused. " Nevertheless, I've been proud of the way I've been
taking care of myself and I don't want to become dependent on a
man to tell me what to do, like I was with Ed. I would feel better if I
wasn't alone when I am faced with this. I want to make all decisions
for myself, though."

"Understood. I'll just be there for moral support. This is your life
and all decisions are yours to make." Martin put his arm around her
shoulders and gave a hug. *It feels good to have a man's arm around
me and not fear he's going to hit me later.*

CHAPTER FORTY-ONE

Parker was sure Addie was leaving, going back east. The year specified in Madame's will, the year she had to live here in order to inherit, would be up soon, and she was moving back to Greenview. She hadn't told him so, not yet, but he could figure it out for himself. It didn't take a genius to tell she was homesick and ready to leave New Orleans after the terrifying experience she'd had.

All she talked about the last several days was her life before she moved to New Orleans — before she found out she was Madame's heir. The impending visit of her two best friends from her old life, Gina and Karen, triggered all this reminiscing. Several times over the past year, Addie mentioned they wanted to come visit her, and finally they set a date.

Addie talked to them at least once a week, so they were aware of her growing anxiety leading up to the arrival of Evie's husband. She kept them apprised of all the preparations she put in place to turn away whatever evil was on its way. She also told them about Ed showing and being killed later, and how she might have caused his death with her spells or juju or whatever the hell she did to turn him away.

Their visit next week was all Addie could talk about. At least reliving the good times with her friends from high school made her stop worrying about Ed's death. "That was one of the best times we ever had together," she said as she and Parker finished their supper at Simon's Place. "The very best."

It was the second or third time in the last week she'd told him about their trip to New York City the three women had taken two years before, each time remembering another incident they from the trip. He also heard about the jaunt to Atlantic City several times, and the time they this or that or whatever, until he was really tired of Gina and Karen stories. Every time he heard another one his heart sank a little more. They were coming next week, and Addie was seeing Mr. Arceneau to sign papers about her inheritance not long after that, so it didn't take a genius to figure out they were coming to help her pack up and get ready to move back home, as she called it.

That's how he knew he was really, truly in love with her. Other girlfriends had moved away, and sure, he missed them for a while, but he didn't know how he could take Addie not being there. Parker even checked to see if his company had a branch in Connecticut, thinking he might transfer. They didn't, and he was too despondent to do anything more, although he thought about registering with a headhunter to see if he could find a good job near Addie.

Parker wondered if part of the reason Addie was moving back was the way people looked at her and talked about her. With the death of Ed Simmons, the man who was now the embodiment of evil in the minds of the citizens of the neighborhood, her reputation was elevated to that of her great-aunt. Madame, after all, had never actually killed anyone. The story of how he treated Evie and how she fled for her life, was now known far and wide. He knew Addie never told anyone about it, yet somehow the story became neighborhood gossip.

Mrs. Lanier made sure everyone knew about the salt and the sweeping and the spitting. The neighborhood had already heard about the magic stones and juju bags Addie, Evie, Parker, Martin, Simon, Dani, and Morgan wore for their safety, about the Fu dogs at the entrance to the shop, and the candles. They marveled at the fact Addie knew in advance something or someone evil was on its way. When Ed died in the accident, Addie's reputation was sealed. Madame turned her husband into a dog, and made people miserable with various ailments, but Addie actually killed someone to protect a friend. Parker had a hard time trying to prevent that tale getting back to Addie, since he was trying to convince her she hadn't caused the death. He enlisted Simon's help to keep that particular piece of news away from her and he hoped they had succeeded, but he wasn't sure.

It was almost impossible to eat a meal at Simon's without being interrupted several times with requests or gifts. In the past week she had been given a jar of candied jalapenos, a jar of green tomato pickles, a sack of homemade pralines, and a jar of pickled peaches plus all sorts of trinkets. The previous night Mrs. Larcade gave her the ugliest ceramic angel Parker had ever seen. He would have trashed it as soon as he was out of Mrs. Larcade's sight, but Addie said she was going to put it on a shelf in her shop so everyone could see it when they came in. Mrs. Larcade beamed at that, and he heard her telling every table she passed, "She's gonna put it in her shop for everyone to admire!"

Mrs. Guidry approached with some item wrapped in tissue paper. "Miss Addie, I was crocheting doilies for my granddaughters and I made one for you, too. I hope you can use it."

"Oh, how lovely," Addie said, after unwrapping it. "I'll put it right on a table in my living room, where I can see it every day."

After Mrs. Guidry left, Parker said, "When are Martin and Evie coming back? Have you heard?"

"Yes, Dad called today, and I talked to Evie, too. They said everything ought to be wrapped up in another couple of days. She met with her husband's attorney and all the business has been taken care of. She hired a local company to handle selling everything in the house. They're going to hold a big estate sale. She's hired a cleaning service to come clean the house, and tomorrow she's going to sign a contract with a real estate broker to sell the property. She said she couldn't have done it without Dad's support."

"I'm glad he volunteered to go with her, and that she let him."

"Yes, I am, too."

"For a while she was concerned about what people would think if she showed up with your dad. She was worried they would think she ran off with Martin when she left her husband."

"I don't think she would ever have gone to see the attorney if Dad hadn't told her that people would think what they want and she couldn't do anything about it. She would have turned her back on the whole situation, rather than dealing with it. She didn't want to ever see her old home again, didn't want to face the people there. Nevertheless, she persevered."

That's just the opposite of Addie, who sounds as if she can hardly wait to see her old friends and her old home again.

CHAPTER FORTY-TWO

Martin glanced over at the sleeping woman in the seat beside him. What a trip. After he volunteered to accompany Evie back to her hometown and help her take care of her late husband's estate, he had second thoughts.

Martin, old boy, what are you letting yourself in for? You hardly know this woman, and you sure don't know what you are walking in to.

But Martin was both a gentleman and a businessman, and he thought Evie needed help getting through all she had to deal with after Ed's death. Evie lived most of her adult life under stress. First was the mental and physical abuse she suffered in her marriage and later from the fear her abuser would find and kill her. After the confrontation with Ed in Addie's shop, he no longer thought that was a bunch of foolishness.

After the shock of Ed's death in the traffic accident, Evie started spilling out the details of her miserable life she'd kept to herself. She told Martin about the beatings and the verbal lashings she had endured for almost twenty years, and Martin marveled that she was able to escape and stay hidden for as long as she had.

"Why didn't you leave him long before?"

"Because of our son, Billy. I could never have run away with a child and stayed hidden. The law doesn't care if a wife runs away, but they would have looked for me if I'd taken Billy. I would have had to deal with schools and all sorts of things like that. Ed or the police would have found us."

"I hadn't thought about how hard it would be with a child."

"You have to know Ed's temper, his need to have control over me. It wasn't so bad at first. It started with small things and escalated over the years. Ed was a respected businessman and he might have gotten custody of Billy if I'd tried for a divorce. I couldn't take that chance."

Over the first few days after Ed's death, Evie consulted with Addie's lawyer, Henri Arceneau, who contacted Ed's attorney,

Franklin Mailer, back in Riverview. What she found out both calmed her and upset her.

Ed Simmon's will was several years old. It had never been changed, and Evelyn was the sole heir to Ed's estate. Mr. Mailer was aware Evelyn had left Ed. Although it surprised him at the time, after seeing more and more of Ed's rage he'd deduced the type of behavior he was seeing was what drove her away. He didn't blame her for going.

Mr. Mailer asked Ed if he wanted to file for divorce, but Ed insisted he was going to find Evelyn and 'drag her back home where she belongs,' so he made no changes to any legal documents. There was a house, paid for; substantial savings; and an accidental death insurance policy, all of which would go to Evelyn.

After much discussion with Addie and Martin, Evie had Ed's body sent back to Riverview, Kansas, to be buried next to their son and Ed's family. There would be no service. Mr. Mailer would submit an obituary to the local newspaper listing Ed's many accomplishments and honors, and requesting that in lieu of flowers, donations should be made to the local abused women's shelter. Evelyn would not badmouth Ed to his friends, but if they inferred something from the donation request that was okay with her.

The thing that upset Evie was she needed to go back to Riverview to dispose of the house and its contents.

"You can have the attorney take care of all that," Martin told her. "You don't have to face that job if you don't want to."

"Yes, I know, but I think I would like to gather some of Billy's things, and photos. These last months, I've thought of several pictures and items I wish I'd brought with me. There's nothing but bad memories associated with Ed, but many happy ones of my son. No one else would know what I would treasure. I need to do that myself."

Martin volunteered to go with her. "Just for moral support," he said.

"That is kind of you, but it's going to take all the money I have to get myself there and back. I can't afford to take you."

"Have you given any thought about how you're going to get there? You said it's a small city, so I imagine there's no airline service. To get there by bus might be difficult. It would take a lot of your reserve money, maybe all of it, to buy a car dependable enough to get you there, and you no longer have a driver's license. Without a license you can't even rent a car."

"I hadn't really thought about that part of it."

"Of course, if you are going to move back there, into your old home, you could go take the driver's test, get a license, and use your money to buy a car so you could move your things back. Or maybe the attorney could send some money from Ed's funds."

Evie shuddered. "No, never. I'm not moving back there, ever. I like it right here. If I didn't have to go back to settle everything, I wouldn't. If it weren't for getting some mementoes of my son, I'd tell Mr. Mailer to take care of it all, even if it did cost more to do it that way." She stood and paced the room. "So how am I going to get there?"

"I can take you and drive you around town to make all the arrangements you have to make. I promise I won't butt in or make decisions for you. I'll just be there — to listen, if you need me as a sounding board."

She stopped pacing and stood looking at him.

"And I promise I'll be a gentleman. I expect nothing from you. Separate rooms. No moves. I promise."

"I still can't afford it. And I'm not hinting that you pay for the trip. I still have some money put back, but I'll have to travel cheap, probably by bus, and I don't think you'd like cheap motels and fast food. I'm not going to ask for any of the money from Ed's estate before it's settled. It makes it look like I couldn't make it without him."

"You've been doing great without him. I have no doubts you would have been even better if you could have been seen out in public and had a job. I'm happy now that you stayed in hiding. All the fears and premonitions you had were true. He did keep on looking until he found you, and he would have hurt you if things hadn't worked out the way they did."

"Mr. Arceneau told me the police said Ed had a gun in his pocket and another one in the glove compartment of his car."

Martin shook his head. How close Evie came to a real tragedy. He shuddered to think what could have happened if Addie had not inherited from her great-aunt and moved there, to give warning, support, and magical protection to Evie and all the friends around her.

"Let me suggest this, then. I have a credit card I seldom use. Let me pay for the trip using it. All the bills will be on one statement. Then, when the estate is settled and your house is sold, you can pay me back out of the proceeds."

"You would do that for me?"

"Sure. Addie considers you a close friend, and that's good enough for me."

"I'll do it on one condition."

"What's that?"

"That I sign a note or something, promising to pay you back."

"All right, if that's what you want," Martin said, smiling.

While driving back to New Orleans, he smiled again, thinking of how strong she'd become the last few days. Evie had been to hell and back in her lifetime. Nevertheless, she persevered.

Ed's burial was already completed, arranged by the attorney, when they arrived in Riverview. Evie made it plain to the lawyer she wanted as little to do with any of Ed's business as possible. The three of them, Evie, Martin, and Frank Mailer, walked through the house together, and Mailer suggested he send an assistant over to gather up all the papers in Ed's study.

"There may be bills that need to be paid, or there may be investment information I know nothing about," he said. Evie readily agreed.

The will was filed in probate court, and Mailer would contact the judge about a quick decision on it. There would be a period of time in which anyone having a claim against the estate could come forward, and until then none of the money could be disbursed, but he saw no reason she could not put the house on the market for sale.

Evie signed a contract with a woman who, for a percentage of the sales, would hold an estate sale to dispose of contents of the home. She was someone Evie knew from church.

"You're sure there is nothing else you want to take with you? Nothing that holds any sentimental memories?" she asked.

"Believe me, there are no sentimental memories here. I have taken a box of items from my son's room, and a box of china that belonged to my mother. Everything else can go."

The older woman touched Evie on the arm. "I just want you to know, everyone at church has sympathy and is praying for you. Several people always thought there was something wrong with the way Ed acted toward you, and we had suspicions about what kind of man he really was behind closed doors. Not everyone put you down for leaving your husband. Sometimes a woman does what she has to do."

Evie, overcome with emotion, patted the woman's hand on her arm, and managed a small smile and a teary, "Thank you."

Next came the Realtor. He walked through the house, measuring and making notes.

"You could get more for it if you have it painted throughout and updated a few things before putting it on the market."

"No. I don't want to do that. If it brings less, so be it."

So he worked up his comparable sales, came up with a price, and filled out a contract. When the estate sale was over and the remaining items given to the thrift shop that benefited the abused women's shelter, he would hire a professional cleaning service to get the house in spotless condition, having the bill sent to the lawyer's office for payment. When the house was ready to be put on the market, he would mail the contract to Evie for her signature and start advertising.

With all business taken care of, Martin and Evie were on their way back to New Orleans. Evie opened her eyes and stretched.

"Where are we?"

"About two hours away from New Orleans."

"Good," she said, adjusting the seat belt and straightening her clothes. "It'll be good to be home again."

"Yes," Martin said, "It'll be good to be home again. I can't wait to begin showing you the town that is your new home."

CHAPTER FORTY-THREE

"That was a delicious meal," Martin said as he placed his napkin beside the plate. "I've been eating Cajun food so much I forgot how good pot-roast can be. You are an excellent cook."

Evie felt herself blushing at the compliment. There had been so few in the last twenty years that each one she received was precious and special. Both Addie and Dani praised her for the way she handled customers. They said she was friendly and cheerful and that was why the customers bought so much from her. A compliment from Martin was special, though, especially on her cooking. Ed always told her she was a terrible cook.

She didn't negate the compliment, though. She took it and tucked it away in her memory to take out later and feel good about.

"Thank you. It was a pleasure to have someone to cook for. Shall we take our coffee into the living room?"

They took their cups and went to sit in the armchairs that were in the main room.

"I want to have everyone to dinner before long. You, Addie, Parker, Dani and Simon. And Morgan, of course. It seems too soon right now, having a dinner party so soon after Ed's death."

"It will seem more fitting to you after a little time has passed," Martin said.

"I want to thank you again for all the help you gave me — the support while I was clearing up Ed's estate. If not for you I think I would have broken down in tears trying to deal with it all."

"I didn't do a thing but listen. You did it all. You are stronger than you give yourself credit for."

"I'm beginning to realize that. It was the voicing things, talking them out, that helped. Once I said my options out loud to you, the choices became clear. Without you, I wouldn't have had anyone to be a sounding board."

"Well, you're free of all that now. At least you can go and do what you want, where you want without any fear. Once the estate makes it through probate and the house is sold, you'll have money to live somewhere else, wherever you want."

Evie looked at Martin, startled. "I can't imagine living anywhere else but here. This is home, and I'm happy."

"Good! That's the important thing. I just thought you might want to buy a house or condo, even if it was here in New Orleans."

Evie sat still, thinking. Finally she said, "No, I don't think so. At least not anytime soon. I'm perfectly content living here."

"Have you given any thought to getting a job? Or are you going to continue with your writing?"

"I have thought about that. I like working for Addie and Dani, but I also think I'd like to work with children again. I don't have teaching certification in Louisiana. I'd have to go back to school to get it. I might do that sometime, but not right now. I'm thinking about my options."

"I hope your options include me," Martin said, carefully placing his coffee cup on the table at his elbow.

Flustered, Evie set her cup on the side table and folded her hands in her lap. "Of course. You are a part of this group of friends. I'm sure I'll be seeing you often."

Martin leaned forward and reached across to place his hand on hers. "I hope you will allow me to escort you places — out to dinner, to the movies, seeing all the Big Easy has to offer. In other words, I hope you will accept a date with me."

"Well, ah…" It had been so long since she had thought about something called a date she didn't know how to respond.

"Sometimes we might be with Addie and Parker. Sometimes it might be just the two of us. But I promise I'll always be a gentleman, Evie. Always."

She sat there silently, her cheeks once again rosy with blush. She felt like she was sixteen again, out of her depth and awkward.

Martin withdrew his hand. "I think we get along well. I enjoy talking with you. But I don't want to give you any reason to think you have to go out with me. You don't have to do what a man wants ever again."

"Oh, Martin. I do like being with you. It's just that you took me by surprise, that's all. I enjoyed dinner with you this evening, and I'm sure I would enjoy going out with you. You'll have to excuse me if I'm still withdrawn. I have become so used to the solitary life it will take some getting used to go out in public again. It was even hard to make the trip."

"I understand. We'll take it easy. Any time I ask you out and you don't want to go, just tell me."

"Okay."

"May I take you to dinner at Simon's Place tomorrow night?"

Evie took a deep breath. "Yes. Yes you may. I've only eaten there one time, the day I arrived in New Orleans and Madame found me there. I'd love to go back."

"I'll pick you up about six o'clock, if that's all right with you."

"Yes, six o'clock will be perfect."

He stood up, "I'd better be going. It's getting late." He started toward the door

At the door he paused. Bending slightly, he kissed her on the cheek.

Someday I'll kiss you on the lips.

CHAPTER FORTY-FOUR

Sounding like squealing teenagers, the three women embraced, their circle of friendship forming an island in the stream of people coming and going at the busy airport.

"My gosh, it's so good to see both of you. I thought you'd forgotten all about me and were never going to come visit."

"As if. We had to come see where all the excitement is going on," Gina said.

"Girl, you are absolutely glowing! Is it facing down a mad husband bent on revenge or is it love that has you looking so good?" said Karen.

"Love. Absolutely. Let's get your luggage and head home. You'll get to meet him tonight."

They retrieved the luggage from the baggage roundabout and chattered all the way to Addie's car in short-term parking.

"It's so warm down here! It's still cold back home."

"I love that outfit you have on. You're still wearing the wildest clothes."

"My friend Dani made it. Her shop is right next door to mine."

"When you told me about her one of the first things I thought was how handy it was for shopping!"

"I'm so glad you finally got the shop you've been wanting. I'm dying to see it."

They used the trip from the airport to Addie's place to catch up on everything that had happened in Gina and Karen's lives in the past year, at least the events that hadn't been covered in their weekly phone sessions.

"Oh, good. There's a parking place right in front," Addie said as she pulled up. "I have parking around back, but this first time I wanted you to enter through the front."

"Addie! This looks like something right out of a movie about New Orleans," Gina said.

"Well, silly," said Karen, "you're in New Orleans, after all."

"Yes, but I didn't think it would look so — so perfectly type cast."

They all laughed as they exited the car.

"Here is my shop, Zappa's. We could go through it to get into my apartment, but I'd rather take you in the other way, through the courtyard," Addie said. She took her key and unlocked the massive iron gate guarding the brick quad.

The two friends gushed over the flower-strewn courtyard, the charming galleries surrounding it, and Addie's antique filled apartment.

"Girl, you couldn't have picked a place to live that looks more like you than this," said Karen. "You must have inherited your great-aunt's decorating sense, as well as all this hoodoo talent."

"I inherited something else, too. Something I haven't told you about yet." Addie guided them toward the far wall. "See this picture?"

"That's one sexy looking woman."

"That's my great-aunt Clotilde. Madame, as the people called her."

"My, my," Karen said, studying the old portrait. "I always did say your hair was as curly as mine. Now we know why."

"And you didn't know she was black?" Gina asked.

"Not until I found this picture, and Parker said, real casual like, 'That's your aunt.' You could have knocked me down with one finger. Everyone around here knew she was black, of course, and no one said a thing. They all thought I knew."

"And they accepted you as you are."

"Yes."

"That's the way it ought to be. Always. Accept people for who they are."

"I was mad a Parker for a while for not telling me, but finally I understood that's what he was saying — he accepted me for who I am. He said he didn't think about it."

"And when are we going to meet this fabulous Parker?"

"He'll be home from work in about an hour. Let me show you to your apartment," Addie said, and led them outside. "That's Parker's flat over there," she said, pointing across the quad, "and Evie lives up there over Parker. You'll be staying in this apartment over mine."

Addie led the way up the stairs and unlocked the door. "Here's an extra key for you to have," she said, handing it to Gina and opening the door wide. "The furniture in this flat is not as fancy as in the other apartments."

"Don't you go apologizing. This looks like something straight out of a decorating magazine."

"There are two bedrooms," Addie said leading the way to the back room, the one over her bedroom, "and the bath for this one is here." She opened the door.

"Look at that tub! I've never seen one like that," said Gina.

"I've stocked both bathrooms with plenty of bubble bath and lotions and stuff. Come this way to the other bed and bath." She led the way back through the living room and kitchen. "This one is over my shop. Since it faces the street, I hope it is not too noisy, but Mardi Gras is over, and since it's Lent, things are kind of quiet around here. Maybe you won't be disturbed. There is no air conditioning, but you can leave windows open, and even the French doors, too. It's perfectly safe, since no one can get into the courtyard.

"I'll leave you now to get settled in. We're having supper at my place tonight, and several people are coming. There'll be Parker, of course, and my father. Evie, Dani from next door and her little boy, Morgan, and Simon, who owns the restaurant in the next block, will all be here, too. All my friends are looking forward to meeting you. They've heard so much about you."

"And we've heard so much about them, we're looking forward to meeting them, too."

"Come on down whenever you're ready. Supper will be in about two hours."

* * *

Several hours later the group was still sitting around the big table in Addie's kitchen.

Karen and Gina had regaled the party with stories of Addie's freaky mystical gifts when they were in school together and afterwards. Evie and Dani had shared parts of their pasts and how they ended up under Madame's protection. Parker related his connection with the old woman and the things she told him. Simon repeated the tales told by the people in the neighborhood, about the things Madame had done, both for and to people.

Finally, Addie noticed the yawns her old friends could no longer stifle.

"You two, go on upstairs and go to bed. We can visit more tomorrow, and you both look like you are about to go to sleep in your plate."

"We need to help you clean up," Karen protested.

"No way," Addie said, starting to gather dirty dishes. "You go on to bed."

"We'll all help," Evie said. "It won't take long. You two run along." Voices of the others chimed in.

"It's just that we had to get up so early to catch the plane, and we're used to an earlier time zone than you are in here," Gina said.

"We loved meeting you all and hope to see more of you while we're here," Dani said.

"Tomorrow night is dinner at my restaurant, Simon's Place. Everyone be there," Simon said as he gathered glasses in his big hands and headed toward the sink.

It was quick work to get the table cleared and the dishwasher started.

"How about a glass of wine for a nightcap?" Parker said. "I'll get a bottle from my apartment and meet you in the courtyard."

Addie said, "Bring glasses, too. Mine are all in the dishwasher."

Everyone trouped out to the table and settled around the table setting on the bricks in front of Parker's flat. Addie brought out a lighter and ignited the three wicks on the big citronella candle in the middle of the table. When Parker returned and poured the wine, he held his glass high.

"I propose a toast. To good friends, old and new. To many more pleasant evenings like this."

"Here here." The voices all chimed in.

Morgan climbed into Dani's lap and promptly fell asleep, his head resting on her shoulder.

"I need to get him home to bed," she said, softly.

"I'll carry him for you in a few minutes." Simon reached over and patted Morgan's head.

"I like your friends," said Martin, and murmurs of agreement came from around the table.

"We need to keep our voices down so they can sleep. I told them it's safe to leave all the French doors standing open, and I see they have done that. They aren't used to this heat."

Voices muted, the gathering rehashed some of the stories Gina and Karen had told earlier. Several times "Did you really...?" was asked, and Addie told more escapades the three girls had together, and quiet laughter bubbled into the night.

Parker was quiet, neither asking nor commenting, and Addie wondered why. Did he not like Karen and Gina? Surely he wasn't jealous of her friendship with them. He didn't seem like that kind of person, and had never begrudged her time with Dani or Evie. She'd have to talk to him about it later, find out if something was wrong.

A short time later, the party started to break up. Parker was gathering the empty bottle and glasses, Martin left to walk Evie to her door, and Simon was about to take Morgan from Dani's arms, when screams echoed through the courtyard.

CHAPTER FORTY-FIVE

Simon was gathering the sleeping boy into his arms when the screams reverberated through the still night air. Thrusting Morgan back at Dani, he turned and raced toward the stairway leading to the upper gallery. Martin, already on the upper balcony, turned toward the cries and yelled back to Evie, "Get inside and stay there."

Martin reached the apartment over Addie's flat and entered the front bedroom through the open French doors. Simon, following ten feet behind, ran into the living room just in time to be hit by a body careening off tables and chairs.

Wrapping his arms around the struggling figure, he yelled, "I've got him. Someone turn on a light."

Parker, right behind Simon, made his way through the dark room to the wall by the front door and flipped switches. The overhead light and the outside light came on.

"Well damn, you're just a kid!" Simon said to the struggling boy. "Hold still."

"What in the world is going on?" said Gina as she entered the room, tying her robe around her.

"Somebody got in bed with me," said Karen, "and I screamed. You — kid — what do you think you were doing, climbing in bed with me like that? He's too young to ... you know, hurt me."

Simon thought about the women waiting in the courtyard below and walked out onto the gallery, still holding the struggling youngster. He adjusted the slight body to get a better hold and the boy cried out.

"Stop yelling! I'm not hurting you."

"Simon? What happened?" Dani looked up toward him.

"This little kid got in bed with Karen."

Morgan, rubbing his sleepy eyes, looked up at Simon and yelled, "That's Renny! That's my friend Renny! Don't hurt him, Simon!"

"Morgan? You know this kid?" Simon asked. He looked down at the crying child and saw the blood on his arm.

He took a good look at the slender figure in his arms and gently readjusted his hold on the boy. His light brown skin was bruised on

243

his arms and legs, and blood was seeping through the back of his dirty shirt.

"Hold on. Hold on, son. Don't struggle. I promise I'm not going to hurt you. No one is going to hurt you."

The boy stopped resisting and collapsed in Simon's arms. Simon, with Martin, Parker, Gina and Karen behind him, followed the balcony around to the stairs and descended into the courtyard, where the anxious women waited.

Morgan wiggled his way out of Dani's arms and ran toward his friend. "Renny! Renny! Are you hurt? Did he hurt you?"

"I didn't hurt him, Morgan. You know I wouldn't hurt a kid."

"Not you, Simon," Morgan said, then turned to Renny, "That bad man, did he hurt you? Aren't you wearing the necklace I gave you?"

Renny shook his head. "I gave it to my mama to keep her safe," he said and burst into tears.

"Let's get inside where we have some light," Simon said.

Still carrying the weeping boy, Simon proceeded to Addie's kitchen. Sitting down at the table, he tipped the tear-covered face up so he could get a better look. Several of the women let out gasps when they saw the eye swollen almost shut and the stripe of raw skin across the brown cheek.

"Who did this to you?" Simon's low voice reverberated with anger and Renny buried his face in Simon's shoulder without answering. "Do you know anything about this, Morgan?"

"It's that man living with him and his mama. He's been hittin' on 'em. He's bad. Real bad. He gets drunk and hits 'em. His mama, she won't run away, so Renny, he runs and hides."

Addie spoke softly. "Renny, is it you that's been hiding upstairs all this time?"

A slight nod of his head confirmed her question. He turned away from Simon's shoulder and spoke. "Madame, she told me a long time ago I could come here if I needed her. Then she died, and I didn't know where else to go, so I hide up there when I have to." He started to sob again.

Addie patted him very gently on the back. "It's okay, Renny. I don't mind a bit that you stayed up there. I'm not mad at all. You just scared the lady who is visiting me, that's all."

"And I'm not mad now," Karen said. "You scared me, but I'm not mad at you."

"How do you get in?" Parker asked. "Up until tonight the doors have been locked."

Renny straightened up and wiped his eyes with his hand. "That iron stuff over the back window is loose. I climb up onto the car shed roof and climb in that window."

"Well, what do we do now?" Simon said the assembled crowd.

Addie said, "First things first. "Renny, have you had anything to eat? Are you hungry?"

"Yessum, I'm hungry. There wasn't nothin' to eat tonight at our house. That's why he was so mad."

Addie got up and went to the cabinet. "Then a big old sandwich and a glass of milk are in order."

"And while she is fixin' that, why don't you tell us how you're involved in this, Morgan," Dani said, turning to her son.

"Well, Renny and I made friends when school first started. We're not in the same class, but we see each other at recess, and we play, when he feels like it. After a while he tol' me about the mean man that lives with them. He didn't want me to tell anyone, though. He's awful afraid of that man."

"Did you know he was hiding upstairs?"

"No ma'am. But I wondered if it might be him when you talked about the ghost."

"There's a ghost up there?" Renny looked terrified.

"No, no ghost," Simon said. "When stuff got moved around, or they found food wrappers they said it was a ghost."

"We found wrappers from hamburgers and stuff up there, Renny. Was that yours?" Evie asked.

"Yessum. I look through the trash cans and find stuff to eat when I'm hungry and Mama hasn't fixed anything."

Addie returned with a fat sandwich and a glass of milk. "Here you are. No one ever goes hungry around here, especially with Simon around. He's the man holding you. Simon, I think you can let him sit in a chair by himself to eat."

Simon reluctantly eased Renny into the chair Dani vacated. Somehow he wanted to keep holding the boy, keep him safe from the world and the people who strike innocents such as Renny.

"So, what's the next step," Martin asked. "We can't keep him here, and we can't send him back. He needs medical treatment."

"The authorities will have to be notified," Evie said. "When you know of child abuse you have to report it."

"I understand that," Dani said, "but I hate for him to have the trauma it's going to be when the police get involved."

"The police?" Renny stopped eating and looked around with frightened eyes.

"See?" Dani said.

"Don't be frightened," Simon leaned close to the boy. "We're just talking now. You aren't in any kind of trouble, I promise."

"We need someone who is familiar with the system," Evie said. "Someone who knows how it works here in New Orleans — who to call and what will happen."

Simon said, "Well, it just so happens I know someone like that. Someone who will know what to do and who to call. She's a real mover and shaker when it comes to children's welfare. Let me call my mother."

CHAPTER FORTY-SIX

"Renny, would you come help me set the table, please? Our friends will be here for supper any time now," Maxie asked.

"Yessum," the boy said as he got up from playing with the toy cars on the floor.

"Pick up all the cars first, and put them back in the box. We wouldn't want anyone to slip on one and fall down."

Renny did as asked and came to help at the table.

"Now, do you remember where to put the silverware?"

He hesitantly placed a knife on the right side.

"Yes, that's right. What goes beside it?"

"The spoon?"

"That's right. You're doing it just right."

His bright smile lit up his face at the compliment, and he went around the table placing the eating utensils at each place. The doorbell rang and Maxie pulled off her apron, hurriedly put it in the kitchen and went to answer.

Soon the living room was filled with people. Morgan, as usual, had been the first person through the door, followed by his mother and Simon. Addie and Parker arrived directly behind them, and Evie and Martin came right on their heels. Morgan and Renny took off to Renny's bedroom, carrying the box of cars with them.

"I'm glad to see Morgan is not possessive with the toys you bought for him," Dani said. "I like to see him share with others."

"I bought more little cars for Renny. I think there are two alike for each kind, so Renny can take some with him when he leaves and Morgan will still have his own when he comes here," answered Maxie.

"When is his aunt going to be here for him?" Evie asked.

"Day after tomorrow, if everything goes according to plan. Children's Protective Services in Atlanta has done the background check and home study, and given the okay for her to be his official guardian."

"Pardon me for asking," Martin said, "but why did that have to be done? She's his blood relative, why couldn't she just offer him a home?"

"Because if he wasn't placed there by CPS, or the court, then his mother could come get him any time she wanted, and her sister couldn't prevent her from taking him. Now, she can't go get him and put him back into the hell he was living in here. Both Louisiana and Georgia have worked together to get this all set up for Renny's benefit."

"Poor Renny. He loves his mother so much, and worries about her," said Addie.

"Yes, all the children like Renny love their mothers, but the mothers just can't seem to stay sober and drug free and take care of their children. Renny's mother is in a rehab program, and maybe, with God's help, she'll be able to straighten out her life. If she does she'll be able to get Renny back."

"Unlike my mother," Dani said. "That's how I came to be raised by my grandmother. My mother couldn't stay away from drugs and bad men. Thank heavens for my grandmother."

"What about the man that was beating Renny? Did he get what was coming to him?" Parker asked.

"He disappeared. He didn't stick around to find out what was going to happen to him," Maxie said.

"After hearing all the stories about what Madame did to people like him, he's lucky she wasn't still alive. She would have taken care of him, all right," Parker said.

Dani said, "We're so fortunate to have you to take him in that night. It was lucky that you were already approved to take in children in need. Thank you for all you've done for him. He looks like a different child altogether," Dani said.

"He's a good boy," Maxie answered. "He's as smart as can be, and polite. Now that he feels safe, and he's clean and not hungry, he's ready to face the world. He's interested in everything around him — hungry for knowledge as well as food. He's been a delight to have around."

"Mom's been an emergency placement home for some time now," Simon told the group.

"Yes, I got approved back when I was a teacher. Every once in a while there is an emergency and no place to send a child that needs a safe, loving home to stay in for a while until a more permanent solution can be found. It started when there was a little boy, much like Renny, in my room, and I asked to take him in. I've had several children since then. I'm glad I can do what I can."

Soon the group of friends was seated around the big dining room table, enjoying Maxie's cooking. "I'm so glad to have all of you here," she said. "In the old days, it used to be like this more often, but since Simon's sister and her family moved away, and so many of the older generation making their exit from this world, it's been a long time since this table has been full like this. I expect every one of you to come back again and again. Don't be strangers now that we're friends."

"Me too?" asked Renny. "Can I come back too?"

"Of course you can, Renny. I hope your aunt can bring you back to visit us."

"I can see where Simon got his cooking skills," Martin said. "Everything is delicious, Maxie."

"I think Simon was born knowing how to cook. From the time he could pull a chair up to the counter he was putting stuff together for us to eat — and it was good, too! He has the knack of combining the right ingredients without having to even look at a recipe."

"He sure does," came the murmur of agreement from around the table.

"And he always knows exactly what a person wants to eat. When I was working, he always beat everyone home in the afternoon and started cooking supper. If I thought that day I sure would like a certain dish, say red beans and rice, then when I got home, guess what he had cooked for supper: red beans and rice. I never knew how he did it!"

Simon shrugged. "I don't know. It just came to me what to cook that day. Like I know at the restaurant how much of what to cook each day — how much is going to sell — so we don't have any left over."

"If everyone is finished eating, why don't we take our coffee to the living room," Maxie said.

"I'm so full I couldn't eat another bite," Martin said. "Everything was delicious."

"Miss Addie? Would you like to see pictures of Simon when he was my age?" Morgan asked when she was seated in the living room.

"I'd love to see pictures of Simon when he was your age, but I've seen the photo album you have at your house, remember?"

"Yes, but there are more pictures in the big one here at Miss Maxie's house."

"Why don't you show them to me, then?"

"He loves those photos," Maxie said to Addie while Morgan went to get the album. "He looks at it every time he comes to see me. I made him that small one of his own, but he still likes to look at the big one."

Morgan fetched the big book of pictures from the bookshelves and spread it out on the coffee table in front of Addie.

"Look, Miss Addie, look at this," he said, and started through the decades of pictures. "Here is Simon when he was seven, and here he was when he was ten."

Renny leaned close and admired the pictures.

"Wow! You've got a lot of pictures there. I don't have any at all of me or my mom."

"Miss Maxie made me an album all of my own. It's at my house. It has pictures of Simon and Miss Maxie, and Miss Maxie's mother and her father." He turned the pages back toward the front of the book. "See? This is Simon's grandmother. Wasn't she pretty? And here is his grandfather. He was handsome. He died in a big war and Simon never knew him."

Addie studied the pictures while Morgan explained the family connections to her and Renny. She glanced through Morgan's photo album, which Maxie started. Dani added photos of herself and Morgan. It gave him a sense of family, she said, as if he had a place in the world that was larger than just the two of them and their little apartment. There were also pictures of themselves on outings to the zoo, on the banks of the Mississippi River, at an ice cream parlor, at Simon's Place, and others all over town.

Morgan never got tired of looking at the pictures and saying, "I remember when we did this!"

Addie paused and studied the pictures, frowning as she listened to Morgan's explanations.

"Morgan, when we get home, I'd like to a closer look at your album. May I borrow it for just a little while?"

CHAPTER FORTY-SEVEN

Parker stared morosely at Addie, who was humming as she placed brightly colored napkins at each setting around her table. She announced this dinner party two days before, saying she would make a big announcement. Parker was sure she was going to tell them she was moving back to Connecticut.

She met with Mr. Arceneau more than a week ago, and ever since, she was always smiling and humming, even breaking into singing. Parker asked her if everything was settled about her inheritance, and she replied, "All in due time, Parker. All in due time."

Parker took that to mean that soon she'd be leaving.

"Parker. Parker," she called. "Earth to Parker. Come in please."

"What?" he said, coming out of his morose phantasm.

"I asked if you would please get the ice bucket and put the bottle of champagne on to chill for me, and get the glasses out of the cabinet and put all of it in the living room."

Swell, now we're going to celebrate one of the worst things to ever happen to me. He carried everything into the next room.

Addie checked on a pot simmering on the stove and tossed the contents of a large salad bowl. Placing it on the table, she leaned toward Parker and gave him a little kiss on the lips. Parker wrapped his arms around her, pulled her up close and kissed her as he never had before, softly, tenderly, passionately. He wanted the kiss to say everything he couldn't seem to say aloud. *I love you. I'll always love you. Please don't leave me. Tell me what I can do to get you to stay. I'll do anything, anything at all, if you'll just love me as I love you.*

Parker wondered, not for the first time, if she had done something to him, fed him a love potion or cast a spell or something to enchant him. Then he thought how crazy it was that he, Parker Hyatt, who didn't believe in such things as love potions or juju or spells could let such a thought enter his mind. *There are no such thing as love potions! There is nothing, not a thing, that she could have done to make me love her. Except be Addie.*

"Ummm. That was a lovely kiss, but I have to cook right now. Keep that thought until later."

Parker released her, with difficulty. He wanted to stand there and hold her, not let her go, but that would be awkward. Guests would be there at any minute.

* * *

Two hours later, the meal was consumed and Addie tapped her water glass with her knife. "May I have your attention? If everyone will move into the living room, I have some news to announce."

The group moved into the next room and settled themselves. Parker settled himself into a chair in the far corner of the room, as if distance would soften the blow.

Addie began to speak. "As you all know, when Mr. Arceneau told me about my inheritance from Madame, he told me I had to live here for one year in order for it to be transferred into my name. If I did not fulfill that provision, her estate would all go to charity. Well, last week the year was up, and I visited Mr. Arceneau."

Parker dropped his head and leaned his forehead on his now fisted hands. *Take it like a man.*

"So now all this, the shop and the apartments, are mine." Cheers broke out around the room.

"But that's not all. Following Madame's wishes, I had not been told about the other properties she owned. She had buildings all over town. Evidently, when someone important or rich came to her for a very big spell, or potion, or juju, or whatever, and didn't have the money, she demanded the deed for a building. She ended up with lots and lots of property, which I now own."

"Good for you,"

"Way to go, girl,"

"Congratulations,"

"What great news."

Words of happiness spilled out around the room.

"That's still not all," Addie said, and they grew quiet again.

Parker sat staring at her. He was happy for her good fortune, but he could not fathom what this might mean to them.

Will she stay here to manage her properties now? A glimmer of hope began to flicker in his chest.

"Morgan, when I borrowed your photo album a couple of weeks ago, I asked if you would bring it back when I asked you to. Did you bring it tonight?"

"Yessum. I've got it." Morgan stood up and retrieved it from the table.

Addie took it and turned to the copy of an old picture. "I looked through Morgan's book when he first got it, but I didn't pay a whole lot of attention to the pictures, until the day at Maxie's house, when Morgan was showing me the originals. When I saw the original of this one," she turned the album toward them so all could see the picture she was talking about, "I thought this picture of Simon's grandfather looked familiar. When I borrowed Morgan's album the next day," she smiled at Morgan, "I compared it to this picture." Addie walked over to a large picture hanging on the wall. An ornate oval frame held an image of three people dressed in fashions of the 1930s.

"This is a picture of Clotilde, Adelaide, and Jean-Paul. The man is the same. Simon, Jean-Paul was your grandfather. We are cousins."

Everyone got up and rushed to compare the two images.

"Would you look at that!"

"That's the same man, all right!"

"Then," Addie raised her voice to get their attention once more, "I rummaged in some boxes where I remembered there being some old photos and I found another copy of the same one that is in Maxie's album. If there was any doubt about it being Jean-Paul, that sealed it."

Addie opened a drawer in a side table and took out an old photo.

"It's signed on the back, 'To my sister Clotilde, Jean-Paul.' "

"I can't believe this," Simon said, then enveloped Addie in a bear hug. "Cousin Addie. I can't wait to tell my mother we know who her father was. Her mother, Francine, would never tell anyone his name."

"Maybe Francine didn't want any connection with Madame," Parker said.

"That could be so. People say Madame had quite a reputation at that time, at the beginning of the war, both as a hoodoo practitioner and as a beautiful woman with many lovers. I think Grandmother Francine came from an especially straight-laced family. They were very upset that she got in the family way without being married. They wanted her to give the baby, my mother, up for adoption, but she refused."

"Well, you couldn't ask for a better person to be related to than Madame," Evie said. "She took care of friends and family."

"And she took care of bad people, too, only in a different way," Dani added.

"Everyone sit back down, please," Addie said. "There's more."

"More?" asked Morgan.

"Yes, sweetie. More," Addie said as she gave him a hug.

Parker knew this was it. *She's going to say she'll be leaving.*

"I told you I now own lots of property all over town. Well, Simon, you know how you've been trying to get in touch with the owner of the building you are renting, the owner of the vacant building next to it?"

"Addie! You own that building?" Simon asked with a grin.

She reached into the same drawer that had held the photo of Jean-Paul and pulled out some papers. "No, not any more. You do. Here is the deed, made out to you."

Simon took the deed into his hands and stared at it, unbelieving. "You're giving me a building? A whole building?"

"Simon, think of it this way. If Madame had known you were Jean-Paul's child, you would have inherited along with me. That deed is for the block where Simon's Place is, which includes the empty store next door that you want for expansion, plus yet another shop, which sits on the next corner. And of course, the space above all the businesses, which could be put together to make one great big super apartment." She grinned, "If you should think of a reason you need a really big apartment."

Simon reached over and grasped Dani's hand. "Yes, I can think of a good reason I would need a really big apartment."

"I thought you would. And the shop on the corner is much larger than the one Dani has now, with a bigger back room for work and storage. That would be convenient, don't you think? Not to be running back and forth up and down these two blocks?"

"Hey! Are you taking one of my best renters?" Martin said.

"Is there room for Spike if we move down there?" asked Morgan.

"The spirits will send another renter, Dad, and a good neighbor for me."

"There'll always be room for Spike," Simon told Morgan, and put his arm around the boy.

She said 'a neighbor for me.' Maybe she's going to stay, after all. The lump in his throat and the heaviness in his heart lifted a bit. For the first time that evening he was able to muster a true smile.

"Simon, when we get past all these changes, I want you to take me around and show me where all the property I own is located. I just have street addresses and photos of the outside of the buildings, but I don't know my way around town well enough to find them all. When you do, I want you to be thinking about picking out another location, in case you ever want to open a second Simon's Place. I'll deed over another property to you."

When Simon stood up to hug Addie again, everyone started talking at once about how amazing it was that Addie and Simon were related, how kind Addie was, and how Madame would be proud of her niece. Parker made his way from his chair in the corner to where Addie was and pulled her into his arms.

"I thought you were going to tell me you were leaving, moving back to Connecticut," he said in her ear.

Addie pulled back. "Is that why you've been so quiet lately? You thought I was leaving?"

"Yes. I was trying to figure out how to talk you into staying, when it was so obvious you miss Karen and Gina so much. I was trying to find a job in Connecticut so I could be close to you, and kicking myself the whole time for being so vulnerable to a beautiful woman."

"Yes, I miss them, but I would miss you more," Addie said as she brushed his hair back from his face. "I'll be here from now on. This is my home. I'm not going anywhere."

Parker's joyous heart jumped in his chest as he pulled her close and kissed her.

"Here, you carry the mashed potatoes, and I'll get the green beans."

"Morgan, you can take the rolls to the table. Be careful not to spill them."

"Simon, that turkey is enormous. Don't you need some help?"

"Mmm. Those candied sweet potatoes look delicious. Maxie, did you make those?"

"No, child, Simon won't let me cook a thing."

"This is a beautiful room, Simon, an excellent addition to Simon's Place. It is going to be a delight to the eyes as well as the taste to eat here when you open it to the public," Martin said as he looked around the new addition to Simon's Place.

"That'll be tomorrow," Simon said as he placed the platter of turkey on the table. "The grand opening of this dining room is tomorrow. I took down the tarp blocking the opening between the two rooms this morning. We're the first people to eat in here."

"Evie, you did a wonderful job on the flowers and candles."

"Addie choose the candles."

"The yellow, orange and green all are good for everything I wish for everyone: abundance, wealth, good luck, wisdom, creativity, security, and attracting good things. And at each place you will find an agate, which is known as the stone of health and good fortune. Take the stones with you when you leave."

Simon brought the last dish to the big, elegantly set table, and then raised his voice.

"Y'all sit down now, please." He remained standing as the others took their places. "As we gather here to celebrate Thanksgiving together, I think it would be fitting to start with each of us saying what we are thankful for this year. I would like to be first.

"I'm thankful for my beautiful wife, Dani, and my terrific son, Morgan."

"Here, here," Parker said, and was echoed by the others.

"And I'm grateful for my mother, Maxie, for her love and support getting Simon's Place off the ground in the beginning years, and is here to see its success and to see the opening of this new dining room. I'm also thankful for her being here for children who need her."

Again the room sounded with ringing voices agreeing with Simon's statements.

"I'm grateful for my new cousin, Addie, for solving the mystery of who my grandfather was. It means so much to my mother and me." He looked toward Maxie, who was nodding her head in agreement. "And I am so grateful to Addie for her gift of this building, this whole row of shops, so I could expand my restaurant and Dani's business could grow too, and so we can have the roomy new apartment upstairs, handy to both businesses. I'm grateful to Addie, too, for the building in the French Quarter, where someday I'll have another restaurant as good as this one. In the meantime, I'm grateful for the rent I have coming in from it." Everyone chuckled at the mention of the incoming money.

"Simon, you'd better sit down and leave somethin' for other people to be grateful for," Dani said and tugged on his sleeve.

"I'm grateful for all the things my husband said," Dani said, her voice trembling with emotion. "But I'm especially grateful for Simon, himself. He led me out of the fears of my past and showed me my future. He's a good father for my son, and I thank him and God for that. I'm thankful for my friends, most especially my girlfriends Addie and Evie, and my mother-in-law, Maxie, who is like a girlfriend and a mother, all in one. I'm grateful my business is growing, and for the fact that Hollywood lady found me and is buying so many clothes from me to put in the movies. And I'm grateful Addie gave me all Madame's clothing from sixty and seventy years ago so I'd have lots to sell to the Hollywood lady. I'm going to be watching for those things in the movies." She stopped and wiped a tear from the corner of her eye. "Look at me, crying, and I never cry. It must be the fact that I…" she paused and looked around the table, "…I, we're pregnant."

"Oh my," said Maxi. "I'm going to be a grandmother." She looked at Morgan. "Again."

"Congratulations!" Addie got up and hugged Dani.

Parker shook hands with Simon and hugged Dani too.

Finally everyone settled back in their chairs and someone said, "Okay, Morgan. What are you thankful for?"

"I'm thankful for the new place upstairs to live 'cause I have a room all of my own. And I'm thankful there is a little yard in the back for Spike to play in while I'm gone to school." He stopped and thought for a few seconds. "And I'm thankful I got a letter from my friend, Renny, and that he is doing okay." He looked to Maxie, sitting next to him.

She smiled at him, "I'm grateful for my new daughter, Dani, and my new grandson, Morgan, and for the other new grandchild I'm going to have." She looked around the table. "And I'm grateful for all the friends I have made. Sitting here at my mother's table once again after all these years has reinforced the idea that all of you are family. Growing up there was always a big crowd around this very table on holidays, and that sideboard where the desserts are sitting held the cakes and pies back then, too, and the same picture was hung over it. Thank you for welcoming me into your lives, for being my extended family."

Evie was next. "I can't express how grateful I am that Madame found me that first day in New Orleans. I'm grateful for her protection, and for Addie's. I've stopped thinking about what might have happened without the protection of those two wonderful women, but I can sleep soundly now, not listening for an intruder, and I can go out and enjoy all this wonderful city has to offer. I'm thankful for my job in the Center for At Risk Children while I'm exploring the possibility of becoming a certified teacher once again."

She looked at Martin, seated by her side. "I'm grateful for Martin. I'm grateful he insisted on being with me when I had to go handle Ed's estate. I could never have done it alone." She paused. "No. That's wrong. I could have done it without him, but he made it easier and for that I'm grateful. I'm thankful that he stuck with me and didn't write me off as a lost cause when I wouldn't leave my little corner of the world because I was so frightened Ed would find me." She turned to him again with a smile. "And I'm grateful he is showing me New Orleans."

She turned toward the rest of the table as Martin placed his hand over hers. "I'm grateful for all my friends here today, especially Addie, who coaxed me from my apartment and helped me feel like my old self, and has convinced me I am a strong woman who will never again be under a man's thumb. I'm grateful for Maxie, who got me the job at the center. I'm thankful I've become acquainted with Parker and Simon, who, as well as Martin, show me constantly that all men are not like the one who hurt me. They show me every day there are good and kind men out there, too."

"I guess I'm next," Parker said. "First, I'm thankful for Madame, who took me in when I saw a "For Rent' sign in her shop window, a sign Madame said never existed. I'm grateful I found this place to live, and because I did I met this woman," he took Addie's hand in his, "who has agreed to be my wife."

Again, congratulations rang out around the table.

When Parker said no more, Addie took her turn.

"I'm thankful for so much we would be here all day if I were to name it all. I'm thankful that my grandmother sent those letters to her sister, so Madame could find me. I'm thankful for each and every one of you, my friends, but I'm especially thankful for two wonderful men, both of whom I would never have met except for Madame's gift. I have gained a father and a future husband.

"But most of all, Madame's gift brought me something much more important, the sense of knowing who I am and why I was blessed with the feelings and premonitions I have — to help others." Addie paused. "Now let's eat before Simon's delicious food gets cold."

* * *

Several hours later Addie and Parker, arm-in-arm, strolled back home.

"I think this is by far the best Thanksgiving I've ever had," Parker said.

"Even though you didn't get to see your family?"

"You are my family now. You and all the others." He patted her hand. "We'll go see my family in a couple of weeks."

"I've never had such a Thanksgiving, either. Before Mom died it was just the two of us, and after she was gone I would go home with Karen or Gina for holidays. They were family, too, in a way, but nothing like this. I finally feel like I'm home, really home."

"You are here where you belong. Life worked out like it was supposed to. "

"Did I tell you Diane came to see me last week?"

"Who is Diane?"

"You remember, that girl I gave the potion to and she fed it to the piano player at Le Chat Noir and he wasn't blind anymore? You remember?"

"Yeah, now I do. Is she still trying to catch him?"

"No. She came to tell me she's engaged to be married, but not to Scott, the piano player. She met the brother of a co-worker and they are madly in love and are going to be married next spring.

She said what you just did. 'Life works out like it's supposed to.' She told me that without all the things Madame did for her, she would never have had the confidence nor be the person she is today, neither would she have met or accepted a date with the man she's going to marry. She credits Madame for that, and she thanked me for the potion that cured Scott's blindness. She said that opened her eyes to what kind of person he was to go off without contacting her. That's when she said life works out like it's supposed to."

Parker put his key in the lock of the big iron gate and pushed it open.

"Yes, and my life, and your life, and our life together, is going to work out perfectly."

As Addie entered the courtyard she raised her head and took a deep breath, savoring the scent of sage and roses.